To Al

A great Cousin!

Hope you enjoy the book!

It could be scary!

David Lafayette

PERIL IN THE WEST:
COLE'S CHALLENGE

DAVID P. LAFAYETTE

ISBN 0-7414-1921-1

Published by:

INFINITY
PUBLISHING.COM

1094 New De Haven Street,
Suite 100
West Conshohocken, PA 19428-2713
Info@buybooksontheweb.com
www.buybooksontheweb.com
Toll-free (877) BUY BOOK
Local Phone (610) 941-9999
Fax (610) 941-9959

Printed in the United States of America

Printed on Recycled Paper

Published June 2004

For

Neil, Geoffrey and Aurelie

ACKNOWLEDGMENTS

When did it begin? Long ago, that's for sure. My brother Robert, in his youth, collected paperback Western novels. I read them at night by flashlight under the bedcovers (he would not have trusted me with any portion of his collections, be it Westerns, matchbook covers, baseball cards or *Sport Magazine*). I am grateful to him for the romantic ideas his novels gave me.

I thank my English teacher at Berlin High School in New Hampshire, Mr. James Dolan, who agreed that English was more than just spelling and grammar. And also Mr. George Daughan, a classmate and good friend since our days at the University of New Hampshire. His comments and encouragement were there when I needed them.

I thank Carol Markee of Nottingham, N.H., who went through an early draft of the novel pointing out where grammar and spelling were important! I thank the members of the Friday-Afternoon-Drinking-Club that met at Legends Sports Bar in Raymond, N.H. Their behavior during and after our sessions dutifully provided raw input for the novel. In addition, I thank my professional editor, Beth Mansbridge of St. Augustine, Florida, who helped polish the final draft into a shape fit for printing.

Finally, I thank my wife Neil, who put up with my absences during the time I spent doing research for the novel.

PROLOGUE

He had bright blue eyes and scarcely a wrinkle on his red newborn face.

"This little man is going to be important," the midwife said, smiling down at the boy. She had never seen such beautiful eyes on a newborn. She could read those eyes so clearly. She carefully wrapped the boy in a fancy blanket and placed him gently into his mother's waiting arms.

She paused over the mother, still looking at the boy. "I borned a hundred of these boys, yes ma'am, least a hundred of 'em," she confirmed. "None had eyes like this little boy." She smiled and said firmly, "Believe me, something sure important's going to happen to this little one."

Through the boy's early years, his mother often recited to family and friends the midwife's prophecy. She was a proud and happy mother and she firmly believed in the power of wise old black women to predict the future.

Twenty-four years later in an area called "the mossy hills" just south of Lowry, Missouri, Randy Denny, the infant fully grown, was shot dead by a metal ball fired from a long rifle. He was riding alone. The shooting fulfilled the midwife's prophecy; it was an important event. Randy Denny numbered the eighth lone rider ambushed and killed near St. Bartow, Missouri, within a six-month period. His death roused John Lawton, the local sheriff, to take on the challenge of finding the perpetrators of these wanton killings.

* * * * *

Randy Denny's father, Sam, was a local artist who hung out and did his painting in the saloons that festered on the low end of the main road through Springfield, Illinois, no matter how hard the church people pressured to stamp them out. Sam was unschooled in his art but had natural talent. He combined that talent with an appealing, entertaining style.

While standing at a saloon bar with one hand wrapped around a glass of whiskey, Sam could scribble out wily cartoons of townspeople looking silly and performing what might be politely called "odd acts." A crowd of drunks would surround him, and laugh and encourage his outrageousness. Sam's art and entertainment brought him publicity, so that later he was able to promote his portraiture work in more affluent surroundings. In addition to a little money he got for the sale of the silly drawings, Sam received free drinks and had a stableful of friends throughout the low-end district.

Sarah, Randy's mother, was definitely quieter than her husband. She was book bent, industrious, and impeccably well thought of in Springfield. Sarah was blessed with her own talent. She designed and made clothes for local businessmen and state politicians who came to Springfield for the biennial sessions of the legislature. If you were in business or politics in Springfield, you were proud to own at least one Sarah-Denny-made suit or coat.

Randy inherited his father's good looks and both his parents' creative talent. From the time he was just a lad, Randy loved to perform. He played lead in school productions and he would bring the house down with his spontaneous humor. Being Sarah Denny's son, he never wanted for stylish, well-made clothes. Blond-red hair, a short-cropped beard, sparkling white teeth, deep blue eyes, a perpetual grin, stylishly dressed and always prepared with a humorous comment . . . that was Randy Denny.

Like many young men in Springfield, Randy's interest turned to hell-raising after he finished school. He would play elaborately staged ruses on townspeople. Once, he targeted Mr. Guntar and it was the talk of the town for weeks afterward. Guntar thought himself a member of the elite in town but he wasn't well thought of, nor liked, for that matter. He was heir to a tree cutting and lumber mill operation. Guntar dressed in fancy Eastern-style clothing and rode about town looking imperial on his big horse. He commanded the horse in a gruff German tongue. Randy made fun of Guntar's German. He passed it around that Guntar's horse was the only creature that understood his German. Guntar, in Randy's words, was "all horse, a hat, and too wide of ass to fit in his fancy riding britches."

One night Randy and friends broke into Guntar's livery and raised his big horse up onto the roof of the stable. The next day when Guntar arrived his horse was on the stable roof looking puzzled and searching for a field to graze in. Passers-by were giggling at the sight.

Guntar cursed in English and threatened anything and everything in sight. He eventually settled down and hired carpenters to rig a pulley and lower the bewildered animal. When the big horse reached the ground, those witnessing it applauded. Guntar was fit to be tied. He knew the source of the trick; it bore the hallmark of Randy Denny. But Guntar also knew enough not to take on Randy. Randy managed always to have the public behind him.

At age twenty, Randy fell in love with Melissa Rhines, the daughter of a local landlord. Like many young people, Randy and Melissa knew their love was perfect. The two visited at the Rhines's house all during that summer. They swung on the back porch and stared intently at each other and talked about such matters as whether Randy's eyes in the twilight were blue or gray. The two were deeply in love and began confidentially making serious plans about their future together.

That very summer a bank was burgled in a nearby town. The burglars opened a passageway between the building next door and the bank's vault and made off with more than a thousand dollars of the bank's cash. U.S. Marshals were called in and they were referred to Randy. Nothing ever came of Randy's interrogation and no other banks were robbed. Mr. Rhines, though, hearing of the marshal's talk with Randy, became concerned for his family's reputation.

He told his associates that Melissa's future with the Denny boy was definitely put aside for the time being.

Not a month after the burglary, Randy was seen riding a sleek black stallion through the back hills and onto the main roads of Springfield. He wore a black hat and he'd hoot and holler like a wild man. The hat bobbed freely behind him and a half-burned cigar jutted from a corner of his mouth. He set tongues wagging.

Thinking back to the bank robbery, most people wondered how Randy could afford to own such an expensive horse. Some, with a grin, thought Randy was practicing a wild look for a WANTED poster. Others thought he looked dashing. And still others thought his behavior was certain proof that the young man had become separated from the community and the protective wing of the church.

At this point, Randy's reputation—already on the edge—took a plunge. A rumor linked him romantically to a whore who hung out at a sleazy saloon on the low end. Rumor spread that he had fathered a child to a schoolgirl in a town north a ways, and that the girl's father was planning to come after him or file legal charges against him.

Therefore, in the spring of 1868, with these allegations swirling and feeding local disaffection, Randy decided to quit Springfield and go west. When he broke the news to Melissa, she burst into tears. He promised her on his grandmother's grave that he'd return. Their plans, he told her, were postponed but not off.

One day later outside a saloon, the road crowded with fellow patrons, Randy jumped onto his stallion, reared the animal back, waved his hat, and charged toward his dream. The crowd cheered. One of its gallant young men was off to tame the Wild West.

Randy planned to travel to St. Bartow, Missouri, a major staging area for wagon trains going further west. Once out West, he'd put in for the free land the federal government was offering to those agreeing to homestead. Or instead of taking up the plow, he'd go on to California or Montana and find gold. Plain nobodies, he'd heard, got rich overnight digging gold in California.

Either way, he promised himself after settling down that he'd send for Melissa and they'd get married and raise a horde of children. He knew that Mr. Rhines would become proud of him again.

Randy arrived in Lowry, Missouri, about ten miles north of St. Bartow, on a hot spring day. Lowry, before the Civil War days, had been a hotbed of Southern sympathizers. Randy didn't know that but if he had, it probably wouldn't have made any difference. He was very excited that day. He craved whiskey and companionship after having spent so many days alone on the trail. He left for town with the intention of getting a peek at his future.

Randy drank a lot that night. At one saloon, he acted out a ruse. He played a Yankee war hero on his way west. He detailed to the crowd how he had done in Rebel foes. The crowd cheered and loved it. He returned to his campsite that night excited about his acclaim. His ruses would be as successful here as they had been in Springfield.

He set out for St. Bartow the next morning. While reliving in his mind his successful debut in Lowry, he saw a reflection of sun on metal down the trail. He slowed his horse and bent forward, peering, trying to discern what was ahead.

The next thing he sensed was being thrown backward off his stallion and a burning pain in his neck. He tried to get up but he could only lie there on the ground in a mess of arms and legs. He tried to let out a swear but only blood streamed from his mouth. The blood squirted and gushed from his neck and ears too. He stared blankly at the crimson color as it crawled slowly across his shirt and onto his coat.

He lay there in a heap for several long seconds, his vision blurring and his eyelids growing heavy. He looked over at his stallion; the big horse turned away. Randy stared up to the sky. The young man was dead at the age of twenty-four.

* * * * *

Jesse Fallon felt blue—bluer than usual. He was standing in a hotel room in St. Bartow inspecting his image in a mirror. Yes, he thought, shaking his head, I look bad, I am aging rapidly. Life is passing me by.

Jesse had lived in St. Bartow for seven years. He wrote news dispatches for the *Chicago Tribune.* He'd won his spurs, so to say, in St. Bartow writing about Indian braves and medicine men, lawmen and gunslingers, and farmers and cowboys. But he was tired of it.

Continuing to look into the mirror, Jesse asked himself out loud, "Is to stay forever in St. Bartow why God graduated Jesse F. number three in his class at Columbia University?" He heard the answer, a refrain that rose straight from his heart, "No. No."

Jesse believed he had done well for the *Tribune.* It was said that General Grant himself, running for President, made a special point of reading Jesse's dispatches in the Washington newspapers. Jesse believed firmly that he deserved a promotion. He wanted to become the *Tribune's* man at the White House or at the U.S. Congress—positions appropriate for a reporter of his experience.

Jesse had come to dislike St. Bartow. In fact, he disliked it with a passion. He acknowledged that the town was exciting but he also believed it was a hellhole and certainly a dead end for a newspaperman. The town consisted mostly of transient immigrants in search of a pot of gold. But there was no pot of gold to find or even a rainbow to follow in St. Bartow. There was only hard work, meager incomes and at any moment a violent death. Jesse knew from experience how the daily existence here wore on people. He was a prime example.

And where is the U.S. Marshal in St. Bartow, anyway? He asked the question of himself as he quickly turned his thoughts back to his current work assignment. Jesse would always do that after a bout of self-pity. Yet he was not likely to self-pity for long. It was how he kept himself going.

Where was the marshal hanging his hat? Jesse needed to interview him. He needed a quote from him for a dispatch, but the big man was nowhere to be found. In fact, Jesse had asked several local sources about the marshal's whereabouts and none had any idea where he was. The situation was maddening for a first-class newspaperman who was always successful in meeting deadlines.

Jesse believed he had his hands around a big story. A crazy person, a sniper, was dry-gulching people in the back-country. For a newspaperman, there were many different issues raised by the sniper. Each of these issues could be highlighted in a series of dispatches. What motivated the sniper? Was he a rancher working to control the land? Maybe he simply didn't believe in making homesteaders of immigrants or Rebels or Easterners. Maybe the sniper was a soldier gone plain loco or unable to accept the War's out-come. Jesse had no idea what the sniper's motivations were; in fact, he didn't really care, but he did need the quotations of an appointed government official to give his dispatch legitimacy. And out here that government official was the U.S. Marshal.

Jesse didn't mind introducing fable into a news dispatch. He would spike a story as quickly as the next newsman. But he needed to satisfy his Chicago editors. Editors would accept spikes in a dispatch but they wanted the thrust of the story supported by verified official quotes. That was the purpose of a U.S. Marshal, as far as the newspaper industry was concerned.

Moving in closer to the mirror, Jesse applied daubs of flesh-colored cream to lighten the dark half moons under his tired eyes. He smoothed down his mustache and slapped his cheeks to impart a little color. That looks better, he thought, checking his image from several angles. He adjusted his hat, straightened his shoulders, and marched boldly down the steps of the hotel and onto the boardwalk of St. Bartow.

Looking around at the activity, Jesse decided on the spur of the moment to visit the local sheriff. He could maybe use quotations from him in his dispatch. The sheriff's comments weren't as acceptable as the marshal's because his authority was limited. First, though, he would stop at the Union Saloon, the hangout of the former Blues. He needed a couple whiskies anyway to do away with the cobbles he was feeling in his belly. Besides, he owed the Blues a visit. He'd spent time at the Rebel Saloon the previous day talking with the Grays about Southern passions being expressed in the New West. Whatever that was, he thought, smiling.

Jesse was a sight to behold, all dressed, parading down the boardwalk. Drunks stared at him wondering how much a hit would be worth. Parents pointed him out to their children. He wore a European-cut plaid suit and a dapper looking black hat with a wide colored hatband and a badge—Press-Chicago Tribune—stuffed on angle into the band. The outfit was not conservative. But Jesse liked the look and feel of it and the reaction it generated—it made him feel successful and important.

An hour later after downing several whiskies and listening to the men's stories, Jesse left the Union Saloon and walked unsteadily in the general direction of the sheriff's office—until he noticed he was in front on the Silver Dollar Saloon. He had never been in the Silver Dollar. The sheriff's office is just down the way, he thought. He decided to try out the saloon first; the visit to the sheriff's could wait.

Jesse pushed through the swinging doors of the Silver Dollar. Sitting at the first table just inside the doors was a man dressed stylishly in very expensive clothing. Well, Jesse thought while surveying the saloon, I'll be able to drink with a cultured gentleman, someone of breeding, no doubt!

"Hello there, sir," Jesse boomed out, "my name is Jesse Fallon. I'm a reporter for the *Chicago Tribune.* Good to see you. May I treat you to a drink?"

The gentleman turned halfway around and rose from his chair.

His face looked odd, thought Jesse. A strange, wax-like substance covered it completely. It obscured his features. The latest from England, he thought. I will have to look into that.

"Good to meet you, Jesse," the well-dressed man said, obviously pleased. "Always a joy to meet another gentleman. Sit down, please. My name is Marchess, Willoughby Marchess. Call me Will. I'm in medicine and I'm from New Orleans. Here, please sit down," he repeated, motioning Jesse politely but firmly to a chair at his table.

* * * * *

Very early the next morning a young road boy, Pete, scuffled his oversized and worn-out boots down a main road in St. Bartow. Pete was looking for anything of value left behind. He had risen early because he wanted to be the first boy out. He knew that first boy out reaped the best pickings.

Suddenly, ahead, he spotted a body lying on the roadside. The body's face was white and bloodless, and Pete saw that the clothes on the body were expensive. Nothing looked disturbed around the body. The body had on a pair of quality boots and Pete hoped the killer had also left other things of value. A fancy hat lay a few feet away and a message saying something he couldn't read was tucked into its hatband.

Pete stared at the body from ten feet away. He cautiously moved closer. The area reeked of alcohol. On the man's neck, two dark purple spots each the size of a half-dollar stood out, side by side. In the middle of each spot was a purple puncture wound. The boy knew immediately that the man's blood had been sucked out. Pete took off like a cannon shot.

He didn't slow his run until he was back in the safety of his hideout deep under the boardwalk.

CHAPTER ONE

The afternoon that Cole Mason rode into St. Bartow the air was filled with fog and rain. Mud was everywhere. Riding his horse Rusty down the main road, Cole tried to avoid the mud but it was a wasted effort. Rusty's hooves kept finding the puddles and churning the mud up, throwing it back at him.

Earlier, when he had realized that the rain would be around for a while, Cole had donned a boot-length oilcloth coat. But the coat did nothing to protect his face from the mud that kept flying up from Rusty's hooves. Some of the mud even worked its way past his lips and into his mouth. He coughed and spit the stuff out again and again. Nasty, he thought, not like clean Vermont country grit. No sir. The stuff is full of horse droppings. "Hey Rusty," he shouted furtively after a bad mouthful, "a little less on the dung, will ya?" His voice surprised him . . . it sounded strong and purposeful above the heavy rain. Not a bad sound for a tired boy, he thought, grinning.

Cole turned his attention back to the town. The air here smelled, he thought. First dung in the mud and now the air smelled. What next? Maybe the people smelled too. Cole looked more closely at the buildings and the people walking the boardwalks lining the road. No, he thought, the smell came from the many humans and animals going through here on their way west. The smell was from the human and animal waste. Got to get used to it, he thought.

Cole had been six weeks on the trail coming from the East. He thought back to the acquaintances he'd made. There was the big Russian and his good friend, Kenzie the Scot. The two immigrants made a lasting friendship coming off the boat in New York. They had worked together to get free of a bunch of gang boys who had attacked them thinking Kenzie was Irish and the Russian a clown, and both deserving a New York beating. The newcomers had turned the tables and gotten away.

Working their way west, the two stayed together with the common thought of finding big riches in the West. They were inseparable after their success in New York. They talked gold from sunup to sundown. They talked about gold relaxing at the campfire. They talked gold collecting wood for a fire or just riding side by side. They talked how deep to dig for it, how big the nuggets would be, and whether nuggets gleamed more at the bottom of a clear stream than in sunlight. They talked about how to keep gold hidden and how to transport it free from thieves.

Kenzie and the Russian were to become millionaires—millionaires just as quickly as they got into the gold fields.

Though Cole was dubious about a lot of their talk, he found it entertaining. He wondered who would do all the work if everyone became a millionaire. He'd shake his head. Life was not that easy, he thought. Especially when dealing with things of high value, like gold. Besides, most of the easy pickings of gold were gone, he'd heard. What gold was left was being mined using high-pressure hoses owned by big companies.

Lennie, the Russian, was a Cossack. He never clearly defined what that was. He was very proud though. He had been born into a family of warriors, he said. When he spoke Russian or Cossack, Lennie sounded more like a prophet coming down off a mountain than a warrior . . . he was loud and sometimes crazy sounding. Most of the other riders on the trail thought Lennie mad. They stared at him when he growled and laughed at his food. Cole decided that warriors in Russia maybe acted like that. When Cole was asked why Lennie growled at his food, he told them it was a mystery, that maybe he didn't like it, maybe it was a habit he picked up in Russia. So, along the trail it was whispered that Lennie was mad. A mad Russian.

Lennie sure liked to drink and dance. He came back into camp one night from a visit to a small nearby town. He was swaying side to side, shouting and singing as he often did. He woke everyone but no one dared say anything. He was crazy. You don't mess with a crazy man. He sang and danced while crouched close to the ground.

Kenzie was always afraid Lennie would take his gun out; he didn't trust him with a gun. One night Lennie, while singing and dancing, did take his gun out. A traveler staying in camp with them shot him dead. He didn't know that Lennie was just a harmless, mad Russian. The guest said he thought Lennie had gone crazy.

Kenzie wept for his friend. They all worked together to give him a proper burial. The man said he was sorry, but there was no bringing him back. Lennie had pulled a gun and died right there.

Kenzie told Cole Lennie had told him his name really wasn't Lennie. He'd said he couldn't use his real name because the czar was searching for him. Kenzie asked Lennie why he thought the czar would bother to search for him in America. Lennie was astounded by the question. After he looked at each person around the campfire one by one as if to read their faces, he pronounced them all crazy and stupid. The czar's agents were everywhere; the czar was like God, he explained. God was everywhere and the czar and his agents were everywhere. He snapped his fingers, closing his case.

Maybe that's who killed Lennie, thought Cole.

The stranger rode off the next morning. Maybe he was an agent of the czar.

"Makes you wonder," said Kenzie, when Cole told him his idea.

They stared at each other for a moment, but neither was ready to believe it.

Cole recalled the two Irishmen he'd met on the trail. The three of them traveled together for nearly a week. The two boys were big, strong, and well mannered. They were on their way West to plant rails for the Union Pacific. They heard there was big money to be made planting rails. They would arm wrestle in the towns along the way to pick up change to pay their way west. The boys were strong as iron nails and mild mannered as a tin of warm sarsaparilla, thought Cole. Passing through Ohio, they made trash of a saloon but only after local boys wouldn't pay off on a wager. The word was that when the two Irishmen left the saloon there were seven or eight local boys laid out in a row, side by side.

Cole looked out at St. Bartow bathed in the rain. The rain was lightening up a bit, yet the mist and fog were as thick as ever. Beyond the road and behind the unevenly built structures he could see an array of outhouses . . . big ones, little ones, abandoned ones, new ones, collapsed and rotten ones. Outhouse buildings told the history of the area. The rotten and abandoned houses told the story of the many people who had come through over the years, quickly moving on farther west. People stayed only for a few weeks or until they secured passage on the next departing wagon train. The newer buildings represented the just arriving flood of immigrants soon to leave, too, and find their way west.

There was no sense of permanence in St. Bartow. Cole could feel that. None at all. He nodded his head, realizing that the values of many of the people in the area would be influenced by loose ties.

Rusty suddenly cantered left, which threw Cole to the right.

"Rusty," he shouted, "don't make it worse than it is. Work with me, will ya?"

Six weeks on the trail talking man to horse, horse to man, your horse becomes like a brother. I'd probably go loco with no one to talk to, he thought, smiling.

Cole heard a gunshot coming from an area just beyond the road he was riding on. It was hard to tell where it came from because of the rain. He quickly stopped Rusty, slid from his saddle and looked around. He was surprised to see that no one on the road acted surprised. No one in town had much reaction at all . . . business was going on as usual. Gunshots, I have to get used to, in addition to the smell, he thought, grinning. What else?

St. Bartow was bigger than he'd expected. The town had a lot of roads, wagons on the roads, boardwalks with people moving about, and many saloons and drunks. Cole read the shingles hanging on the storefronts . . . people selling or wanting to fix things, foreigners' names on signs, immigrants, half-breeds and the like. They didn't look American, either. He had never heard so many different tongues. More foreigners here than in the whole state of Vermont, he guessed.

Plenty of noise, too, even in the rain. Hammers on nails on buildings, hammers on boardwalks, muleskinners cursing. Cursing loudly, he thought. He heard a driver coming up fast from behind and cursing a blue streak. Cole glanced back over his shoulder. The driver was just a form covered up from the rain with a tarpaulin. Cole heard blacksmiths banging on anvils, and again, guns shooting in the air. The gunshots made the town sound like Virginia in the War, between skirmishes . . . never quite gun quiet. Yet the excitement in the air caused Cole to smile. He felt the excitement welling up inside.

He heard a disturbance in the road ahead of him. It sounded like a serious squabble between two people. It was coming from his left. He looked over and picked out an elderly man who was apparently being needled by two road boys. The boys were probably after the man's money, he thought, or looking for a little amusement in the rain.

Along the trail Cole had heard about the reputation of road boys. The old man was dressed in a suit too fancy and too small, and wore a bowler pulled down over his ears. You get picked on when you dress silly, thought Cole.

"Old man," the bigger boy shouted into the man's ear, "what's that, a bugle boy outfit? Were you born in it? Anyone ever tell you that you done growed out of it? Did you know that?"

Both boys were enjoying the encounter, laughing and dancing about on the wet boardwalk.

The old gentleman was looking around for support. Several passersby watched but no one offered him assistance.

"Young men, I'm a doctor, a doctor of medicine. I am here to help—"

The bigger boy broke in again. "Help? Bet you're from 'lanta. Bet you're a Rebel. Bet General Sherman cut you loose, right? Bet you cure itch and pull teeth painless, right? We ought to pull *your* teeth. Treat you right, old man."

Cole looked at the smaller road boy. He didn't look right. He looked as though he wouldn't know the end of the rifle the ball comes out of. One minute the boy stared blankly around, the next he danced about in loops. He had trouble focusing his eyes.

Possibly born stupid, thought Cole.

"Just look at yourself, Reb," hooted the boy as he stepped forward, threatening to shove the old man.

Small medicine bottles rattled in the man's pockets as he jumped away.

He must really be a medicine man, thought Cole. I hear that those guys aren't field daisies. 'Fore long he'll pull a derringer from his coat and shoot himself a dumb kid.

The old guy struggled to convince the youths of his worth.

He didn't deny being a Rebel, though, Cole noted.

The old guy began again. "Young men, my medicine has a long history of curing the worst ailments of the human mind and body—"

"Hey, you," Cole shouted at the boys, "leave the old guy alone. Move on. He's not bothering you."

The boys looked over at Cole.

They aren't used to having their play interrupted, thought Cole.

"Well, Pete," the bigger boy spoke while leering at Cole, "we have us here a big man with dung on his face on a short fat horse, wanting to worm into someone else's business. I think, Pete, that dung-face needs a lesson."

Cole rose in his stirrups, pointed at the boys and hooked his thumb over his shoulder. In any language, that said "Move on."

The boys now moved quickly against Cole.

"Okay, trail trash," said the talker, "we'll learn you to mind your business. You gotta be a Rebel too. Do ya hide corncob pipes in your saddlebag, like your brothers, right?"

Both boys laughed.

Cole acted instantly. He swung from his horse and using it as a shield, he sidestepped the first attacker, grabbed the leader and threw him through the air into a mud puddle about ten feet away.

Several passersby roared approval.

The young man pulled himself up. He began shaking and scraping off the mud that clung to his face and clothes. The other boy joined him and almost on signal, they took off together up the road.

The older boy paused at a nearby corner. "You rotten Reb," he shouted with little emotion. The two boys disappeared around the corner.

Cole moved quickly to mount Rusty as the old man ambled toward him.

"Thank you, my good man. Not many would help an old gentleman nowadays. You are a true Samaritan."

Cole looked closely at the old man. His face looked vacant and transparent. It appeared even to glow some. His hair and tiny mustache were out of place. Must be painted on, Cole thought. What is this thing? What did I save?

"Well, sir," Cole said, "got no wash with Rebs myself, but it isn't right, two young ruffians. . ."

The old man flashed anger. "Sir, I'm no Rebel." Saliva flowed from a corner of his mouth. His eyes were beady and he raised his hands as if ready to fight. "Not by birth or sentiment. I'm from New Orleans. My granddaddy fought alongside Andy Jackson and they beat back the British. My father's a planter down there. We have always supported the Union. My daddy and his loyal darkies fought alongside Abe Lincoln. My sentiment, sir, was then, is now, and will be forever with the government in Washington, D.C. Yes, sir."

Wow, thought Cole, that's quite a line.

"Please," the old man said, holding up a hand, signaling a truce, "let me treat you to a nice glass of spirits. Least I can do for you." He smiled, confident that Cole would accept.

Cole realized he had insulted the old man by implying that he was a Rebel. He should have a drink with him. He wiped the mud from his brow and tasted the road caked to his tongue.

"Sounds good, sir." Cole smiled. "And I'm sorry about that Rebel stuff. I should've never listened to those puffed-up kids. A drink of spirits will clear my whistle. But tell me, sir, you have no disappointed customers around, do you? I choose to do no more people-throwing today."

The old man grinned.

That smile was an ordeal, thought Cole. The man's face looks waxed and a grin could be the last straw.

"Only one disagreement a day, my Good Samaritan, and I just had it." He cackled loudly at his line.

Cole smiled kindly at his strange benefactor. "Cole Mason," he said, holding out his hand. "I hail from Vermont."

The man shook Cole's hand. "As we say out here, howdy, Mr. Mason, I'm Willoughby Marchess. Please call me Will. And by the way, any man that can throw another the way you just did can be a friend of mine any day."

Willoughby's cold hand surprised Cole as much as did the strange wax substance on his face. His hands were unusually cold. He's walking around embalmed, thought Cole.

"Well, what do you know," exclaimed Willoughby, turning toward the boardwalk, "we have a saloon right here. The Lord provides."

As though he doesn't know it, thought Cole. What am I getting myself into? Oh well, one drink and one drink only.

The two walked together up the stairs and through the swinging doors into the smoke-filled air of the Silver Dollar Saloon.

CHAPTER TWO

Cole was six weeks on the trail before arriving that rainy day in St. Bartow. He had started from his home in Franklin, Vermont, and followed a well-used east-west trail he picked up in western New York.

The day he departed, light flakes of snow were falling. A big storm was expected, but it did not dissuade him at all. He had planned the trip for some time. As he walked his horse out of the barn, his family was waiting outside the farmhouse ready to wish him good-bye and safe journey.

Cole went to his mother first. He could see the disappointment on her face.

"Cole," she said, "why this? You have a fine life ahead of you at Mason Farm and we want you here." She hugged him and waited, not expecting a reversal of his decision. Cole was always searching for change and excitement. Leaving Mason Farm and going west was all a part of what Cole was.

"Yes, Mother," he answered as cheerfully as he dared, "I am going to miss you too. Mason is a great farm and a great home." He spoke with deep affection. They had always understood each other; there were few secrets between them. He hugged her closely.

"What about Angela?" she suddenly asked and looked at Cole seriously. "She loves you, Cole. It'll break her heart." His mother looked away, head bowed.

Angela had been Cole's girlfriend since school. She had waited for him four years while he'd been in the Army of the North. Cole knew that his mother cared little for Angela. It was a secret she couldn't keep from him.

"Trust me, Mother. Have I ever disappointed you?" He hugged her again and flashed his little boy smile . . . the smile that disarmed her. She smiled her understanding.

"I'll miss you so." She hugged him closely. "Take care of yourself. Do nothing silly. Promise me."

"I pledge. I'll make you proud." He patted her arm affectionately. It was the same good advice she had given him five years earlier when he had left for the War.

He moved rapidly down the line of family members, reassuring each in a personal way. He thanked his father, shaking his hand.

"You've been a good son, Cole," his father said sternly. "We'll miss you on the farm."

Always stern, thought Cole. "Thank you for all you've taught me, Father. I will miss you too, and your advice and counsel." Cole smiled warmly and moved on.

When he had completed his good-byes, Cole swung up onto his horse. He looked around one last time . . . at his mom and dad, at Tom and Little Pete, at his other brothers and at his sisters, at the round barn he'd played and worked in . . . and at the farmhouse that had always been his home.

He turned his horse to the west, waved and rode away.

* * * * *

Deciding to go west had not been easy for Cole. He had returned from the War expecting to marry his sweetheart, settle down, begin farming, and raise a family as the Masons had on the land for generations. But he quickly became restless. He decided he no longer loved his girlfriend Angela. He had to tell her of his changed feelings. He felt guilty. She had waited for him while he was at war. He came to realize that the quicker he left, the better off both of them would be. His "make-believe" around her made him feel dishonest.

Cole also came to realize that farming in Vermont was not for him; it did not capture his interest as he had imagined. Talking with fellow soldiers during the War, he heard of the many new forms of industry and ways of farming and transportation being introduced into the country. He wished to be a part of that change, not tied to a farm in Vermont.

Another experience was pushing Cole west—something that had happened in the War. He hated to think about it. He feared that someday he would be accused of having done something terribly wrong and having to defend himself against the charges. Any time a stranger came through Franklin, Cole grew anxious, suspicious, and fearful for himself and for his family's reputation. Making public the false charges could cause his family to suffer.

Cole remembered as though it was yesterday the sounds and smells of the day it happened. He had been a soldier for fourteen months. On this warm autumn day, broken clouds in the sky allowed the sun to shine brightly on leaves just beginning to turn. He hunched on the battle line, rifle ready and bayonet at his side. His body was protected somewhat by a large rock. Several horses lay dead behind him, having been struck by fragments of artillery shells. They smoldered there covered in black crusted blood, thick of flies and wavering in maggots.

Cole felt the fear of war. A Rebel attack was imminent. His legs felt frozen. He peered across the field in front of him. The stench of burned powder and rotting horseflesh filled the air. The screams, cries and explosions of war were all around.

A Union captain made his way up the battle line. He picked three soldiers, including Cole, to patrol a section of land between the two battle lines. The three soldiers began their mission after dark. They successfully penetrated the Rebel line and picked up useful intelligence. But when they attempted to return they were overrun and cut off by an advance of the Rebel forces. All three of the Union soldiers were taken captive.

The three were immediately separated by the enemy. Cole was taken to a nearby farmhouse to be interrogated. He was left alone and was mentally exhausted by the time his interrogator arrived. He had never anticipated being captured and knew nothing of what to expect.

“Good day, soldier! My name is Beaudin. I am a captain in the Confederate Army and a graduate of West Point Academy, class of 1862.” He held out his hand.

Cole shook it. Beaudin had a singsong way of talking. His voice was different and pleasant. Beaudin kept smiling and looking at him like he was a specimen. He was short in height and wore a red scarf tied around his neck.

He looked ready for a parade, thought a sullen and scared Cole.

“Well, suh,” Beaudin said while looking down at a paper in front of him, “you have nothing to fear. Your name is Mason and you are a farmer. We have a lot in common. You are a Protestant and a farmer, as I am, and I am a member in good standing in the Masons.” He laughed at his humor. “We’ll get along famously.”

Cole remained silent. He didn’t know whether he should talk innocently or keep quiet.

“Loosen up, man,” the Captain spoke loudly, still smiling at Cole. “We cannot become friends if you continue a schoolgirl sulk.” His eyes never wavered from Cole’s face.

He began by asking Cole simple questions. Beaudin sat ramrod straight. After each question, he would beat his left foot on the farmhouse floor.

Cole thought the action peculiar. Was his behavior a matter of inquiry or of injury. Beaudin’s questions were intended to make them friends, Cole decided. He interspersed questions about Cole’s war experience with questions about Vermont. He seemed to be genuinely interested in Cole’s answers.

The questioning went on for a long time. Cole felt himself dozing several times. Beaudin would bang his left foot on the floor and laugh when he saw Cole’s eyes glaze over. After about three hours, Cole became increasingly tired and Beaudin apparently became less interested in him.

Beaudin said, “I’m sure your leaders don’t tell you this, but it is not hard-working farmers like you, Mr. Mason, that the South fears and fights. No sir, it’s the masses of immigrants that form the core of your army and the moneyed class of officers that lead them. That, Mr. Mason, is what we fear. Why do we fear? We fear because your intention is to change our way of life. A way of life guaranteed by your Constitution. A life that the South is peacefully satisfied with."

The statement confused Cole. "Captain Beaudin," he replied, "I know of no brigades or armies of immigrants that make up the Union Army. The army is made up mostly of farm boys like me."

Beaudin was frustrated, Cole knew. He realized that after three hours of interrogation, Beaudin had little information of value from Cole. Cole felt that Beaudin had decided he was ungrateful.

Beaudin's pleasant, singsong Southern lilt became tough and threatening. "Look sir," he said, still sitting at attention, "you credit yourself well here today. You are proud, and your country and commanding general, they are proud of your behavior. You have played the game honorably. And I have helped you." He paused, waiting for a sign from Cole. "Now you must help me." Wham! Down went Beaudin's left foot.

Cole jumped. "Yes sir, I know nothing of what you ask," Cole said, trying to be polite.

Beaudin shook his head. A look of disappointment fleeted across his face. Cole felt sorry for him. But he didn't know whether that feeling was right.

"We bring an end to this, suh. Come here to the window."

Beaudin stood up and led the way, limping to the window. "See your friends out there?"

He pointed to a willow tree. Cole saw his fellow soldiers hanging by ropes from branches, extended by their arms and feet. They were being tortured. He could hear the soldiers moaning. Maybe this treatment was normal in war. He was surprised he didn't feel outraged; all he felt was powerless and exhausted.

"You could be out there too. I saved you from that suffering," Beaudin said, sounding hurt and angry with Cole. He threw both his arms up in desperation.

Cole's mind was numb. The two soldiers were suffering but he couldn't decide how badly. Their faces were bright red, eyes sunken into their sockets. Cole knew not at all what he should do, if anything. The choices given by Beaudin were not clear to him. Blood rushed from Cole's head, he began to shake, and his mind went blank.

"I'll give you a final chance, Mr. Mason," intoned Beaudin. "Give me the information and your friends will be released. Otherwise, your friends will remain hanging and you, suh, you will be treated with privilege. Yes, privilege, right in front of them." A smile wafted across Beaudin's face. Wham went his left foot again.

Cole jumped. He stared at Beaudin, too scared and helpless to say anything. He wanted his mother.

"You know, suh, those two will dog you to the gates of hell. That is, if they remain alive. The war will never end for you. You have only one minute to choose the honorable course. My advice, suh, save your honor, save your countrymen." Wham went Beaudin's left foot in its recurring cadence.

Cole later found out that the two prisoners had been told that he had cooperated with the Confederates. The prisoners were taken down from the tree, battered and beaten. Yet, in their misery, they could easily see that Cole was accorded favorable treatment.

During a Union artillery assault a few days later, Cole escaped. The gate on his prison door had been left unlocked. He ran wildly through woods and over ravines, cutting his arms and face on the sharp brush. His mind felt hot and without thought—only fear. His body just moved, seemingly without command. In pure panic, he didn't care where he was running to, as long as it was away.

Somehow, after an unknown period, he found himself back on the Union line. In the confusion of a Rebel counterattack, no one asked where he was supposed to be or where he had been. In fact, he fought so hard in the group he joined, that he was commended by the commanding captain. He was confused by the commendation but pleased that he had been accepted, and that his panic was gone.

Cole's experience as a Confederate prisoner upended his confidence. He became bitter about the War and always fearful of being accused of a wrongdoing—a wrongdoing he doubted he was guilty of. He feared meeting up with the two prisoners in the trees he believed he might have caused to be tortured. He vowed never to reveal to anyone the ordeal he had suffered.

* * * * *

Cole labored for six more long months on the Mason farm. He saved money and toughened himself on the work. For the trip west, he bought a horse of mixed blood with a strong strain of Morgan. He named the horse Rusty. Rusty was small but his strength was remarkable. Of good breeding, the horse had leg power and unusual quickness and stamina.

Cole rose early the morning he departed for the West. He'd travel to St. Bartow in Missouri and find a job traveling west. Once out there, he'd get the free land being offered by the federal government to those who chose to homestead.

"Cole," Angela whispered as she caressed him the night before he left, "do you understand what you're giving up?"

Not only did her fragrance excite him, but her breasts were pressed firmly against his body. He did not waver; his decision was firm. He'd miss her as he would miss his family but he must experience more of the country and gain back his confidence.

The morning he left, Cole had two hundred dollars tucked into his boot, a bedroll, fifty pounds of supplies, a six-gun in a saddlebag, and a rifle in his saddle scabbard.

He worked his way slowly through the East and the Midwest until he arrived in St. Bartow on that wet day.

CHAPTER THREE

Cole walked behind Willoughby into the saloon. Willoughby motioned him to take a seat at an empty table. The strange little man continued on to the bar at the back of the saloon.

He's familiar with the place, thought Cole, shrugging. Maybe he's sold an elixir or two here. So what, he thought, slumping into a chair.

The smoke and foul air made it difficult for Cole to see in the one-room saloon. He squinted to look around at the four walls, a beat-up floor, a leak-stained ceiling with scattered bullet holes, a bar made of castaway lumber, a collection of cobbled-together tables and chairs, a big grandfather's clock behind the bar, and a dusty, black upright piano sitting in a corner. That was it. No fancy red velvet saloon with dancing girls like the soldier boys used to describe. A grin spread across Cole's tired face.

In the smoke, Cole could barely make out Willoughby getting drinks. Two rough-looking men at the bar were standing and talking together. Two other tables in the saloon were occupied, each by a couple of men whose glasses had been refilled since Cole sat down. They would bang an empty glass hard on the table for service. The patrons were dressed as cowboys or workers; no one was remotely dressed like his benefactor.

Willoughby returned to the table carrying two drinks.

Cole took a sip of the one handed him. Strong, he thought, but not bad. He smacked his lips and took another sip. "Thank you, sir," he said, smiling, "I've been waiting for this. The long trail makes drinking men of even abstainers, you know."

Willoughby looked as though he was trying to smile at Cole's comment.

He didn't do a good job, thought Cole. He must have something on his mind. Willoughby looked stranger up close. When he spoke, the lines in his face made no effort to flex. Even his stronger feature, his lips, looked make-believe in the darkness of the saloon. Cole looked away. He didn't want the old man to catch him staring, but he found it difficult not to stare. He must know how he looks, Cole reasoned. He had been told of it many times and probably not always nicely.

"So, why you here, Cole? Drawn to the West? Looking for wealth? Problems back East? Tell me be still if it's private." Willoughby laughed, hollow and anxious, as he peered through the smoke across the table.

Cole continued to survey the saloon. The two bartenders, both short men, were trained to respond when pointed at, motioned to, or banged at with a whiskey glass. Both had black hair, slicked down and parted up the middle. They wore identical black aprons. They looked a lot like Willoughby, but without the heavy wax. Are their hands cold too? Cole wondered.

Cole answered, "No, no specific or personal reason for being here. No big reason. I want to see the West." He chuckled softly. "I want to see the opportunities we hear about in the East. I'm not afraid of hard work. I like to write. Maybe I'll chronicle people coming West." Cole grinned again and shrugged.

Willoughby ignored his comments. "Son, this place can make you wealthy. It's up to you. You have a way with words and you're thoughtful, honest and good looking. That's mighty important out here."

He hadn't touched his drink, Cole noted. Maybe it'd heat him up and wreck his complexion! Cole noted the drink was helping him relax. He always got funny after a few drinks.

Willoughby continued, "My advice, use your strengths for yourself, don't work for somebody else. Don't herd steers, manage a store, drive a wagon, guard a rich rancher, no sir. You don't get rich, Cole, using your strengths to help someone else. You get rich using your strengths to get people to work for you." He cackled a laugh that sounded to Cole as if it had begun back in the Dark Ages. "No charge for that advice, my good man."

The whole piece sounded rehearsed, thought Cole. Probably he's used it on other men new to the town.

"Never thought about it that way, but you have to start somewhere, right, Mr. Marchess?"

"Yes, sir. But when you have talent like yours, you don't start at the bottom. Sales are a natural for you, Cole. You have word power, good looks—and you look honest. You can easily get into buying, selling and trading. People will trust you. Ten thousand people go through St. Bartow each year, thanks to the government's offer of free land." Willoughby banged his glass for emphasis, his drink spilling over the edge. "That, my friend, is your potential pool of sales. It's a big group, a transient group and, I add from my experience, an ignorant group."

"An interesting point, Mr. Marchess, but I don't see myself selling medicine."

"Call me Will, please, Cole. Mr. Marchess is too formal for friends."

Cole could feel Marchess trying to worm his way closer into his life. He drank and listened.

"Medicine may not be it for you, Cole, but selling medicine is a very good teacher. Puts you face to face with your customer. You learn to come up with reasons why the customer can't live without your product. You make him feel guilty for not owning your product for himself or for his loved ones. After you get those principal methods down, you apply them to whatever you choose to sell. I chose medicine because it's an easy sell. Everyone is a potential buyer. Everyone has or knows someone who has some kind of ache or pain."

Willoughby's soaring, thought Cole. Still, there was no color in his face, not even sitting in the heat of the saloon. He had a peculiar odor about him too. Like mildew. A rancid mildew. It smelled as if he might do his sleeping in moldy haystacks. Maybe out here people smell like that. Cole shrugged. Maybe out here all the people sleep in haystacks. The town had an odor, so why not the people? Cole shrugged again. He was feeling lightheaded. His eyes were heavy. He wondered if something had been placed in his drink.

"Listen," Willoughby said, again demanding Cole's attention, "the staging area here in St. Bartow helps you organize sales. It brings transients together in one place. Some have items they can't transport west. Others need things they don't have. So you step in. You stage panic sales, buy from one wagon owner and sell to another."

Cole was about to respond, but couldn't.

"And," Willoughby added, "you can cut the wagon boss in on the deal. The boss tells an owner that something he owns is too heavy to carry. He creates panic. You step in, buy it cheap and sell it dear to a wagon owner up the way. You could even take orders, Cole." Willoughby laughed heartily at his scenario. He looked at Cole for a moment and then added, "You know what I mean, old boy." His vacant eyes tried valiantly to twinkle; they came close but never made it.

Soaring like an eagle, thought Cole. The guy should've been born with wings! "Yes, Will, but it sounds crooked, doesn't it?" Cole looked off again around the saloon.

Willoughby acted hurt. "Cole, you don't do it that way all the time." He paused and renewed his appeals with a new round of vigor and earnestness: "You could help me sell medicine. Double my sales," he added, "honest-looking guy like you."

Why does he keep referring to how I look, Cole wondered. How does he know I'm honest? I can't remember anyone telling me three times in ten minutes that I looked honest. This drink is affecting me. I'm getting silly, tired and irritable.

"Consider this, Cole. An important part of getting wealthy is knowing how to hide your money. You can be successful but if you become a target for thieves . . . it's all over. You spend your effort guarding riches instead of making more riches. Medicine is a perfect way to hide wealth. I am telling you this because I trust you, Cole. Medicine bottles don't take up much room. Did you know there's as much value per pound in medicine as in gold and silver? Well," he added, "almost as much. But thieves don't bother you if they think you're carrying medicine . . . how about that?"

Cole interrupted brusquely, "Does the medicine work? Is it good?"

Willoughby shot back, "Cole, it's a family recipe, passed generation to generation. It's good for heartburn, liver trouble and wart removal, aches and pains and to be frank, if you rub it on in the spring, it'll keep mosquitoes away."

Cole laughed pleasantly. That answer was sure prepared, he thought. He was feeling high but he didn't want to offend Willoughby. He was beginning to find the conversation funny, maybe even silly and a little boring. Either the whiskey was strong or he'd become more susceptible to alcohol after six weeks on the trail.

"Does it work?" Willoughby's voice reached a new height. "It works for some people and on some ailments. But it's a small amount of money to invest in a cure that could rid you of a major ailment and change your life favorably forever. Every one of God's children is different, my friend. That's what God wanted and that's what this new country is all about."

Gosh, thought Cole, he's recited that before. "I appreciate the offer, Will. Darn kind of you. I'll think on it, but I do want to look around first. I really have my heart set on farming, getting land."

Willoughby tried another approach. "Do you have the money to begin farming? Expensive business, you know, farming."

"Nope, that's why I'm going to look around." Cole spoke firmly, telling Willoughby in the tone of his voice that the discussion about his future was ended.

But Willoughby talked on and even picked up speed.

Is he trying to overwhelm me? Cole wondered.

"The best way to get west and get money to start farming is to take on a partner and work a gimmick like my medicine business. The two of us could work our way west, stop at wagon train sites, soldier forts, railroad camps, mining villages . . . create a ruckus, create a crowd and sell our wares. Hey, Cole, let me tell you, there's beautiful women out there." Willoughby's eyes went side to side and an elusive twinkle tried again to break out.

"The most dangerous way," he continued, "is to do it alone. You can get lost, attacked by wild animals, renegade Indians, and killers are loose out there. People going alone get shot and killed every day. You can hire a gunslinger to protect you but . . ." Willoughby raised his arm and rubbed his thumb and middle finger together signaling the great amount of money it took to buy protection. "And then if you are successful, your guard may shoot you and steal your money." Willoughby laughed loudly at his description.

Cole had enough booze and enough of Willoughby. He pushed his chair back and stood up. As he got up, a bartender waved a finger at him and pointed to a patron walking toward his table.

"Howdy," said the man, "I saw you throw that mouthy kid. It surprised him, I'll say. My name is Al Witham." He grabbed for Cole's hand before it was offered.

"Well thanks," said Cole, grateful for the interruption, "appreciate it. I'm Cole Mason from Vermont. Meet the ruffian's target, Will Marchess. He's a medicine man from down Louisiana way."

"Oh ya," said Witham, ignoring Willoughby, "that young one deserved the thrashing you gave him."

"You know those kids, Al. Are they bad ones?"

"I don't know. They hang together on building corners like locusts. They pass gossip and lies and then start spitting at each other like wild snakes. They hire out for anything except killing, and that I'm not sure about," he added, shaking his head.

Witham continued. "Say, Cole, come see me at the Circle W staging area down by the river if you need a job. We dispatch a train at least every four days. We can always use another tough guy. The pay's competitive."

"Thanks," said Cole, pleased that Willoughby saw that he had another offer, "I may come visit you."

"Be looking for you." Al smiled, tipped his hat, and walked toward the door.

Medicine drummers don't have an excess of prestige out here, thought Cole. Or Marchess has a reputation I know nothing about. Or Witham is a man of few words. He ignored Willoughby.

Cole got up and headed for the swinging doors. Willoughby tagged behind him.

He's quiet, thought Cole. Is it because I refused his offer? Can't take refusal? Witham ignored him. Did that quiet him? Odd behavior for a person who prides himself on being a salesman.

Outside the saloon Cole held his hand out to Willoughby. "Thanks for the hospitality, sir, and for the advice. I'm going to visit the sheriff and get his ideas."

Marchess said nothing.

Dropping his hand, Cole saw the medicine man glance at the sinking sun. Maybe it's getting late for him, or he has another meeting. He's sure given up on me. If I'd accepted another drink, we'd have been there all night. Cole held out his hand again.

Willoughby ignored it a second time.

He'd turned icy silent and wanted to go, Cole figured. He wants nothing more to do with me.

Without another word, the two men parted. Cole noted that Willoughby's eyes had never looked at him directly, nor had he spoken since Witham showed up. He has pressing business elsewhere, Cole decided.

CHAPTER FOUR

Once free of Willoughby, Cole felt a heavy weight lift from his shoulders. What an experience. What a strange little man . . . the rancid smell, the cold hands, the waxy face. His effort to control was truly strange. And the idea that working with him would position Cole to meet and get women—one of his big points! The man had obviously never known a woman. Cole shook his head in wonder at the man's boldness.

Where does he get his confidence? More than his statements about my honesty, his offer to help me get women must be his real opinion of me! Cole raised his eyebrows and shrugged his shoulders.

He swung up into the saddle. As soon as he hit leather, Rusty jumped. . . . A sign of fear, Cole thought. Probably he felt ignored. First time we've been apart for a long while. Poor critter is feeling abandoned. Yeah, for Willoughby. Again Cole shrugged and smiled. He patted the horse's shoulder as he started down the road. I'll make it up to you, old boy, honest, he whispered.

The sheriff's office wasn't hard to find. It was the only building nearby with barred windows and a double-planked, siege door. A sturdy sign on the front wall read: John Lawton, Sheriff, St. Bartow, Missouri.

Cole tied Rusty to the rail running the length of the building. Must make it a short visit, he thought. He looked up toward the horizon and then back along the roadside. Shadows had begun to creep up the buildings on the east side of the road. Sundown's pushing in fast, be dark before long.

He rapped twice on the big door. He heard a movement inside and what sounded like a "Come in," so he swung open the door and pushed it in. The room was of adequate size, no more. Two holding cells made up the back section and both were empty. The sheriff—Cole assumed he was the sheriff—was sitting behind his desk being shaved by a short, fat man with broad shoulders dressed in a white barber's smock. A mirror was rigged so that the sheriff could follow the shaver's progress without effort.

"What can I do for you?" the sheriff asked loudly, his eyes steady on the mirror.

"Don't want to interrupt," Cole said softly, laughing. "Didn't know I came into a barber shop."

The sheriff swung around and the man in the smock jumped to avoid cutting him.

"What are you," he questioned after a pause, "some kind of traveling funnyman? You from around these parts?" he added quickly.

"Meant no offense," Cole said, "just took me back. Hang, I knew a guy back home that used an outhouse for a library. No kidding, an outhouse for a library. You go in there and you had to be real quiet."

The sheriff let out a deep, booming laugh. "You got a wit about you, kid. I'm too busy to shave myself," he said, moving his head to get a better look at Cole. "Besides," he added, "Harry here cut hair in Kansas City 'fore he came here. He's up to date and that does my image well, right, Harry?"

Harry grinned and resumed his shaving, "Yes sir, Sheriff, up to date."

"Before you tell me what you'd like of me, let me explain I have two jobs hereabouts. The fine people of St. Bartow elected me sheriff, but I also do the marshal's job. I don't mind my job, but why a do-nothing marshal was appointed in this active territory by that bureau of saps in Washington is another of those Washington's mysteries I'll never understand. You know, on the same level as keeping Fort Sumter undermanned, undersupplied and undergunned." The sheriff looked at Cole with suspicion and asked, "You aren't a Reb, are you?"

"No, not that," said Cole, a smile spreading across his face. He was still in his humorous stage. The whiskey had loosened him up for sure. He thought he'd better watch himself.

"I don't generally bitch, especially 'bout another in my line of work," the sheriff continued, "but my boys and I are overworked and tired. The marshal is never here. So if you're coming about a problem out there in Rabbit Hollow, try the marshal's office and if he ain't there, good luck."

The two other men in the office, both wearing stars, were quiet and grinned proudly as the sheriff talked down the marshal.

With the shave completed, Harry dusted off the sheriff and helped him into his vest. A big, shiny, bright silver star stood affixed to the sheriff's leather vest.

The sheriff looked over at Cole. "You're big and impressive, young man. What's your name, where you from, and what can I do for you?"

The sheriff was big himself. Over six feet, trim, and he wore his gun even while being shaved. His staff respected him, that was clear. Not much dust settled on the guy, Cole concluded.

Cole introduced himself to Lawton and his deputies, and told them of his intention to go west, probably to homestead. He asked the sheriff his opinion of the safest way to get there.

"Well, Mason," the sheriff answered, "let me tell you. There's no safe way. That's why people pay money to ride on one of those wagon trains. There are renegades out there who'd just as soon dry-gulch you as wave at you. I've been out to investigate five sniper killings at least in the past few months. There is no indication that an organized group is doing it, far as I can tell, and I can't discover a motive. Money seems not to be an issue. The victim's valuables and his supplies are always intact."

The sheriff downed the remaining black coffee from a mug. He stood with Cole near the desk. "There's another situation out there. Kind of a crazy, wacky thing. I made a trip up Chilson way the other week in my role as marshal. Town's not a day's ride north of St. Bartow. Some friggin' animal attacked a young boy up there. The boy and his father work a farm there." He paused and shook his head sadly. "Darn it, really weird, the kid had pinholes in his throat. Bigger than pinholes, really, big as nail holes, probably. Small nails. At first I thought gunshot wound. No one's going to attack someone with a nail. But the holes were too small, I decided. Maybe a hungry animal. But what kind of grisly thing just sucks blood. Most animals I know want a little flesh too."

Sheriff Lawton gestured Cole to a straight-backed, wooden chair as he sat in his well-worn leather-cushioned office chair. "Then the father tells me that from a distance he saw a bat sitting on his son. He thought his son was taking a nap. That's when he rushed to the boy's aid. Not a buzzard, mind you, the farmer saw a lousy, screeching big bat. Well, that's another problem, Mason," he added, "you better be on the lookout for a bat that wants your blood."

The sheriff held up his hand to stop a comment from Cole. "The story ain't over, Mason. Baffled, I looked around for clues. I discover that a wagon likely crossed the area at about the same time the boy got killed. So, I got it. It makes sense to me now," he said seriously, "the kid got sucked dead by a bat that came by driving a wagon." Sheriff Lawton paused to let that sink in.

"Just a taste, Mason, of the mysteries out there. In addition, of course, you have to fear the lone thieves, gangs of crooks, army deserters, rustlers, renegades, savages, rattlers, bears, wolves, and just plain mean bastards who decide for some reason or other that they hate you and want to do you in. To head off alone would be irresponsible unless you know how to survive like a mountain man." The sheriff stopped to assess the effect of his story.

He's exaggerating, thought Cole. Those are the problems you could run into but it doesn't follow that in any one trip you'd run into all of them. The guy admits to being tired and overworked. He sketches quite a picture, though. Cole looked closely at the sheriff: frontier look, trim, tough, dark complexion, small mustache, slight belly, in good shape for about forty-seven years. He carries a tied six-gun and shows the confidence to use it. He's sure impressive looking, thought Cole.

"I am considering going it alone," said Cole. He knew he sounded silly. "About the bat, sucking human blood. I have to say it sounds like a fairy tale. I have no answer for that risk. About the dry-gulcher, that sounds like a possible big problem. Tell me, are there ways to protect yourself from a sniper, Sheriff?"

"If a yellow-belly got it in his craw to kill you, a yellow-belly can, and the odds of his success are on his side. You can reduce his odds by traveling west when the sun is in his eyes. And always keep your eyes peeled for reflections on metal. Once you see it, you got yourself a split half-second to get yourself the hell out of a bullet's way. Practice rolling off your horse. It's pretty simple once you get the hang of it. Tough to cut the glare off a rifle, and a killer isn't interested in that detail especially if he's been successful killing a few times. Also, try to jockey your horse side to side. Don't ride in a straight line. Jogging side to side causes the sniper to shift his rifle to follow you. The thing is heavy, you know. Typically, they keep it in a tree crutch to steady it. Maybe lay it out on a rock up high. Not many snipers are steady enough to be able to hit a target while holding the heavy thing in their hands. If he gets a shot off, it's past you by the time you hear it. Remember that. When you hear it, he's trying to get you back in his sights. Once off your horse, roll like crazy or even run until you find cover. If you're successful up to this point, the odds may be shifting a little in your favor. He may panic and run. Those guys aren't brave, they're cowards. If he does run, you can hear the sound of his horse's hooves beating in the distance."

Cole noticed the deputies nodding in agreement.

"Mason, I hope you're around here for a while. We could use your freshness. You have to meet two of my crew. Anything I forget about outlaws, they remember. The big guy, he's quiet but don't let it fool you. He's Jack Stilkey. The dark guy to his left, that's Brave Nelson. Brave's a half-breed tracker. Most full-bred Indians can only struggle to match his ability. His mother was pure Indian, his father was a white man. I ought to let Brave tell you all this. He understands white behavior well." The sheriff laughed. "This office has come to feel that outsiders understand our own people better 'n we do." The sheriff laughed again.

Brave grinned proudly.

"And speaking of Brave, he has an uncle that's a full-blood medicine man. From talking with his uncle, Brave has some unusual theories of what killed the farm kid. According to legend, bats, part-man, part-animal, may exist in the human world and live off human blood. We haven't yet asked Brave to catch one. But we may, if it strikes again." The sheriff laughed lightly.

Brave's face was frozen. He stood straight, expressionless, black eyes on Lawton.

"You can tell by Brave's accent," added Lawton, "that his father ministered to the Indians. He was university educated back in the East. Brave's been asked numerous times to speak over at the little church, but he hasn't agreed to it yet."

Everyone laughed, including Brave.

The sheriff turned back to Cole. "Mason, I know I mentioned the marshal is never in town. He has an office here but forget it, the man is always away. Saw him two or three times in two years. When I did meet him, he acted above me. In fact, he acted above everyone. 'Keeping peace in the countryside,' he says over and over again. Bull. Unattended problems in the countryside are what comes to roost right here in St. Bartow. No town is quiet if you don't have a quiet backcountry."

"These two boys," the sheriff said, motioning to Brave and Stilkey, "they keep order in town. I handle the countryside. I spent five years in the Union Army, Mason, the last two as a decorated colonel." The sheriff stared at Cole for a second, his eyes half-closed as if in deep thought. "Were you in the military, Cole?"

"Four years in the 11th Vermont Infantry. Mostly protecting Washington and in Virginia, sir."

"Good to hear, Mason. Happy you were one of us."

"Yeah. Not many Vermont boys were Johnny's," Cole answered wryly. That was a dumb response, he thought. The booze from the Dollar is still making me silly.

The sheriff ignored Cole's comment. "Mason, I know I've been talking nonstop for twenty minutes at least, but I could use you, a big guy, dependable, I hope. I don't know whether you're looking for work. Most people are that show up here. I have no salary to offer. I can deputize you a bounty hunter. There has been a $400 reward for the sniper, dead or alive, to be paid through the territorial office. My experience is they live up to their reward offers. It may now be higher after the kid from Illinois got killed the other day in the Mossy Hill section. If you work with us and we get him, the $400 is yours. As law officers, we aren't supposed to put in for it. I'd sign a document to that effect. I don't believe you'd have a problem collecting."

Cole's temperature soared. "Sounds interesting. What would be my contribution?"

"Well, it'd be risky, that's for sure. The federal government doesn't pay you $400 for anything but taking a big risk. You'd help flush the sniper out. We'd bring him in or snap his neck at the site, one way or the other. It's a dead or alive situation."

Cole liked the offer. His experience with Beaudin came flooding back. He felt overwhelmed, unable to make a decision. Free land was fine, but he'd need money to develop it. Willoughby was right about that. Four hundred dollars amounted to ten months of wages.

"Appreciate the offer, Sheriff. Can we meet on it tomorrow? Assume my answer is yes, but I'd like to sleep on it."

"Fine, son, we'll meet tomorrow morning. If you decide to join forces, we'll draw us a plan with you in it."

The men stood up. Stilkey and Brave smiled as they shook Cole's hand. They acted pleased he'd be joining them.

Cole departed the office. The sheriff's offer was a plow down his furrow. There'd be risk in it but he'd be working with top lawmen. And there'd be reward money. Well, reward money if they got the sniper. The risk was great, as he knew from the War. His mother would be upset if she knew what he was considering. Cole shrugged off that concern.

When he reached Rusty, he decided to check the horse over. As he went through the motions, his thoughts turned to risk. In the War, he'd experienced great risk. He was used to it. Maybe taking on the sniper would be good, help him forget the War—help him bury the Beaudin thing. It was still affecting his sleep. Those soldiers hanging helplessly, faces contorted. Attacking the sniper would seem low risk after that terrible situation.

Cole was thinking deeply as he climbed onto Rusty and galloped off. I've never searched for a campsite in the dark. I better get moving or I'm going to discover what it's all about.

CHAPTER FIVE

The short man hitched his way aimlessly along the boardwalk of St. Bartow. He was dragging his left foot behind him as if it was an overly long tail and he was a very slow-moving animal. A handkerchief was pulled down over his head favoring the right side of his face. The handkerchief had a hole large enough for an eye to peer out. But on the left side, there was no hole, and no features showing.

Anyone bothering to look could see that the little man was disfigured. The wound around his eye had healed, but the original wound must have been bad. The man must have encountered a large explosion during the War. Men crippled in the War often chose to head west and scratch out a living begging or performing simple jobs rather than returning home, showing off their broken bodies.

No one paid the man any heed; he was just another casualty of a brutal War. After all, many of the maimed passed through St. Bartow. The man hitched down the boardwalk unhurried and undirected. In the fading afternoon light, he was thinking about a place to stay that night. He carried a bedroll of rags strapped on his back. He stopped in front of the sheriff's office, and casually rolled and lit a cigarette while resting his body against the boardwalk railing.

He took several puffs on the cigarette. He then walked his way warily down the boardwalk steps to the muddy roadway below. When he reached the road, he stretched his arms and body, fighting off a surge of afternoon fatigue. He looked around and suddenly ducked under the boardwalk. He had been cautious and no one had seen him.

In the semi-darkness under the boardwalk, he laid himself out on his back and pulled and dragged himself backward, using the joists for leverage. His arms were strong.

Inch by inch, foot by foot, he pulled himself along toward the underside of the sheriff's office. Barely four inches of space separated his body from the joists supporting the boardwalk and the sheriff's office.

He worked his way along until he was directly beneath the office. He knew he had reached his target when he heard voices above. It was like the War again, he thought. He was positioned near the battle line, waiting to strike.

He listened until he heard what he needed to know. He had been told right; the sheriff had been a colonel in the Union Army. The big, young kid had been a soldier for the North. The little man was very satisfied with his cache of information. He chose now to rest his tired body. He dozed and dreamed of his past.

* * * * *

He found out his unit surrendered when his leader marched them into an open field and read a dispatch. The Confederacy had been dissolved. It was no more. He could have fought on. But he was tired and wounded. He had no choice but to surrender. His captain read the surrender terms word for word, very slowly.

They milled around for two days, not knowing what to do. Some of them found parts of uniforms to put on so that if Yankees showed up, they wouldn't think them guerrilla fighters. The Yankees would be tough on guerrilla fighters. A number of soldiers shook hands good-bye and took off for home. The captain turned his head. He acted as though he didn't see them.

Yankee soldiers arrived and formed them into lines. They were required to rip off battle ribbons. One by one, they came off. They stared at each ribbon and rank mark before discarding it. They ripped off stripes and even brass buttons on uniforms. We could have had the Union soldiers rip them off. Hardly anyone did.

A Union soldier nicknamed "paymaster" by the disgruntled soldiers gave out ten Yankee greenbacks to every Confederate soldier. “Go home, Johnny,” he said, grinning like a donkey. “No more soldiering for you. Go pick cotton.” He laughed each time he said it, each time he gave out the money. “You be thankful for General Grant or you be walking yourself, not riding a horse home,” he said seriously.

“Where’s my horse? I don’t have a horse to go home with,” said Bellows. He was serious.

The Yankee soldier stared at him. “You think General Grant gonna give you a horse if General Lee wouldn’t give you one? You kinda stupid, boy. You one to walk home, Johnny.” The Yankee soldiers laughed.

Bellows looked disappointed.

The soldier in front of him in line was with them for several months. He gave up his ten to Buggar Johnson. Buggar was bad off. Both legs gone. We were carrying him in a wagon. Clyde was taking Buggar home. Buggar didn’t want to go. He cried. He never made it home alive, I’m sure.

One soldier tried to give me his ten dollars. I wouldn’t take it. I stared him down. No way I was going home, not looking like this. And no way I’d take his ten dollars either.

Killed eleven Yankees. Hit one from one hundred yards. Got to feel and understand the rifle and the breeze to score at that distance, yes suh.

Sitting up there in a tall tree. A bluejacket pranced by, saluting, smiling, and slapping the rifles held up to welcome him. My loins heaved with excitement as I watched him get closer. My breath bottomed and grew still. I checked the breeze. He stopped his mount. I squeezed the trigger; no jerk, smooth. Powder popped. Smoke tickled my nose. I knew that I had him. The Yankee slumped. The troops paused, frozen.

They ran to the bluejacket as he crashed from his horse.

I’m home now, as a child. At Mr. Bartis’s plantation, niggers cringed when they saw Daddy. Daddy was overseer. Daddy’s niggers got plenty to eat.

A bugle sounded, medals and buttons were ripped off. “War’s over, here’s ten dollars. Go home. Go pick cotton!”

CHAPTER SIX

Cole found high ground a about a mile and half from town to set up camp. There was drinking water nearby and plenty of grass for Rusty. He slept well and the next morning he was surprised to discover that he'd picked a spot half a mile from where a wagon train operator was training drivers. After preparing coffee, Cole sat back and watched the drivers perform.

A grizzled old trail hand was doing the training. He rode up and down the line of wagons shouting commands and advice. He looked and sounded like an army sergeant. From what Cole could hear, his choice of language was rich in profanity. One driver made the mistake of failing to stop his team after the trail hand signaled halt. He nearly crashed into the wagon in front of him. On its own, at the last minute, his team of horses reared up and nearly toppled backward onto the shaken driver.

After that, the driver's wagon was continually out of step with the other wagons. Any confidence the driver had built up slipped away. A meeting between the trail hand and the driver turned into what looked to Cole like a series of physical threats amidst profane shouting. The driver ripped his hat off and threw it into the back of his wagon.

Cole decided to see if he could help. He climbed onto Rusty and rode bareback over to the wagons. At Cole's arrival, the driver threw down his reins and stared maliciously at the trail hand who had wisely decided to exit the scene.

Cole smiled at the driver. The driver talked to him in a foreign language, throwing his arms up and pointing at the departing trail hand. Cole motioned that he would climb into the driver's box and sit by his side. As he climbed in, Cole glanced backward into the wagon and was surprised to see a girl sitting there. Her bare feet were dangling off the tailgate. He had missed her amidst the confusion. Her beauty startled him.

The girl wore a colorful gingham dress and her skin was a light tan. Her body was muscular, more so than Cole would have expected in a young woman. She looked questioningly at him and then looked away, intentionally ignoring him, he decided.

The driver noticed Cole looking at the girl and yelled something that Cole did not understand. It was obvious, though, by her response what he had said . . . "Go find something to do. This man is helping me!"

Cole smiled and winked at the driver. He took up the reins and showed him how to back a team into line. The driver tried it several times and became successful. He smiled at the young girl in the back of the wagon. She ignored him and continued staring off at the horizon. The driver shrugged, as if to say "What can I do?" They both turned to look at the girl. She turned toward them and with her face remaining serious, she stuck her tongue out and quickly looked away. Everyone laughed, including the girl.

It was a cute trick, thought Cole. There must be a lot of independence and respect for each other in this family. It made him think of his own family back in Vermont.

His immediate task over, Cole jumped onto Rusty and started off back to his camp, only to be stopped by the old trainer.

"Howdy, young man. Good work. I got to get this train ready day after tomorrow. Thanks for the help."

"Happy to help," said Cole, smiling. He reached over and grasped the man's hand. "Must be tough for them, not knowing much English."

The trail hand laughed. "Don't believe it, son. They know English better 'n you and me. They just don't want to show it. You scream, they act. I saw it myself. That's the secret, son, of dealing with or training foreigners. Scream at 'em loud." The trail hand rubbed his chin. "You're big, and you know what you're doing. I need help. These immigrants know nothing. They get off a boat in New Orleans, get ferried up here, and buy supplies and a wagon and head west to homestead. And I take them. I gotta be loco for this job." His eyes rose to the top of their sockets.

Cole let the reins drop and waited for the proposal that was sure to come.

"I need help. Mr. Witham, the owner, says I can hire whoever I want for what I want to pay, within reason of course. Right now, the pay's good. How about it?"

A man of action, thought Cole. "Well, sir, I just arrived in St. Bartow. I just started looking around for work. Thanks for the offer. I'll think it over."

"There is another job open son, pays a little more. It's security. It pays more 'cause you can get killed." He laughed from the belly. "Watch out if someone offers you a high-paying job." He laughed again and his belly jiggled again. "You get paid more out here if you get killed." The old guy chortled this time.

Cole saw the driver that he had helped returning.

A shy smile covered his face. "That was good, sir, thank you. Come for food, breakfast. My wife or daughter like you," the man said in passable English.

I guess I should scream out my response so he'll understand, thought Cole, laughing to himself. His wife or his daughter likes me, he wondered. I hope it's his daughter. "Yes, sir, I'd be happy to. I'm camping over there." He pointed across the grassland. "It'll save me cooking. Not my favorite job. Thanks for the offer." Cole told him he'd be right along.

The trainer laughed. "You're in for it now. You saw his daughter. She's a beauty. Sonia. Sonia Josephson. Two men working for Mr. Witham are trying to court her. The old man, he watches her closely. He knows he's got a husky there. Probably will use her to get himself a bigger slice of free land." Again, the trainer rolled his eyes and hopped his belly.

Sonia Josephson. Cole looked over and found her watching him. She quickly turned away.

He thanked the trail hand for the job offer, said goodbye and headed for the Josephsons.

* * * * *

The breakfast was simple but satisfying. Cole missed the family gatherings he was used to. The kidding among the Josephsons was endless.

Mama Josephson turned her attention to Sonia. “She is a joy as a daughter and exciting, Mr. Cole. I think she make good wife too. What do you think?”

“Oh, Mama,” blurted Sonia, covering her red face with both hands of open fingers.

Mr. Josephson added, “But she see things, Mr. Cole, things not in Sweden.” He chuckled lightly and drew smoke through his morning bowl of tobacco. Mr. Josephson stared straight ahead.

“Papa, I don’t make things up. I saw what I saw. It’s scary. And I thought you should know.” Her eyes flashed. “Why bring this up to company if you don’t believe me?”

Mr. Josephson rolled his eyes, smile gone. “Mr. Cole, they grow giant birds here. I think they feed on poor settlers.”

Sonia stood up and pointed at her father. “Daddy, you are making me look silly. Mr. Cole doesn’t want to hear how silly you think I am.” She glared at her father and got up, ready to leave the circle. “Leave me alone,” she said.

Cole was listening with increasing interest. “Wait, Sonia, please tell me what happened.”

She frowned at Cole. “Okay, Mr. Cole. But don’t laugh and please keep father quiet. That will be a difficult task.”

She sat down. “In the evening, I take my dog, you see him tied up over there, out for a walk, just before dark, always. One evening I got no more than out of sight of the wagons when three big birds fly over. Two landed in the bushes, but the third I think landed in the dark just out of my sight. That third one comes back toward me and it is a man, not a bird. The big bird has turned into a man.”

"Did the man speak to you?" asked Cole.

Sonia looked surprised that Cole was treating her story seriously. "Yes, the man said I was very beautiful," she said, blushing. "He said I could be a queen if I came with him. I was frightened. He sensed it, I think, and he told me he'd protect me. He said he had a beautiful piece of jewelry in his pocket and that he'd give it to me. He came over to show it. I could see even at a distance that the jewel was sparkling and beautiful. I actually began to believe I could become a queen if I had that beautiful jewel."

"How did you get away?" asked Cole. He was finding that the story had similarities with the sheriff's story about the young farm boy who had gotten killed up near Chilson.

"Mr. Cole, I found I really wanted it. I almost think I was going to go with him. But my dog started to bark. He pulled on his leash, wanting to attack the man. The man pulled away. He hissed at the dog—a frightening hiss. I never heard a human hiss like that. It scared the dog to death. He took off and I ran with him back to the wagon."

What is this? Cole wondered. These beasts, if that's what they are, are aggressively gathering in threes to attack a beautiful immigrant girl. Cole was alarmed and dumbfounded by the tale. What was going on?

"See, Mr. Cole, silly, silly," Mrs. Josephson said with a sweep of her hand. "Maybe after she becomes a queen she can get someone to help me keep the wagon clean, yes?"

"See, Mr. Cole, they don't believe me, and you probably don't believe me either. Well, I saw the man the next night, and the dog barked at him again. We ran off together back to the wagon. If I didn't have my dog to protect me, I'd probably be dead."

Cole saw tears in Sonia's eyes.

"Or a queen," said Mr. Josephson, thoughtfully, continuing his puffing.

"Daddy!" screamed Sonia, jumping to her feet, angry and ready to cry.

Cole didn't want to scare Sonia or the Josephsons but did want to make them aware of the seriousness of the situation. “Look,” he said, “don’t any of you go out alone after dusk.”

“What you mean, Cole?” asked Mr. Josephson, his chin dropping.

“A kind of beast has been sighted in the St. Bartow area. It is said to be possibly both animal and human. It targets humans, as far as is known. It can imitate human speech.”

“Cole, you mean Sonia is right, she was in danger?” asked Mr. Josephson. He dropped his pipe, jumped up, and ran to his daughter putting his arms around her.

“Yes, I’m serious,” Cole said firmly, “I’m very serious. I believe what Sonia says she saw. I want you all to promise that none of you will go beyond the perimeter of the wagon train after dusk. Do you all agree?” He looked at each one of them.

The Josephsons were taken aback. They hadn’t expected Cole’s reaction at all. The family members all nodded. They were ready for bed and with a lot to think about.

Cole said good night and gave Sonia a special look of support. She didn’t turn away this time; she gave him a look of gratitude that showed a warmth he had not noticed before.

Cole swung up onto Rusty and headed back to camp. He wondered what the beasts were, how many people they were stalking, and how many beasts were out there.

CHAPTER SEVEN

Sheriff Lawton rose early the next morning. Another day, another set of problems, he thought as he poured himself the first of several tins of coffee he'd have that day. Lawton was a disciplined man; he led his life by a series of simple rules whenever possible. Some would consider those rules compulsions but to Lawton they gave his life structure, assured his survival, and were a source of pride and a trademark of his life.

Lawton slept six hours each night—exactly six hours. He'd go to bed at ten and rise at four in the morning. He knew that his mind and body required six hours of sleep to function at peak level. Sleeping for a longer period was a waste of time, and taking a nap in the daytime was a waste of life.

Rising at four in the morning was not just a routine calling for Lawton. He enjoyed it, as he had come to enjoy many of the other activities he had initially begun by rule. He really enjoyed making love to Mrs. Lawton at four in the morning on Tuesdays and Sundays. He believed that she had come to appreciate it too. Lawton found that his lovemaking schedule freed his mind from random thoughts of sex and helped him keep his mind concentrated—an essential quality for people in his field.

Lawton also prided himself on what others considered his unusual ideas about law enforcement. Take the subject of lawmen: Most persons, including lawmen themselves, thought a quick draw was the defining quality of talented, effective lawmen. "Bull," Lawton would say. "True only if gun battles were the beginning and the end of a law officer's work." They weren't. Deadly force was infrequently needed and when it was, it represented a failure at peacekeeping efforts.

Skilled lawmen could anticipate gun battles and maneuver to avoid them. Intelligence, good character and flexibility were the traits of really good lawmen, Lawton believed. Good lawmen worked to conciliate differences before a confrontation turned lethal. Lawton would accept deadly force but only as a last resort.

Towns with quick-gun lawmen generally had the most killings and were not safe, by any means. Lawton didn't believe that to be a coincidence. Killings by lawmen or by outlaws or citizens in vigilante groups were all just that, killings. Killing in some towns became the major way to solve problems and it created fear and an expectation among the population. Lawton pointed to Dodge City as a town where violence was rampant and lawmen's behavior was not a small source of the problem.

The house suddenly felt stuffy. I guess I've philosophized enough, he thought. Lawton went over and opened the front door. A light breeze blew up from the river, stirring the curtains and swaying the multicolored flowers. Mrs. Lawton worked hard planting the flowers and took pride in watering them and picking spent buds. Her interest in the appearance of the house pleased the sheriff. She had created a lovely oasis for them here on the edge of town.

Lawton sat down and resumed thinking. Most lawmen strove to affect a deadly image, and many got killed because of it. He tried hard not to go down that path. There was the time Krugger came to St. Bartow. Lawton had been sheriff for only a few years. When word arrived that Krugger was on his way, the good citizens panicked. Krugger was one of the fastest guns around and had a well-deserved reputation for killing.

When Lawton received confirmation about Krugger, he followed his regular plan, without deviation, for the next few days. He had planned to go up into the hills to look into some rustling, so he did just that. When he returned, Krugger had been drunk for several days and had scared the hell out of the town. Lawton disarmed and jailed the drunk Krugger.

Once the gunman was in jail, Lawton made sure he felt the weight of the Lord on him.

Other lawmen would have tested mettle with Krugger. Going off to do work in the hills would have been seen as cowardly. Bull, Lawton would say. I'm alive and Krugger is out there in the forest searching for a soul, and none of the citizens under my protection are pushing daisies. That means I won.

Lawton's thoughts turned to the sniper. How could he use his strengths to end the sniper's terror? The sniper bothered him more than he let on. In his thinking, Lawton saw a direct relationship between being disciplined and being virtuous. But from what he could observe, the sniper used discipline to kill innocent people; in fact, people without any meaning to him. To Lawton, such behavior was an ethical contradiction.

The sniper had to be insane. He might be into religion or politics, be a former soldier, a local crazy or a lonely immigrant. But if he kills for anything but wealth or love, he's insane.

Developing a plan to take down an insane dry-gulcher was simple, he thought. There was risk in it, though, for the person chosen as bait. For that, he needed an aggressive man without "fear on his sleeve" and young enough to not quite understand his mortality. The new young man, Cole Mason, was a perfect candidate. To get the sniper, it was necessary to collapse his freedom of action, either in time or territory. Make the bait so enticing that the sniper would act immediately. And limit the territory where the bait would be available . . . like setting a trap for a rat in your front room using a strong trap and a piece of smelly fatback.

The sniper was a big problem, larger than most realized. The townspeople missed the big picture. They thought themselves free if the sniper didn't aim his long rifle at them. But a sniper could do worse; he could tarnish a town's image. Businesses would stop growing. Homesteaders would choose other towns to depart from. They'd take their wealth to these other towns. St. Bartow could die. There were dead towns all over the Midwest for one reason or another, not the least one being a steady rise in violent killings.

Nowadays with newspapermen embedded in towns up and down the edge of the West, the awareness of violence was more widespread. Reporters using telegraph wires sent descriptions of violence throughout the country. That was particularly true of investigative reporters like that Jesse Fallon, the *Tribune's* in-town drunk. That guy sniffed like a fly after bear dung. Well, he's dead now. Wasn't really a bad guy. Brave's monster picked that target well. Lawton smiled lightly.

The sniper thing has to end. Publicity will bring in the army. That's all he needed . . . a company or two of battle-scarred soldiers on a Saturday night. Lawton poured another tin of coffee. He'd better slow down. The wife will hear me and think it's Sunday, four o'clock. If she sees I'm not there she'll start getting ready for church. He laughed to himself. He heard her stirring now in the bedroom.

Time to head for town and relieve Brave. He's a good man, that Brave, for a half-breed. Strange how animal killings set him off. His eyes gloss over. Terrible way to go, regardless of what's doing it. The animal must hide in the caves up there behind Surley Hill. Those caves are deep and connecting. Never been explored, far as he knew. Once, the town thought the guerrillas were making headquarters out there. Maybe townsmen can organize themselves and go through the caves carrying torchlights. Flush the thing out. Seems as though there were some stories from down New Orleans about bloodsucking back a few years ago. Probably should get a dispatch out to them. Gotta use that new technology.

The sheriff grabbed his hat and walked out the back door. He looked hard around the barn and adjoining woods. He saddled his horse and swung onto it. He touched his mustache. Another rule. It was smooth. Appearance was important in law enforcement.

Lawton was not eager to get to St. Bartow today. It was a beautiful day . . . a break from the rain. The air was clean. No odor. Unusual.

Lawton glanced up behind him to the hill—another behavior by rule. He saw a reflection. Sun on metal. Instantly he dove off his horse, hitting the ground lightly and rolling and grabbing for his holstered gun. Lawton had practiced that roll many times. He heard a sound of whistling air pass close to his ear. A split-second later he heard the crack of a rifle.

CHAPTER EIGHT

Soon after leaving the Josephsons, Cole departed for St. Bartow and his meeting with the sheriff. While riding into town, Sonia filled his thoughts. Rawboned, blonde and outspoken Sonia. What a saucy and beautiful woman, he thought. Such a difference from women in Vermont. She was definitely part of a new breed, those women learning to survive in the New West.

Sonia was Swedish and that made Cole curious about the world beyond the Union. He was not sure where Sweden was but he knew it was in Europe and that girls there had hair as yellow as corn. He was deeply concerned about her welfare. Her story of the three birds and the strange man was ugly and scary. He wished he could stay close to her and protect her. Fortunately, her dog and parents were there to keep her safe.

Cole arrived in St. Bartow at about nine. The town was awakening. Most of the windows in the houses and doors in the businesses were closed. Although the rain was over, puddles still pockmarked the roads. A few buckboards were out bouncing around making early deliveries. These people get up late, he thought. He was anxious for the meeting with the sheriff. He hoped the sheriff hadn't had second thoughts about taking him on. Cole had decided he really wanted the job.

While riding along waiting for the town to open up, Cole saw the two boys from the day before. They were walking toward him. "The Mouth" and "Mr. Crazy," he thought. What a couple of odd ones. He owed the two something more than a toss in the mud puddle. They had obligated him to protect Marchess, which in turn had led to his having to accept a drink from the old man. Some big, horrible penance is due those boys, he thought jokingly.

Cole watched the boys meander side by side down the road toward him. He didn't want to be blindsided should they have deviltry left in them. Road bums get up early, he thought. Probably have no place to sleep. The dumb one was grinning and was wearing a white dunce's hat and silly pants, too short by at least an arm's length.

When they got close to Cole, the bigger one, the talker, raised his hand in a peace salute. "Sir, we want to talk, that's all, just talk."

They look harmless this morning, thought Cole. Maybe they want to make amends. It's too early for another brush, anyway. Cole yelled out with authority, "Look, get smart. Don't pick on an old man. He was a doctor and old enough to be your grandfather. Find someone your own age to pick on." Cole hoped by taking the initiative the two would be set back on their heels.

"Mister, we didn't pick on that man, no, not at all," said the talker.

"You didn't? It didn't appear you were passing time, that's for sure."

"He paid us to tease him. He saw you riding up and he offered us money to make his life miserable. He wanted you to save him. Honest as honest is . . ."

What is this? Are they crazy? Road thugs and lousy liars too? Useless, lost kids. They hang out on corners, fight, spit at each other, and hit on passersby for coppers. Cole anticipated another battle,

"You're aiming for another ride into a puddle. I can see it coming. This time for lying."

"No sir, not again. Right, Pete?" The bigger one turned to his sidekick. Pete grinned, displaying a mouthful of black and broken teeth.

Pete agrees to anything, thought Cole. He's probably a moron. He'd probably agree to a flat Earth. Cole decided the fight was gone out of the boys. They wanted forgiveness or acceptance. Maybe he could get information out of them. Here I go, he thought, using them to get something, like everyone else. "Well, okay, I accept your explanation. Besides, I'd hate to have to toss you after a single tin of coffee."

"Mister, what are you? Where are you going? You're not a trail hand, or farmer, or a wagon driver or lawman or gunslinger. What are you, and how'd you get so strong?"

Cole grinned. "If we're friends, tell me your names. My name is Cole."

"Carl, my name's Carl," said the leader, "and soon-to-be toothless here, he's Pete."

Pete punched Carl hard on his shoulder and scampered to safety a few feet away.

He's not all dumb, thought Cole. He understood that and he knew enough to run off! Cole grinned. "Well, I'll tell you my secret. Hard work on a farm and a stint in the Union Army, that's how I did it. But my horse, Rusty, he's really a tough guy, not a thoroughbred but he's got a strain of Morgan horse blood in him. He was born strong. He worked on a farm but never spent a day in the Army. In a weight-pulling contest, I'd put him up against any horse in the county."

"Can you lift a wagon by yourself?" asked Carl, more awed by Cole's strength than by Rusty's.

"Sure, as long as it's small," Cole said, and smiled.

The two boys grinned.

"We got something to tell you," said Carl. "Won't cost you anything."

"Ya, the guy's a bird," said Pete, tonelessly.

First time he's spoken, thought Cole. He can talk. Looks serious too. "Who's a bird?" asked Cole, looking at Pete.

"Wait, you," said Carl. He elbow-shoved Pete. "Let me talk. The guy, Mr. Medicine, pays us to find out where certain people live, things like that. And when he saw you on the road, he paid us to tease you."

"And he's a bird," screamed out Pete.

Pete looked frightened. Carl was center stage. Pete kept trying to shove Carl so he could talk.

"Mister, we didn't choose to pick on the man," Carl continued, jumping about and warding off Pete. "He paid us. He saw you coming and he wanted you to save him, we think. That's the truth, so help me, Mr. Cole."

Cole was puzzled. Why would Marchess do that? Are they lying?

Pete broke in now. "Ya, medicine man disappears. Up in the sky."

"Ah," said Carl in disgust, "let me tell it. You can't talk. Pete here said he saw the old guy turn into a bird, a bat, he says. Some kind of bird, right, Pete." Carl laughed. He put his arms out and waved them up and down imitating a bird while circling Pete and laughing and cawing like a crow.

An angry Pete chased after Carl. Carl continued to dart about around Carl and in front of Cole with hands flapping and crow sounds coming from his mouth. Pete reached down and picked up handfuls of mud and threw them at Carl.

Pete may not be sitting on a tied saddle but he sure wants to make his point, thought Cole. He saw what he saw and it's worth a fight to make his point.

"What a show," Cole yelled. He pulled several 2-cent pieces out of his pocket and tossed them at the boys. The boys grabbed as soon as the coins hit the mud. They were digging furiously as Cole rode off. He was still chuckling when he arrived at the sheriff's.

Swinging off Rusty, Cole thought of Willoughby. Willoughby . . . counting people and flying like a bird. What was that all about? And turning into a bat, a crow of some kind? That was the third time he had heard birds mentioned in an evil way—the sheriff's tale of the farm kid, Sonia's tale, and now this thing from Pete. Was Marchess involved in this?

Cole tied Rusty to the railing in front of the sheriff's office. Back home, you'd hear these tales in front of a fire on a cold night. He shrugged and headed for the sheriff's door.

CHAPTER NINE

Natalie lived at the Talbot House in St. Bartow for three years. Lady's, as it was called, was a whorehouse, the most highly regarded in St. Bartow. The girls at Lady's were clean, appealing and well dressed, whether lounging in the house or strolling the boardwalks.

As fitting its status, the house charged the highest rates in town, as much as six dollars per session, and the chosen lady expected a generous gratuity too. This policy succeeded in excluding as clientele everyday riffraff and in sustaining the house's reputation.

The women at Lady's performed an array of functions not usually associated with brothels, like helping patrons bathe, barbering, shaving, and washing clients' clothes. If you behaved and one of the ladies thought you a good tipper, she might even rustle up nibble food for you from the kitchen. The word across Missouri was that there was nothing in Kansas City that Lady's didn't have right there in the little town of St. Bartow.

The owner of the house and the business, Lady Talbot, was very proud of her creation. She gave the house her first name, Lady. Rumor had it, probably accurately, that Lady had been born in Liverpool, England, where she started as a whore before opening her first house. Like many others of her day, she came to America from England seeking greater opportunities. Arriving on a ship in New York, she worked her way west plying her trade until she reached St. Bartow. She settled there and began her new business.

Being English, Lady was fastidious in her personal ways, and her ways became standard for all the girls in the house. Each of Lady's fourteen girls bathed at least once a week and several, two and three times a week. This standard was enforced by Lady and her manager, which was no easy trick.

As would be expected, Lady Talbot was a good businesswoman. Her record with the sheriff's office was unblemished. Rarely was the law called upon to remove a patron for drunkenness, for smashing something, or for threatening a girl or behaving just plain nasty. Part of her success came of course from patrons' fears of being excluded from the house for the remainder of their lives if they acted improperly.

Natalie was the only Negro woman employed at Lady's. She came to Lady's after being freed at the end of the War. She was considered by the clientele to be beautiful and sexually attractive. Her presence at Lady's soon became legend.

To be clear, Natalie was not now a whore at Lady's. She started as one, however. Before she arrived in St. Bartow, Natalie's first moneymaking job was as a saloon dancer and singer. The position was a disaster and she walked away from it. She was sick when she arrived in St. Bartow and didn't understand why she always felt so badly. (Later she found she had reccurring bouts of melancholia.) With nowhere else to turn, she applied for a position at Lady's. She decided there was no other kind of work for a Negro woman that would give her greater independence.

She began at Lady's as a prostitute but failed miserably. Men's wild nature aggravated her melancholia. She couldn't abide drunk and wild behavior. She couldn't have sex with men she didn't feel safe with, even if they behaved well. After a month of agony she decided she'd had enough.

Lady Talbot was a shrewd businesswoman. She wasn't about to let this striking, intelligent, tall and beautiful black woman out of her employment. Lady's prestige had been on the rise and she knew that Natalie was one of the reasons. To keep Natalie, she offered her the position of house manager.

Lady had observed that Natalie was good with numbers and got along well with the girls. Lady offered her a fair salary and promised her that prostitution was not a part of her work. Natalie trusted Lady's word. She took the job and it wasn't long before she decided she enjoyed it. Natalie found herself developing confidence for the first time in her life.

Natalie would arise early before the traffic grew heavy so she could watch the town come to life. She would look out her window, across the road, and see light in the sheriff's office. The light gave her security.

She watched Deputy Brave leave each morning on his rounds. She liked Brave. He was sensitive and thoughtful. He never patronized Lady's and she was pleased about that. She wondered sometimes how it would be to make love with him. She'd blush about that thought, which surprised and pleased her too.

This morning it was still dark outside but with enough light to see the few wagons moving along the road. Usually Natalie had the parlor next door and the window to herself, but this morning several of the girls were up. Laughter came from the parlor. It was Pony and her wild laugh. Natalie smiled, shaking her head. Pony was a dear.

"The guy was little, like a dwarf." Pony couldn't control her laughter. "How else could he be going to it like that and I be able to feel his tongue on my bellybutton! I don't know what he thought he had a hold of!" She laughed again. "Short men are attracted to me," she continued after laughing subsided.

She was enjoying lead role, thought Natalie.

"They like my thighs," Pony concluded with a flash of serious pride. She lifted her knees and her robe fell open, exposing shapely thighs.

"S'not your thighs, Miss Po," interjected Fancy, "it's your name, 'Pony.' Men want you 'cause they want to ride you low and hard and have no risk of falling."

Laughter filled the room again, including a new burst from Pony.

"Hey, ladies, be quiet, you're upsetting my dwarf," a voice called from beyond the parlor.

There was another round of uncontrollable laughter.

"Better lock up your bellybutton, Victoria," Pony called to the back room.

The girls are being silly, thought Natalie. Business must have been slow.

Half-listening to the girls in the next room, Natalie began an assessment of her life. The girls were coarse here, but honest, and the money was good. Lady Talbot was fair. Natalie felt secure for the first time in her life. Before St. Bartow, she had tried working as a singer and dancer. On the plantation, she stayed awake dreaming of her coming fame as a singer and dancer. And then she had an opportunity to perform in a saloon in New Orleans. She found she couldn't handle the men. She'd be taunted and propositioned, her breasts felt for, and her private areas grabbed. Unlike some entertainers who were able, she couldn't respond in a way to get the men off her back. She simply became terrified.

She came to believe that she did not understand men at all. When sober, they were shy and polite, but when drunk they were wild and aggressive. Saloon owners were no better. They saw no difference between a dancer and a whore. She often had to sleep with an owner to get the money she had made as a singer.

"I can bathe on a single bucket of water," Folly confided. "That includes washing everything, right, Napie? Napie says he enjoys helping me bathe because it means he has to lug just one bucket from the well, right, Nap?"

Napie was the inside security man, cook and handyman. He was preparing food up the way in the kitchen. "Ya, Fol, that's right, whatever you say," he replied. "But I think you don't reach the far places. I think you'd need another six or seven buckets for that."

The listeners soared out their laughter again.

Folly was hurt. "Thanks, Nap, the smell didn't seem to bother you the other night," she shot back.

"Don't worry, Fol, since I been in St. Bartow, I can't tell smells no more anyway," Napie deadpanned.

Another round of laughter came from the parlor.

Natalie grinned. The smell was often offensive in town and Napie's jokes about it were funny. One way the girls acknowledged his help was by giving him free services. He enjoyed the girls. He played no favorites and they all treated him well.

Natalie turned and looked back at the road. It was lighter now and the traffic was getting heavier. She thought of the killing down by the river. A woman had been found dead there last week. She was a street whore, a heavy drinker. Natalie hadn't known her. According to a client, her blood had been sucked out. Her neck was punctured in two spots, each one purple colored and the size of a half-dollar.

Natalie thought of the plantation upriver from New Orleans; it was never far from her mind. And stirrings of melancholia, a weakness in her stomach, and abject fear accompanied these thoughts. It seemed so long ago but it was only four years. The owner of the plantation was a beast. He was known to kill the same way the poor woman in St. Bartow had been killed. Could the beast from New Orleans be loose here in St. Bartow? Possibly. But hadn't the guns from the Yankee Navy put the plantation up in flames? Was she ever to free herself of paralyzing fear? Feeling the pain of the past, she bowed her head and closed her eyes.

After a few moments, she stared out again at the muddy road. She didn't feel free today. The sun was striking the tops of the trees and would soon begin its trek down the buildings. She saw a man riding down the road. His horse had short, powerful looking legs. He was big and strong looking himself. She imagined him as handsome, polite, clean, intelligent, sensitive, and on his way to meet her. He stopped and talked to two young men on the road. She had seen those two before, always up to no good. Tough road boys, she thought.

The rider laughed as he talked. He was enjoying himself. The boys began chasing each other, sometimes playfully, sometimes not so playfully. They spit at each other.

Well, that is the progression. First fists, then spit, then rocks. What wonderful behavior, she thought sarcastically.

The rider reached into his pocket and threw something to the boys. Probably a coin or two, she guessed. Young road boys were always needing money for something. Probably they had sold the nice-looking man the location of Lady's. She grinned at the idea.

The boys scurried after the coins.

The rider rode off laughing. His hair was long but combed like they do it in the East. He rode to the sheriff's office.

A lawman, she guessed. Her breath warmed and her cheeks reddened.

The rider knocked on the sheriff's door, waited a moment, and walked in.

Natalie suddenly felt very alone. She caught movement out of the corner of her eye. Was someone else watching? She looked to her right and saw an odd-looking old man standing under the protection of the eves of the Silver Dollar Saloon. He was short and dressed in a fancy suit and a bowler hat. She realized he had been watching the rider too.

Her sixth sense told her that the man was sinister. She trembled and gasped. She must warn the rider of the danger he was in.

"A lady your size," Dolly was explaining, "needs more than a bucket of water to get clean, Fol, she needs a river."

Natalie shut her mind to the talk from the next room. She concentrated on the strange, bowler-hatted figure recessed into the shadows of the saloon. She watched as the man raised his arms, flapped them and began to turn into . . . a bird . . . no, a bat.

Oh, it's him, he's here! Her mouth flew open. The beast is here. He's found me! She felt drained. She saw the bat flying toward her. It flew deliberately, as if in slow motion. It knows I've been watching, she thought in terror.

The bat turned its head toward her as it flew by.

"It's my master's face," she whispered and cowered in fear.

"Girls like you, my Marsha, drown their body in sweet powder," Daisy was saying.

But Natalie didn't hear her. She heard nothing more. Her mind was fixed on the bird. The sun would soon be up. That would save her today. She watched the beast circle overhead.

He must have a lair nearby, she thought. Natalie yanked shut the red satin tarp over her window. She grabbed a hat and shawl from her closet, ran out her door and down the steps of Lady's. Out on the boardwalk she looked up at the clear sky. The bat was nowhere. The sun was now hitting the very tops of the taller buildings. She must warn the rider of the evil that had been watching him. She walked toward the sheriff's office as quickly as her legs could carry her.

CHAPTER TEN

When Cole pushed open the door and walked into the sheriff's office, he half-expected to see the sheriff sitting at his desk being shaved. But instead Cole found himself face to face with a wide-awake and serious Deputy Brave. The sheriff was not in.

Brave was a shorter man than Cole had realized. Sitting at the sheriff's desk, his feet barely reached the floor. He was husky, though, with a broad chest and muscular arms. Probably he stood five feet eight in height, Cole guessed, and weighed maybe two hundred pounds. His high cheekbones and dark coloring came from his mother's side, he decided.

"I came to see the sheriff," Cole said, smiling. "We talked a few minutes yesterday about a job. Do you know when he'll be in, Deputy?"

Brave was dressed in black. The only other color about his apparel was the white clasp on the handle of a gun strapped to his waist. He wore a black buckskin shirt with black leather frills. The whites of his eyes stood out against the dark clothing and complexion. A tough, good-looking man, Cole concluded, a person you'd think twice about, before crossing.

"Lawton should be along any minute. Should have arrived an hour ago." Brave shrugged as if to say his lateness wasn't unusual. Brave walked over to another table in the office, sat down and began to clean a rifle. The rifle was new and up-to-date—a pump action that expelled a spent shell while automatically pumping a new one into its chamber.

"Well, I'll wait for him," said Cole, "if it's okay with you and seeing he'll be along shortly."

"Suit yourself," Brave said, "and grab yourself some coffee." He pointed to a pot steaming in the fireplace. "Ain't Mom's but it serves the bill."

Cole poured some into a tin and took a sip. Brave was right, it wasn't Mom's. Brave gotta be a better lawman than coffee maker, Cole concluded. He spread himself out in a chair not far from where Brave was working. "Sheriff was concerned yesterday about killings around St. Bartow. You got thoughts on that, Deputy?"

Yeah," said Brave, glancing at Cole. "Can't figure it. There has to be something wrong here." He kept cleaning his rifle; having finished the barrel, he moved to the stock.

Cole took another sip of coffee. "Seems there's two kinds of killings, right? One, the killer lies in wait and shoots a passerby from a distance. And in the other, the victim has his blood drained through the neck by a bat or by some other animal. Is that the way you see it, Deputy?"

"That's about it," said Brave, his voice a pitch higher. He glanced again at Cole.

A strange look came over him.

Brave was turning gaunt. He suddenly appeared prepared for battle, like an Indian warrior.

Is war paint forming on his brow? wondered Cole. Am I imagining this? It must be the shadows.

"How many people do you think were killed the second way, having blood sucked out?" Cole continued sipping his coffee, fascinated by Brave's changing appearance.

"Twelve in a two-year period that we're aware of, eight men, four women. All young. Seven bodies were found out in the country, five right here in St. Bartow. Victims here in town were killed at night. Bodies were discovered the next morning. Those killed outside town, we don't know when they were killed. Likely the same, killed at night."

Buffing the rifle stock, Brave's hands moved in a fervor. He glanced up at Cole again.

This time, Cole felt he was primed for battle. Brave looked into the distance, far beyond the end wall of the room.

The man's a warrior, thought Cole, and ready for battle. Cole recalled a memory from years ago near Petersburg in Virginia, looking across the field for Rebels. He felt then like

Brave looked now, ready for battle. Cole wondered whether he too had looked battle ready.

"The victims offered no resistance as far as we could tell," Brave continued. "Most had been drinking heavily. One was a top hand for a cattle outfit moving through the area. According to the report, he had left town drunk with a lot of cash on his person. He had quit the drive. The money was still there on his body. The sheriff believes money isn't an object in these killings. That's why he tends toward 'the animal did it' theory."

Brave surveyed his cleaning job, then said, "The killing the other day was of a newspaperman, Jesse Fallon. The man was around town for a long time. His body was found near the Silver Dollar Saloon just up the road. He had been drinking pretty much from late afternoon. The telltale markings stood right out on his neck. His hat was a few feet away. Fallon wasn't a favorite of the sheriff's. The guy drank a lot, was real nosey and forever behaving like an Eastern know-it-all. He liked to build himself up in his stories, I guess. Lawton thinks his newspaper—it's big back East—will tar the town for his killing. Lawton is concerned how these killings make St. Bartow look. Worried about the appearance. Reflects on him, you know."

"And I understand you believe a human did these killings, right?" asked Cole. "A human that sucks out and drinks blood?"

Brave looked away. When he turned back, his eyes had narrowed. His appearance had begun to change again.

This is strange, thought Cole. He could swear that war paint was appearing on Brave's cheeks and forehead.

"Not a human. What I believe is not understood. My background is different. I am half-Indian and lived in an Indian village north of here until I was seventeen."

"No, I didn't know you lived as an Indian. How has it affected your understanding of these killings?" asked Cole.

"I have experienced different truths. My uncle is a medicine man. He is smart and has great knowledge of human behavior. He told me stories of men who changed into animals and behaved in evil ways." Brave was trembling now. "In fact, I heard tribal elders speak of soul-like creatures who lived in a world midway between life and death. The creatures represented the dead and they returned to the human world, but only as evil."

Brave pulled a large handkerchief from his pocket and mopped his forehead. "How they got to the middle world, I do not know. How they returned, I do not know. Why they returned only as evil, I do not know. When they arrived they took on different forms: as bats, as wolves, as humans. My mother's people believed what returned represented a concentration of the evil that existed in varying degrees in all humans. The form of the appearance of the evil, animal or human, depended upon the form the evil chose to be in at the time it was seen."

Cole thought of poor Sonia; she was never far from his mind. Should he ask Brave to interpret Sonia's experience with the bats and the human who wanted to make her a queen? He thought better of it. Brave might think he was taking his side of his disagreement with Lawton. There was nothing to be gained by talking with Brave about it now. He would keep the information handy.

"You know," said Cole, "there are many disturbances going on. A lot of them right here in the West. The War, slavery, immigration, new religious sects, hatred among sects, fights between ranchers and farmers, immigrants with odd religions, some with loyalty to Rome, battles with Indians, and Indians massacring whites, and whites slaughtering Indians, torture as a tool by practically every group, and on and on and on."

Brave concentrated on the rifle and didn't look at Cole.

"What I mean," Cole continued, "I see a lot of evil. I see it on sides that are supposed to be right and sides that are thought to be wrong. It's impossible to believe that one individual or group is solely responsible for the evil. In fact, sometimes you can't see which group is the real evil . . . the evil that is out there or the evil that is trying to destroy the evil out there."

By now, Brave had put the rifle down and was gazing at Cole, who felt inspired to continue.

"If there is an ability to exist partway between life and death and it concentrates the evil in human behavior, there is no shortage of the supply of evil in people today—intemperate behavior is all over the place."

Cole held his hand up to stop Brave from interrupting. "That's far from saying, Brave, that I agree with your tribal elders. But it does admit confusion. We live in a world of great uncertainty. Machines are coming out that will change even more greatly the world we live in. I'm sure it'll make it possible for even more forms of evil. What I'm saying, I guess, is that I want to remain open to all possibilities."

Cole believed he had impressed Brave with his observations, and frankly, it was his true opinion.

"A significant point here," said Brave, "is that Indians and other so-called primitive cultures accept that evil can take a human form, although the way it becomes a human form may not be understood or agreed upon."

"How do you catch and kill a beast?" asked Cole, starting in a new direction.

"It's difficult," Brave answered. "You find its presence or body, if you will, in the daylight. It will be asleep, in a trance. You drive a wooden spear through its heart."

"Ouch," said Cole, his eyes growing big. "I take it this is tribal knowledge."

"Yes, tribal knowledge, as you put it. You can burn beasts too. A beast can't survive fire or direct sunlight, unless it's protected well by a thick coat of wax. The wax protects a beast from daylight, but not from fire. Wax works for beasts well into mornings and in late afternoons. It works not so well in the direct sunlight. It is easy to identify a beast when it's in human form with wax protection. Not all beasts have access to the wax, though."

That sure describes Willoughby, thought Cole. He must have gotten hold of a mother lode of wax. He was wearing so much of it he looked silly. So I shared a whiskey with a beast! Cole shook his head, feeling lucky to be alive. "Are there outward signs of a beast, like horns or something? You can't just throw a spear into people sleeping, hoping you kill a beast."

"No, no," said Brave. His rifle rolled off his lap. "A beast can't wake up if it's daytime. There's a smell of death about a beast too, a rancid, moldy odor. You couldn't misjudge a human sleeping, for a beast in a trance."

Brave's upset by my thickness on the subject, Cole thought. But what does a Vermont boy know about beasts? A beast to me was my father when he was getting insistent about performing some work I wasn't ready to do. Brave described Marchess perfectly. It's hard to believe that runty little man is a beast. I'll have to think about that one. "How about his hands, when a beast is out in the daylight protected by wax, are his hands hot or cold?"

"I don't know," said Brave, puzzled.

Cole thought Brave might suspect he knew more about beasts than he was letting on. "Brave, I can see why the sheriff has trouble grabbing onto this. I find it interesting, though. How can these—"

A rising level of yelling and cursing came sweeping into the office from outside. To Cole it sounded like a horseman, or horsemen, riding at full speed and unaware of the rules of the road. Whatever it was, it was scattering the wagons and everything in its path and raising a chorus of curses.

Cole decided it was a single horse as it came to an abrupt stop in front of the office. Brave looked at Cole, drew his gun, and moved to the door. Before he reached it, Sheriff Lawton burst in. He looked out of sorts to Cole; not the cool man he had witnessed yesterday.

"The bastard tried to dry-gulch me! He was sitting on the hill behind my cottage. I saw the sun reflecting off his barrel. If he'd been in the shade, I'd be buzzard meat. I dove off my horse, the ball missed. I chased the bastard for ten miles. Lost him in the rocks up near Colton's spread."

Lawton threw himself into his chair. He quickly leaped up and poured himself a tin of coffee. His hands were shaking as he dropped back into his chair. His shirt was open, sleeves torn. Dirt was smeared across his face and hands. He was hatless. His sharp appearance of the day before was gone.

"I'll get a posse together," said Brave, moving toward the door.

"He's long gone, Brave, don't bother," growled Lawton. "But I did pick up a useful lead. It'll help." Lawton raised his middle and index fingers, forming a victory symbol. "A big lead. I know the source of the rifle he uses. And maybe a motive."

"What?" said Brave.

The sheriff paced the room as he spoke. "I've heard the sound of his killer rifle before. It's a large bore rifle made specifically for the military. Made in Springfield, Massachusetts. Because of its length and the size of the charge it takes, the sound it makes is unique. You won't forget it. I heard it at Shiloh. Reb snipers used the monster to cut down high-ranking Union officers."

"How did Rebs get a rifle made in Massachusetts?" asked Cole.

"Easy," said Lawton, staring at Cole like he didn't understand the purpose of the question. "The coast was like a sieve during the War. The Rebs used blockade runners. They'd unload into smaller boats out at sea and haul the stuff in. That's how they got the bulk of their weapons. It's business. This is the era of business. War is just another opportunity for commerce."

The sheriff plopped down again into his chair. His eyes turned to slits. "I was aide to Brigadier Smithson. We were on a hill overlooking the action playing out below. Suddenly Colonel Johnhower, a fellow officer, was struck dead by a rifle ball in his neck. I heard the rifle. You never forget a sound like that. This morning I heard it again. The rifle had the sound of reverberations in a hollowed-out cannon."

The sheriff paused and squinted at Cole. "Mason, right? This a social or business visit?"

"Business. Sheriff, I want to be a part of your effort to put an end to that sniper."

The sheriff's face lit up briefly, then he frowned. "Look Mason, I'm pleased at your offer, but let me be frank. The job's extremely dangerous. The dry-gulcher killed at least twelve persons, maybe more. That's one every three, four weeks. He's crazy. He gives no warning. He's disciplined. That's what makes him so effective. Hell, you might be a little silly, be out on your burro, and the bastard sees you coming down a trail and he drills you. Killing's his satisfaction. Doesn't want money. Really crazy." The sheriff wiped his forehead with his torn sleeve.

"Sheriff, the risk is my concern. I can take it. I feel I have a responsibility too. We all have a stake in taming our new country."

"Very gallant, Mason," the sheriff answered sarcastically. "The firearm you carry, is it for rattlesnakes and decoration or can you use it?"

Cole felt blood rush to his face. "I can't outdraw a fast gun, Sheriff, but it doesn't sound like that's what we'll be looking for. As far as rifle shooting, I am good, very good. Near the top in the Vermont infantry. I've never shot a man close up but I feel confident I have the courage to kill a dry-gulcher."

The sheriff looked pleased. Cole believed he gave the right answer. He defined his weaknesses but emphasized his strengths. The sign of a balanced personality, he thought.

"I must remind you, there's no room for you as a paid deputy. The town and the merchants fund me. What I get pays for two deputies. I have two and I like them."

As if on cue, Stilkey opened the front door and came in. He took a look around and knew something was amiss.

The sheriff nodded at Stilkey, then turned to Cole. "There is a way I may be able to pay you, though, and I told you about that."

"What the hell's going on?" Stilkey's voice boomed. His eyes were on Lawton.

The sheriff proceeded to fill in his deputy on the close call.

"Darn it," said Stilkey, "this guy ain't afraid of anything. Let's get a posse and get him. Give me a shot, I'll put a vent in his outhouse, I guarantee it." Stilkey went over to the wall and grabbed a rifle. "Let's go." He started toward the door.

"Hold it, Jack, he's gone, escaped. Long gone," said the sheriff. "I want a break, time out. Then I want to get together—tonight would be good—and draw up a tight plan."

Lawton turned to the group. "I want you all here. Cole, Brave, and Jack, we'll draw us up a plan tonight and give each of us duties, and get that miserable man once and for all."

CHAPTER ELEVEN

Cole was first to leave the sheriff's office. He left confused. The dry-gulcher's choice of the sheriff as a victim didn't make sense to him. It didn't fit the picture of the dry-gulcher they'd been discussing. Lawton was anything but a "silly old man on a burro," as the sheriff himself had described a likely target. The sheriff was a somebody. He was the government and the law. Did the killer have an agenda other than "silly old men on burros"? Was the sniper instead attacking legal authority? If so, this was a different operation than what they'd been thinking about.

And why had the sniper come into town? That made no sense either. Operating in town, he lacked the natural security of the backcountry. Cole couldn't imagine a sniper trekking a big rifle through this town. So why, he asked himself, did the sniper come into town? One thing for sure, he wasn't cowed by those looking for him.

Cole concluded that their picture of the sniper was inaccurate. The sniper's move into town muddled some of their other assumptions, too. They thought the sniper operated alone, without assistance. That idea was probably wrong. If he operated alone, how did he know who the sheriff was and where he lived? Difficult information to get if you hang out only in the hills. Maybe there were two snipers, not just one—an in-town sniper to get information and set up in-town targets, and a backcountry sniper for the hills. You'd need a lot of information, intelligence, and planning to undertake an in-town sniper operation. All those functions would simply be too much for one man.

In Missouri during the War, there had been extensive guerilla activity. Guerilla fighters were local citizenry who fought as military combatants. These fighters fought by their own rules, which often meant no rules at all. Most guerilla fighters dressed in civilian clothes or in the uniforms of the adversary. Maybe the dry-gulching was a continuation of guerilla activity. Maybe a group of Southern diehards was behind it.

For sure, Sheriff Lawton must be prepared for a sniper assault at all times. Cole must too, now that he had joined the battle.

He looked up and down the road as he walked toward Rusty. Traffic had picked up since early morning . . . it was fairly bustling now. A wagon stood broken down on the north side above the sheriff's office. The driver was apparently fixing a broken wheel. Cole watched the man closely. A few hours earlier he would not have bothered. He untied Rusty and slowly swung up into his saddle.

"Sir, I must talk with you."

The voice was from behind him. Alarmed, Cole turned toward it. A woman was standing alone in the shade of the sheriff's office. She was tall, dark-haired, her body the color of a deep tan, and she was looking directly at him. She was dressed fashionably and stood straight and proper. She was poised, like a woman of the city. And she was beautiful, exceptionally beautiful.

"Ma'am . . . I'm sorry . . . were you speaking to me?" he stammered.

"Yes, I am sorry to take you by such surprise." She walked up to him out of the shade and stopped short by a couple feet.

She came much closer to him than a woman would have back home, he thought, particularly before a formal introduction. Cole could only stare at her. Her eyes were dark. His face turned red and he could feel heat as he realized she knew he was staring at her. Something was hidden in her eyes, though. Was it concern? Fear? Vulnerability? That was it, he thought, vulnerability. But even that look added to her beauty and mystery.

He waited for her to speak again. She was about his age, he guessed. Why was she standing here by the sheriff's office?

"I must warn you, sir," she said softly, "a man was watching you this morning." She paused. "I know this man. He means to do you harm."

Cole was taken back. Was it the sniper? Was the word out that he'd joined forces with the sheriff? Was he being set up for an ambush? Who else could it be? Who else would bother watching him? It had to be the dry-gulcher.

"Ma'am," Cole said, feeling the heat of the sun, "there's no place to talk in comfort here. May we move over here to the shade?"

"Of course, sir," she said simply, "where we talk is not important. My mission is to warn you of danger."

She spoke with a mellow accent. The words had an aristocratic ring. A touch of the Southern way was in her speech and in her words and in the way she moved her body. He recalled the accents of Rebel officers captured in the War. Her speech was similar but more mellow.

Cole dismounted, retied Rusty, and led the lady to the nearby shade.

"So, ma'am, who was watching me and from where?" He asked casually.

She was sharp in her reply. "I feel you don't understand the danger you're in. I also don't believe you understand the risk I took in coming to warn you. The man I speak of is pure evil."

Cole felt rebuked. After a pause, he said, "I'm sorry, very sorry. I didn't mean to make light of your warning or your effort. Please excuse me."

She started over. "I'm confusing you. Let me tell my story and if you think it of little matter, we can part neither the worse off. Is that agreeable?"

Cole nodded. "Sounds good." He was unable to suppress a small, friendly smile.

She smiled back, then her expression turned serious. She said, "I was a slave as a child. I lived on a plantation owned by an evil man. On weekdays he remained in his plantation house. But on weekends he traveled to New Orleans to prey on humans. He'd attack men, women, and children. It didn't matter to him. He needed blood to survive. He attacked humans anywhere . . . in alleyways, rooming houses, along the waterfront, in villas, apartments. How did he go about it? He'd use deception or manipulation to work his way into a victim's good graces. When he succeeded in obtaining trust, he'd fall on him and kill him by removing his blood. Why didn't we report him? Sir, we could not. He was white and protected by white society. If we reported him, he would find a way to have us killed for lying or rebelling. White plantation owners were very powerful lords."

She paused a moment to search Cole's face for a reaction, but there was none. She continued. "I would never have revealed this story, sir. Because of this, I have lived in fear my whole life. But this morning I saw my plantation master's face here in St. Bartow and you, sir, you were of its attention."

Cole was silent. A few days ago he would have laughed at it. He thought back to the conversation he'd had with Brave and with Sonia about the man who promised to make her a queen. That certainly was an attempt at manipulation. Cole held up a hand while forming questions in his mind. The woman stood patiently.

He said, "You saw a man today and his face resembled that of your old master on the plantation, right?"

She nodded. "I saw a form of a beast out the window where I live. It was dressed in a suit and a bowler hat. It stood in the shadow of the livery down the road. You were riding into town from the other direction. I think the form became agitated, for some reason, after you talked to the two young men. The creature's neck began to extend, its body shook and quivered, and its head began to change into a bird, then a bat. I realized right away that I was watching a beast changing form."

While attempting not to show his emotions, Cole wondered if he was being taken in. Was he being manipulated or deceived himself by the woman? She was as beautiful as a queen. But by her own tale, she could be a beast in disguise. He said, "Go on."

"The creature sensed something was watching it. It quickly turned form from a man into bat. I was repulsed. The bat began to fly away toward me. Its fangs were working up and down grotesquely. As the form closed in on me, I saw its face. Or the face it wanted me to see. It was the face of my old plantation master."

Cole was skeptical and she sensed it. "Sir, listen. The beast is going to attack you. He wants me to stay out of its way. That's why he flew toward my window. My days are numbered," she cried softly. "He will come for me. He has wanted me since I was a child."

Her world was unfamiliar to Cole; there was nothing in her story he could relate to. Was Willoughby her old master? Those cold hands, Cole recalled. This is a nightmare. But has my life been sheltered or are people out here crazy?

"I'm sorry, ma'am, but these things you speak of are not of my life. I mean, they are not of my upbringing. I believe you are telling me the truth, as you see it, but it's not of my experience."

He sensed anger rising in her.

She struck back. "You never were a slave, either. Your father was never pulled from you and sold, and sent far away because he no longer was strong enough to bend to the work in the fields. No, sir, such things were not of your experience. But these things happened to me and to others like me, and you have just completed a war over these matters. Hasn't the War made these things a part of your experience? If it hasn't, what did you learn from the war? Has the war been a failure? If it was a failure, I ask for your sake…learn from my experience."

"I'm sorry." Cole held up his hands in surrender. "I didn't mean to question your sincerity or to fail to understand because of my ignorance."

She appeared to mellow; she looked almost contrite. "Thank you. I'm sorry I was angry. I'm so concerned. I know not where to turn. And I thought maybe you—"

Cole asked, "Did you see the human form turn into a bat, did you see the process? Or did you turn back and see a bat where the man had been standing?"

"Actually, I saw it changing," she said thoughtfully. "It spread its arms out and a black web grew from its torso. It began to shrink down in size." She shuddered.

"Did anyone else witness the sighting?"

"No, it was very early morning, as you know. Hardly anyone was out. Everyone in my house was in another room."

"And," he asked, "why do you believe that the beast has targeted me?"

"You were coming up the road. There was no other activity out there. There was no other reason for him to be out there except the two boys. I concluded that he was upset that the boys were talking with you. I cannot shed any more light on that."

Yet she added, "I can also tell you that beasts have been known to hunt well-formed bodies . . . well-developed human bodies. These bodies provide superior nourishment. When superior bodies are unavailable, the beasts will shift their attacks down the chain. The lowest and least successful beasts live off the blood of rats and field animals, the very bottom of the chain."

Cole blushed. That shows what she thinks about me.

"The sheriff has told me that there has been a series of killings around St. Bartow. The victims had their blood sucked out. Is it possible that the creature you knew in New Orleans is in St. Bartow and active here?"

Tears welled up. "It's happening, yes, I know." Her hands flew up to her cheeks to catch the tears running down her face. "A woman was killed that way the other day down near the river."

Cole felt her anguish. Her feelings were sensitive and strong about these beasts, like Brave's feelings. Brave wanted to attack the beasts so badly that war paint formed on his features.

"The killings here," Cole told her, "have been of drunks and children and of women, persons less physically able to defend themselves. I don't believe I fit those categories. Do you believe the beast is getting bolder, or is there a specific reason why it may be targeting me?"

Cole saw confidence return to the woman. "I don't know. The beast may have lost strength during the fires down in New Orleans. Maybe the killings here have nourished and strengthened it. I don't have an answer."

He touched her arm. She smiled and lowered her head modestly for a moment. Her perfectly formed breasts whisked his thoughts away from the killings; he imagined the joy of having her love him and making love to her.

"My name is Cole Mason," he said, holding out his hand. "Thank you for coming to warn me."

She shook his hand. "I am Natalie," she said. "I do not have a last name." She smiled at him.

Cole wondered what she meant by that. Later he learned that former slaves often did not have last names. Some took the last names of their masters. "Where do you live?" he asked. "I'll walk you home."

She raised her shoulders slightly and looked lost. He looked up and down the road for a place where she might live.

"I live at Lady Talbot's," she said, "Lady's." She pointed across the road. "It was from the window right in front up on the second floor that I saw the beast."

A surprised look fleeted across Cole's face. "I thank you for the warning," Cole said, smiling warmly, forgetting he had already told her that. "Perhaps we can see each other again." He nodded and removed his hat.

That was a stupid thing to say to a woman who just told me she lives in a whorehouse, he thought. She can't be a prostitute. Maybe she owns the house.

Cole took Natalie's arm as firmly as he dared and guided her across the muddy road. They walked in silence, both shy at the occasion. She smiled gratefully when they reached the other side. She turned her head, waved gently, and walked up the steps leading to the boardwalk at Lady's.

CHAPTER TWELVE

Natalie. My beautiful slave girl. Framed in red in a window. I have longed for her for so long. My loins beat wildly. My lips quiver.

I lost my Natalie on my plantation. I've found her. Found her in a whorehouse. Such a waste. I will bring us together. We will live together forever.

In the dark tonight, my beautiful Natalie, I will rescue you.

I go off to dream.

* * * * *

Natalie had a thin nose, high cheekbones and flared nostrils. She walked with a regal step. She was born proud. Before the sun rose, she walked to the fields to be with her mother and her father. She did no field labor. Her beauty had been recognized at a young age. Natalie would work inside.

From behind pulled drapes I watched her. She knew I was there. Her body movements were not meant to go unnoticed.

The first time I saw her, my temperature rose, my face turned white, my neck pulsed, my tongue itched, and my lips quivered. My lust cried out for her blood. Her hair was straight and long and held together at the shoulder by wisps of colored cotton cloth. I wanted to ride with her on that cloth. Simply . . . I had never experienced such profound lust.

She was a virgin. I knew that. Her black eyes looked out from large white oval sockets. As she grew older, her beauty enhanced, as did my lust for her. Was I in love? I do not know. I wanted to obsess her. I wanted her to obsess me. We would live and hunt together forever. If that was love, yes, I was in love.

On weekends I traveled away to satisfy my lust. Beautiful women and men lived there, sons and daughters of growers, merchants, shippers and businessmen. But none of these people possessed the raw appeal of my little slave girl.

My field hands knew of my passion. They took money to keep me informed of her activity. When she blossomed at fifteen, the son of my overseer sought her affection. He teased her and jostled her outside my window.

The boy was simple. He had a flat face and craggy eyebrows—a facial structure signifying low intelligence. His body was developed but his mind was short in range. I couldn't bear to think of Natalie and that boy lying together. I trembled in rage. I knew I must destroy that boy.

I'd sworn never to strike on my own plantation, never to soil my lair. But I decided on an exception. I'd kill the boy and hide the body so that the father would never find it. He'd never know that I killed him; he could not seek vengeance on me.

An event interrupted my plans. A destructive war between two sections of the country, the North and the South, spilled into the area. Naval forces of the North bombarded New Orleans. The warships started up the Mississippi River. The ships bombarded crops, animals, plantations, homes and buildings. The naval forces announced to the slaves that they were free, that they could leave the plantations.

Freed slaves were as dumb as field tools. Most returned to their shelters and waited for freedom to arrive. There was no next day of work for slaves after the fields were destroyed. There was only suffering, idleness and hunger.

I watched the contemptuous destruction of the land. It was on the scale of Pompeii. But in this case, the people brought it upon themselves.

One day soon after, I heard artillery close by. The naval ships had made their way up the river from New Orleans to my plantation. The smell of smoke pained my nostrils and unnerved me. I knew I must escape. It was time to evacuate.

I decided I'd strike the overseer's son and exit the plantation with Natalie. We would live and hunt together in New Orleans. There we would be safe. The line separating white and black, master and slave, was obscured in New Orleans at high levels of society. Beautiful black women could live in harmony in aristocratic surroundings with wealthy white men.

Cannon fire in the sky foretold the War closing in. The noise anguished the slaves. They moaned at the coming terror. I packed steamer trunks with gold and jewels and papers of credit. I kept one trunk free to hide in during daylight hours. I turned the plantation over to the overseer, the simple boy's father, and drove off. I hid my wagon nearby in the woods and made my way back to strike down the boy and get my Natalie. I was excited and anxious to feast on the boy's blood.

My plans unraveled. The boy and Natalie had run off in the confusion of the navy's assault. Together or alone, I do not know. Either as a diversion or as an act of war, the plantation house and buildings were afire. I saw the flames whipping across the roof timbers.

I was terrified, and too close to the fire. My body temperature rose critically. I began to drip fluids. The booming cannons on the river upset me. I ran to the wagon and left for New Orleans. I decided to hide the wagon in an abandoned building during the next daylight. The next night, I dashed for New Orleans, closed out my affairs, and started north to Missouri.

I continue my long life. I will be with my Natalie soon. My lust is abiding and cannot be unrequited. We will have a new life together.

CHAPTER THIRTEEN

The sun was in the final leg of its voyage when Cole started back into town. He was anxious for the meeting with the sheriff. Mindful of the sniper's attack that morning, he chose a roundabout trail into town. He'd arrive in St. Bartow coming in from the east rather than from the west.

As he rode, he closely watched the terrain. He practiced the approach suggested by the sheriff, looking right and left and then up onto high ground. He searched for telltale reflections on metal. It was not a carefree ride; it reminded him of standing alert on a battle line and watching for Rebel infiltrators. His situation had changed full round since he'd arrived in town just yesterday. He had been so lighthearted then and felt so secure.

Rusty helped in the effort to outwit a sniper. Cole jogged Rusty left, then abruptly right. Rusty decided that the changed direction of the jogs was a game. He'd guess the timing and direction of the next jog and without a command, he'd begin the jog.

"Smart horse," Cole said smiling and stroking Rusty's sleek neck, "you'll save my life some day, old buddy."

Cole's thoughts moved to Natalie . . . beautiful, poised and intelligent. Shyness was not a trait of hers. Was her behavior a part of her personality or of her culture? She'd had a lot of experience with people. But was she a whore? Did she develop that confidence by whoring? Though he thought it silly, he allowed that he didn't know much about the trade and that it might affect different woman different ways. He blanched. She was too well spoken to be a whore. He must have misunderstood her. Maybe she rented a room at Lady's.

He turned his thoughts to the beast. Natalie confirmed Pete's sighting. Both said Marchess transformed himself into a bird or a bat. There had to be truth in those separate observations. The two were unlikely partners in deceit. Evidence of the presence of beasts was piling up and becoming compelling. But how could it be? He shrugged his shoulders.

Assuming beasts were in the area, was there one only? Unlikely, given the number of sightings and killings. If there were conditions for one, there could easily be more. Did all the beasts look like Marchess when in human form? Natalie and Pete both described a beast looking like Marchess. It seemed unlikely that there was only one beast. Okay, he thought, two confirmed sightings and both looking like Marchess. But both dressing like him too? A too-short suit and a dapper hat? Unlikely. There must be only one beast, unless there's a clothes exchange for beasts in the area or they bought their outfits from the same tailor. Cole grinned. This isn't funny, he reminded himself.

How about lairs? Was there more than one lair? Cole shook his head. The more beasts and the more lairs, the more difficult to rid us of them.

He thought back to his experience in the saloon. As odd as the little guy looked, it was difficult to think of him as a beast. His behavior was deceitful and manipulative. He kept picking my destiny for me. But the guy was not a classic beast like the troll under a bridge. That thought shows the limits of my experience with beasts. Willoughby was informed about life in the near West and he had reasonable ideas and followed a profession. He smelled bad. If smelling makes a beast, he was one hands down. If we'd drank more at that saloon, he may have tried to take advantage of me.

Why did Willoughby pull back when Al showed up in the saloon? He didn't say another word. Maybe he decided he couldn't entice me away from my surroundings. Brave said beasts look for a weakness. They attack the old, the drunk, women, and the lonely—people less capable of defending themselves. Was I a "lonely"? I was new to St. Bartow. That could be it. He saw me riding with a saddle roll and stuffed bags. He assumed I was new to town and expected me to be lonely. Cole shrugged.

He wondered how a beast stood with the law. It was a stupid thought, but did a beast possess rights? If Marchess changed into a bat and a bat subsequently killed a human, would the law have to prove that the killer was Marchess and not some other beast? Were beasts like humans—not guilty until proven so? If a beast limited his victims to field rodents, would he be guilty of anything? Maybe down the way humans would have to get a Supreme Court decision on the rights of beasts. This is all pretty silly, he decided. What it comes down to is: What are beasts?

Let's go in another direction, thought Cole. Are we unwittingly opening up a path for beasts to return from the beyond? Brave and Natalie talk freely of beasts like I talk of the Duncans living down the road in Vermont. Are such thoughts creating a sinister kind of force that provides entry for evil to come back from the beyond? There are masses of immigrants going through St. Bartow. Perhaps some of them also have beliefs that give beasts a role. Could these immigrants contribute to this passageway too?

Cole arrived at a stretch of trail leading into St. Bartow. He guided Rusty down it. On the way in, he'd seen no sign of a sniper. In the near-darkness, the shadows around the outlying buildings would make good hiding places for beasts. Probably better hiding places than for dry-gulchers.

Lanterns were powering up in the outlying buildings. The pungent odor of the town again assailed his nostrils. In a few days, the odor will become so familiar that I won't even notice it, he thought. And beasts will probably become a part of my world too.

Cole rode up to the sheriff's office and swung off Rusty. He tied the horse and headed for the office door.

CHAPTER FOURTEEN

"They drive 'em right through the water holes!" Stilkey's voice exploded Cole's solitude as he walked into the office. "They don't give a darn if it destroys the holes. Cow dung and mud everywhere! Darn it, Sheriff, I don't blame Johnson for wiring off his holes. I'm surprised he didn't shoot the cows when they broke through. And they didn't clean up the holes either, when they moved on. A darn shame, the whole darn thing."

Cole found himself in the midst of a fierce discussion. He was taken back by Stilkey's strong stand. He sounded like he was about to pop a vein.

Lawton was hunched at his desk, hands folded and feet resting casually one by the other. He stared at Stilkey, his face relaxed for a man encountering fierce opposition.

He's used to Stilkey's strong positions, thought Cole. The sheriff is letting Stilkey talk on. At least Lawton is relaxed, not like this morning after the sniper attack.

His entry seemingly unnoticed, Cole stood on the side listening. He learned that outfits from down Texas were driving cattle across open land near St. Bartow. Land used intensively by local ranchers. The Texas outfits were gutting and fouling up the water holes used by the ranchers. The local ranchers were upset and had begun forming associations to work to drive off these outfits and anyone else that used the water.

The government's position was that rangeland was open and the water free to all. The Texas crowd was moving through the area for honest reasons. They were moving their herds to train-loading platforms as quickly as possible. These platforms, like the railroads themselves, were moving inexorably farther west and were now not too far from St. Bartow.

Cole gathered from the talk that the number of herds coming through was increasing. That day, Stilkey had apparently put himself at risk quelling a near-war between Texas cowboys and a local rancher.

"Yeah, Jack," said Lawton, seeing Cole and trying to cut off the discussion, "it's tough but it's a situation in which we have no choice. This is open range. You let water holes get barbed off and next it'll be the land, and then we'll have a real range war quick as you can say Abe Lincoln. Farmers want to come in and squat too and wire off land. We don't let them do it unless they got that piece of paper. That's the law and the law's the law."

Stilkey raised his hand, wanting to continue.

"Look, Jack, the law says no one owns open land." Lawton's voice was rising. "That's the law. We enforce the law. If you want to get into the right and the wrong, we have no control over the cause of the problem. They want more and more beef back East. If there is a solution not of current law, it's got to come from up the ladder, Jack, probably from as high as the courts or the Congress in Washington."

Brave butted in. "If you're in search of a real fair solution, Jack, consider the Indian situation too. Farmers and ranchers and trappers and hunters and miners have been invading Indian land with the same kind of disregard that the Texans are showing here. How 'bout their rights?"

Lawton held up his hand to end the discussion. "That's enough, men. We'll talk about this again later." Lawton grinned at Cole. "Welcome, Cole, to one of our more exciting disagreements. You're in time!"

Stilkey was not going to give up. "You're putting me on, Sheriff. Local ranchers have used these water holes for generations. The water's theirs. These big outfits come in and give them no due. The law isn't right if the powerful have rights to beat up on the weak, no sir. Besides, Sheriff, the local ranchers help pay our salaries. The Texas outfits just give us grief on Saturday nights."

"The law is the law, Jack, that's it. We don't make the law, we enforce it." Lawton was trying his best to end the discourse. "You can't fence off what you don't own and you can't keep people from using what's free. There is no limiting the use of open range and water holes, period. That's a federal law. If I enforced the wishes of those who pay my bills, I wouldn't be the sheriff here, Jack, I'd be a dictator of sorts."

"You watch, Sheriff," Stilkey said, "ranchers here gonna hire an army of gunslingers to do their bidding. We'll have cowboys and gunslingers here, drunk as hell, thinking they're a reincarnation of Yanks and Rebs."

"You guys don't have a moment of rest, do you?" Cole cut in, hoping to quell the argument. "First a sniper and now this."

"One thing for sure," Brave said, "we need more lawmen. Things are getting out of hand. Too many killings and too many people needing protection for the number of lawmen we have."

"What do you mean?" asked the sheriff, turning to Brave and looking puzzled.

"Unrest is in the air, Sheriff. You can see it and you can smell it. Killings, fights, disturbances over land use and ownership, conflicts among religious groups, and Rebel and Yankee soldiers. There are more disturbances in a month than there used to be in a year."

"Hey, Brave," Stilkey yelled out, grinning ear to ear, "that ain't unrest you're smelling. You need to get back to Indian land, out of this town. That's where the smell's coming from. It's worse this year than it's ever been."

Everyone laughed.

When the laughter subsided, the sheriff asked, "Okay, Brave, but what's your point?"

"We need more lawmen here, Sheriff. With more lawmen we could catch problems before they get loose. There'd be more respect for the law, making our job simpler. That's all I'm saying, Sheriff."

"I agree. But we have enough staff for the responsibility we have here in St. Bartow. The problem is, as I have said repeatedly, we have to spend at least half our resources for the town on the backland. We don't have any support in the backland. The marshal has a federal allocation of four people and himself. Do we ever see them around? Take right now. The sniper has been the marshal's problem for the last year! Who knows if the sniper came into my town actually because he got a free pass in the backlands from the marshal? We need a working marshal in this territory. An active, working marshal. I'll continue to work to have the guy replaced but I can't push too hard. Remember, he's a political appointee. If I push too hard, the territorial office will think it's sour grapes on my part. In the meantime let's concentrate on the dry-gulcher."

The sheriff looked over his men. "I'm beginning now. Let's forget everything unrelated to the sniper. How much agreement do we have on the sniper? Let's find out."

CHAPTER FIFTEEN

"Okay," began the sheriff, "I say we have two killers here . . . a sniper and an animal, er . . . not necessarily an animal, but a killer who kills by sucking the blood out of a victim. The killer may be a human. But it behaves like an animal. Either way, human, animal or both, do we agree that the blood sucker is not the sniper?"

The room was silent. Stilkey grinned as he looked over at Brave. Brave and Cole looked straight at the sheriff. They finally, one after another, nodded their agreement.

"Does anyone disagree?" Lawton asked again, sweeping his eyes over the group.

Silence reigned. Not even the scrape of a boot or the creak of a chair was made.

"We agree then, two different killers," said Cole, breaking in. "If we're going to speak to the sniper, I want to say something about how we may go about figuring who he is and how we can get him."

"Go ahead," said Lawton, settling in his chair. "I want to hear ideas."

"We should search for things in common among the targets he's chosen. If he selects victims for convenience only, it'd be unlikely, Sheriff, that you'd be selected. Choosing you was specific and risky. You are the law. We should look for things that you have in common with other targets. Also, the attack on you may have been a watershed. It signals a change in strategy. The sniper targeted someone in town for the first time. Something in your background sheriff, might tell us something about the sniper and his motives."

"You make some good points, Cole," said the sheriff, nodding. "I don't want to take anything away from them, but how do you think he gets his information? If he targeted me for a reason, he had to get information about me from somewhere. Either that, or he is targeting me simply because I'm a sheriff. But why target a sheriff? Does he get information on the boardwalk? In a saloon? In a whorehouse? Wherever he gets it, it's good information."

Cole suggested, "Maybe he needs no source of information about you, Sheriff. Maybe he lives or hangs out here in town."

"I agree that we have to look into the 'why and how' of the killer," Brave chimed in. "If there's no specific reason why he picks a victim, we might as well pick a good spot for a bushwhack and wait for the guy to set up his ambush."

"Spoken like the true son of a university-trained man," the sheriff said, and smiled proudly, as did Brave in return.

The sheriff truly enjoys his staff, observed Cole.

"I'll tell you," Stilkey blew out, "with all the foreigners coming in here, one of them is crazy enough to do this, that's my feeling, Sheriff."

"Let's concentrate on the similarities in the targets. Then we'll move on to where and how he gets his information," said the sheriff, cutting off discussion of whether the killer was an immigrant.

Stilkey's feelings were hurt. He groaned, making it obvious.

"Jack," said the sheriff, turning to Stilkey, "we can't begin by limiting our search to immigrants. If we do, we have limited our search to a group because it looks or acts differently. We cut out everyone else, which is about ninety-five percent of the population. Actually, most of the immigrants look pleased to be here. I don't see a motivation to attack people. I just don't want to limit our search that way. We could say the bushwhacker is a former Rebel soldier. We could start a witch-hunt for a Rebel. I don't want to do that either. Let's look at possible motives, access to and sources of information. If it works its way down to immigrants, we'll go there."

Stilkey bristled but said nothing.

There's goodwill between those two, regardless of their many conflicts, thought Cole.

"I think he's among us," Brave broke in, trying to change the atmosphere and get a point across too. "Someone we see every day. He's gotta carry a rifle, a big one. And he's gotta get it places fast. One minute, Lowry, the next, St. Bartow. Maybe he moves it around by wagon. He lives by that gun. It's a part of him. He can't stash it away in a field and take a chance someone will find it. It would kill him to lose it. Like losing his legs. Maybe if we asked around town whether anyone saw a guy traveling fast between these towns in a wagon or something big enough to hold a rifle, we'd get ourselves a lead."

"Let me make a list of things to look into," said Lawton, reaching for a piece of paper.

"He's a loner and he's loco," said Stilkey, shaking his head. "Who'd hang with a bushwhacker? If you're crazy as a loon, you can't hide it. Only another crazy or his mother hangs with a crazy. I'd look around for people who look or act differently. That's why I talked about foreigners. Another point, plain sucking air costs money. He's getting money from somewhere to live on, unless he had a lot to start with. Having foreigner friends to hide you out and feed you is the same as having money to live on."

In his own way, Jack was making good points, thought Cole. Several of his points supported a conspiracy or a two-sniper theory. He was right, too, in implying that they didn't know whether foreigners or religious sects or former Rebels had a bigger goal than just starting a new life in the West. But he agreed with Lawton that it was best initially to keep their search open.

"Okay, I got my paper here, let's make a list of what to look into." He posed a question, scribbled it, then moved on to the next one. "Was anyone seen moving something heavy and coming fast down the trail from Lowry? Was anyone seen moving rapidly between Lowry and St. Bartow? Was anyone moving through the saloons, whorehouses, and stores asking questions about people in the area? And what do the sniper's targets have in common? How does that sound?" he asked.

“Sheriff, you were in the War, a decorated Union officer. I wonder, do any others of those targeted have credentials like yours?” Cole asked.

The group turned silent. Stilkey began to drag his big boots slowly across the floor. The big man straightened in his chair and towered over Cole.

Not a sound in the room. What have I said to bring on such silence? wondered Cole.

“The guy killed up in Lowry, up the road, he was the right age for the military,” Lawton began. “Doubt he was an officer—a little young from what I hear. He may have been decorated, though. He’d just got into town.” Lawton’s voice trailed off.

Cole was watching Stilkey from the corner of his eye. Stilkey’s breath was coming in gasps, like from a wounded bear. The conversation was obviously painful for him.

Looking anywhere but at Stilkey, Brave said, “Maybe one of us should go up to Lowry. Check out the investigation and see what information the boy gave out around town before he got killed.”

“Good, good, but can we work it in?” the sheriff asked. “How about it, Jack, can you work it into your schedule?”

“I guess, Sheriff,” Stilkey responded, teeth gritted, “if someone takes my rounds for a couple days.” He shook his head. “I don’t like the trail this is on, Sheriff. I think we’re going to decide the thing is being done by a crazy Reb. That’ll be the conclusion based on one sniper killing and a wide shot at you. It’s a thin reed to stand on for such a conclusion. If we looked into more killings, these findings might be just bullshit.”

The sheriff was irritated. “Jack, don’t take the shot at me lightly—‘wide shot, thin reed, bullshit findings.’ ”

“I’m trying to be a part of this, Sheriff,” Stilkey ground out, equally upset. He peered at the ceiling. “I think you want to blame a Rebel, a John Wilkes Booth come West. You don’t go around telling everyone you were a Yankee colonel, Sheriff, how come the guy knew? Seems more likely that he'd be from around here and know your history, including that as sheriff."

The sheriff spoke in a measured but firm tone. "Being a colonel in the Yankee Army is important to a lot of people, Jack. Besides, he could be from around here and have Rebel sympathies."

"You all know," said Jack, turning to Cole, "you don't, Cole, but my family in Virginia went two ways, Blue and Gray, like a lot of families did in Missouri. Look, I am tired of Yank-Reb talk, hearing decisions about events and people today drawn from what side they supported or fought on. Because some people were Rebs doesn't mean their beliefs and behavior was crazy or that they're stupid. We got to get over it. And I think this talk isn't helpful."

Jack's torched, thought Cole. He's right, though. The War is in all of us. We gotta find a way to get rid of it.

The sheriff moved to calm Jack. "Jack, I'm not trying to pin this on anyone. The War was violent. There were many losers and some of them believed firmly in their principles. But a few losers may not be good losers. I want to be even-handed. I want you to go to Lowry and look into the circumstances of the killing up there and come back and report to us. I ask now that we move on. That we together draw up a plan to end the reign of this sniper."

Cole thought anew about Stilkey: a quiet man but loud when he should be. A big man and a man capable of deep emotion. He was someone you could count on. He was six-foot-four at least, and weighed 280 lbs. easily. He could probably stop a bullet in flight, but he could also end a fight just as quickly. He was big enough and strong enough to move a house. The sheriff needed a strong man like that on his team.

The room was quiet.

Cole said, "Sheriff, for the sniper to do his shooting in Lowry and get down here to attack you, he'd have to start immediately. When he's in Lowry, maybe Jack can look into whether anyone was seen riding hard this way carrying a weight. He'd have to have had the gun with him. He'd unlikely have two of them. Jack, when you're up there, you can look into whether a stranger was hanging on a corner and happened to disappear at the same time as the killing."

Stilkey was silent.

The sheriff averted his eyes. "Let's keep moving," he said, "I see progress."

A murmur of agreement arose.

"The sniper's rifle," the sheriff said, "the sound of it, very important. That rifle was a part of sniper activity on both sides in the War."

"I agree, the sniper was likely in the War," said Cole, nodding. "Probably got training there."

"Yeah, even if he bought the thing or stole it," added Stilkey, "he knows how to use it."

Stilkey was rejoining the group, Cole noted. The meeting had turned businesslike.

"Another thing," Brave said, "he has to keep that gun handy. It's impossible to transport the thing without giving it away. Maybe he stashes it in town and picks it up before he takes off."

"Possible," said the sheriff. "Well, we've talked enough. We have consensus and information enough to draw a plan."

The group nodded.

"Okay," said the sheriff, "let's fill in the blank spaces."

CHAPTER SIXTEEN

Cole liked the plan and was pleased with his contribution. Before leaving home he'd worried about finding a purpose in the West. Walking toward Rusty, he heard his heels beat a sound of confidence on the wooden boardwalk. The War and Beaudin were beginning to fade from his memory.

It was dark. The plan called for him to proceed to the Union Saloon. There he'd play a fun-loving, recently discharged Union soldier passing through on his way west. The plan presumed that the boy from Illinois shot down in Lowry behaved in that way. As best he could, Cole would make public his departure time and expected trail. The way he chose to do this was up to him. The sheriff hoped the sniper would pick up the information. If he did and he acted upon it, the sheriff and his deputies would be ready for him.

Cole swung up onto Rusty. The horse acted strangely, he thought. The Morgan snorted and bounced its head from side to side.

"Whoa there, Rusty, take it easy, boy." Cole reached down to calm the horse. What's spooking him? A predator coming down from the hills? Cole saw nothing through the thick darkness. He could hear the music of a piano rippling through the night air. Lady's was awash in light. His mind turned to Natalie. He pictured her singing and swaying beside a piano in Lady's front room. She's thinking of me, he thought. He grinned and felt his face redden.

At the Union Saloon, Cole would talk about his Yankee background.

"Expect to get tested," the sheriff had warned. "Some of those boys been without women for 'least a year and been on alcohol since morning, maybe yesterday morning. They got to test you before they accept you. We'll go in to help only for big trouble. You're pretty much on your own."

Cole listened and sniffed his way up the dark road. Fine music and ripe air. Is it romantic, scary or just plain smelly? He was excited and pleased to be involved.

Cole reviewed parts of the plan. At dawn, Deputy Stilkey headed off to Lowry, where the last victim was gunned down. He'd look into the victim's activities there and see what other information he could dig up. He'd return to St. Bartow the next day and share his findings.

After that, Cole would leave for the West. As a cover, the sheriff would find him a job working on a wagon train. If the sniper acted to form, he'd attempt an ambush of Cole. When he did, the sheriff would cut the guy down.

Rusty snorted and danced sideways. Strange behavior, thought Cole. Is he sending me a message? Is something prowling out there? A mountain lion, maybe? That'd be it back home. Animals can smell a fight. They prepare by freeing themselves—like tossing a rider. Cole smiled, and reined in Rusty some.

"Sir, you, Cole," a voice called.

Cole tensed. The voice came from the boardwalk ahead. In the dark Cole saw nothing. Suddenly he made out a man standing on the boardwalk, just beyond the Silver Dollar. How does he know my name? Cole wondered. He yelled back, "That's me, yes."

Rusty cantered sideways, putting distance between them and the voice. The horse acted truly skittish now.

"I got a message for you," the voice called out, "from a friend. He needs you. He needs help."

"Go ahead, I can hear." Cole hoped he sounded annoyed.

"Carl sent me. He's around the corner, next road."

"Why send you if he's around the corner? Who are you?"

"He can't come. You two talked about this, I think that's what he said."

"Well, what is it?" asked Cole, sounding annoyed again.

"Look," said the voice in an impatient tone, "I agreed to look for you. I don't know what it's about. I'm just a messenger, get it? I help people I know. Carl, he's one of them."

Cole guessed the man was fifty feet away. If he rode in a semicircle, he would keep the man roughly the same distance away. If the man was interested in ambushing him, fifty feet was a pretty long distance for an accurate gunshot, particularly in the dark. Cole felt like he was being set up.

"Look, friend," Cole called out, "tell Carl I'll see him tomorrow. I'm on a mission now, very busy."

The man hesitated. "Okay, I'll tell him. We'll meet again."

What does he mean by that, 'We'll meet again'? Cole kept his distance, and was now past the place where the man had been standing. Not comfortable, Rusty sped up on his own. Can't blame the poor horse, thought Cole.

He looked over his shoulder, expecting to see the man swinging into his saddle or walking away. But no one was there. No person was there, nor was any horse. The man had vanished!

Cole turned Rusty around and rode back to where the voice had come from. There was no one there. The horse was not upset now, thought Cole. But how'd he get away? Cole saw no sign of him. But wait—something caught his eye. Something glistened in the reflected light of a lantern attached to a building.

Cole got on his knees and stared closely at the planks on the boardwalk. He saw six or seven pools of liquid on the planks and several large puddles farther up the boardwalk. The liquid hadn't seeped yet into the worn boardwalk. Too thick, or it hasn't been there long enough, he thought.

Had the man been wounded? Was he maybe dripping blood from his hands or mouth? Cole's muscles tightened. Should he report this to the sheriff? There was no way to report it. The sheriff had already left for the Union Saloon to back him up.

Cole mounted Rusty and headed toward the saloon. He must put this thing out of his mind for the time being.

CHAPTER SEVENTEEN

Cole knew the saloon was nearby when he heard the raw, untamed bedlam. The air was charged with it: indescribable noise was flowing up the road—voices yelling, cursing, and screaming; furniture twisting and crashing; and boots banging on the floor in a crazy sounding drumbeat. All of it was bathed in the merriment of a wild, off-key piano. And a single, unrestrained, infectious laugh kept burrowing up through it all.

Cole smiled at that particular sound. In military hell-raising, there's always a soldier with a shattering laugh, yes sir.

Cole guided Rusty to one of the few open spaces at the hitching rail. Tonight is going to be interesting, he thought, swinging down.

"It'll be hell there." Those were the words of Sheriff Lawton, Cole recalled. The sheriff had good appreciation.

Cole straightened his mustache and made his way up the boardwalk and through the group of drunken patrons hanging on the boardwalk rail.

He pushed the swinging doors open and walked into bright light and dense smoke.

A man wearing a worn infantry hat was standing just inside the doorway. His hat was askew and pulled down to his ears. "Hey soldier," he mumbled, eyes focusing with difficulty, "I know you, yes sir, where was it?" He shook a finger at Cole. He tilted his head back and to the side in his effort to recall that meeting place of long ago.

Sitting at a nearby table a man loudly answered Cole's greeter. He was wearing blue military suspenders and a blue shirt, and was sitting with three others of similar appearance. "Hey Anson, be still. You've seen someone someplace else at least twenty times tonight. You got three drinks out of it.

Get new eyes or a new brain or a new approach, will ya?" The man winked broadly at Cole. Everyone at the table laughed.

Cole coyly saluted the "greeter" who still was trying to remember where that fateful meeting had taken place. On this mission, Cole told himself, make no enemies. He worked his way through the near-full tables and chairs to the bar at the back of the saloon and politely pushed his way up to it.

He ordered whiskey, smiled at the bartender, and looked around. The scene brought back memories. These were the hell raisers, the cream of the army. They'd go into battle with no whine or whimper. He looked the saloon over closely. He could pick out separate groups of hell raisers. Some were the plain losers; they were unmotivated and unskilled, except at finding ways to dog it. In the Vermont 11th the doggers had the nickname "third buglers." They'd move into battle cautiously, unless really pushed by the sergeants. They would make it usually only after the outcome was certain. They typically waited for a third bugle, a bugle they hoped would never sound.

Looking through the saloon, Cole decided the men here were in general the good soldiers, the good hell raisers. Very few third buglers were present. Those guys were probably back home telling War stories, he thought.

Union Army officers were another group of patrons, standing apart from the hell raisers. They were gambling; poker was the game. They looked like they were playing five-stud draw, a favorite of the Midwesterners. They were dressed alike in black waistcoat suits, string ties, and wide-brimmed, flat Western hats. The officers' mustaches were uniformly trimmed and neat looking. These soldiers stood out in another way too—to a man, they had bright red faces.

Rouged up, thought Cole, dance hall rouge. Don't remember that in the military. He decided the rouge was a new thing from Europe or England. It sure wasn't Western. Maybe it's big-town Western, he thought. The gamblers were drinking tamely and without fanfare.

Cole saw another group he identified as farmers. They sat together, dressed in frayed overalls, worn boots, torn flannel shirts, and faded hats. A lot of labor had passed in those boots. Several of the burly farmers had set aside tables for arm wrestling. They groaned and screeched as they plied their strength against each other. Showing their tools, thought Cole. A lighted candle was placed so that the loser paid dearly—no halfway losers. Few of the farmers carried guns and even fewer appeared to be drinking. They trusted their security to their wrists.

Tables of wild cowboys were interspersed. They wore chaps. They kept them on even away from the range. Probably a badge or something, thought Cole. He noted they beat their spurs into the wooden floor as though they were still out riding hard. Quite physical, these cowboys, he thought. They shouted loudly. They banged friends' shoulders and backs for emphasis almost after each spoken word. They drank heavy and had endless itches that required attention. They looked edgy. Like at any moment disaster could befall them. They were prepared to draw a gun, pull a knife, or throw a fist at any real or imagined provocation. Lawton had warned Cole to give cowboys a wide berth. His advice was well founded, thought Cole.

Cole stood relaxed at the bar, sipping his whiskey and observing the patrons. No one looked or behaved like a sniper. But if one were here he'd probably hang near the hell raisers, Cole decided. That group took to strangers and passed information easily in banter. Picking up a partially filled shot glass, Cole moved to where the hell raisers were deep in play.

"Mike," a freckled face with a wild, blond beard yelled out, "my woman told me a guy with a real short staff, a 'bitty thing' she described it, came by to see her, wanted help on whether the thing was working, I guess. I thought of you, Mike. Was it you looking for advice from my woman?"

"Is that so," came a concerned response. "She doing testing now, is she? I thought she a regular whore. A tester, well. She must get big staffs or little staffs, a mix of staffs, in that work. That's interesting! Bet her men go home pleased with or without a score."

Laughter rose from nearby tables.

Mike continued. "Not me, though, Jon. I'm a satisfied soldier, a beans and hot bread guy. Maybe it was Hiram. Old Hi has to test his stump now and then. I've seen him leaving town late at night, kind of testy. He gotta make sure his works . . . gotta be ready to hose down his campfires, yes sir. Don't want no prairie fire."

More laughter.

"Wasn't me, my staff's real big. I know that. Don't need no testing. No mistakin' that," toned Hiram in response, "When I first tested the thing, eleven years old, the lady next door said it was a monster. Like scared her to death, yes sir."

"Bet you a real animal, eleven years old," a voice yelled out, laughing. "Bet it was as big a monster as General Bobby Lee, yes sir."

More laughs erupted.

Maybe the humor won't end, thought Cole. I gotta work myself in somehow.

"Maybe Phil went for a test?" suggested Hiram, trying to get the bug off his back. "Rumor is that he's bitty staffed, like the size of a little toe or finger. I know he'll say no, but we all know how guys from Jersey lie. Tell people they're from New York, things like that."

"You guys are funny," said Cole, smiling. "You must of known each other for a while to know all about each other's stumps." Cole took a drink from his whiskey glass, smacked his lips and turned around to the men. "You all in the War together?"

The men looked surprised and puzzled.

They're not used to interruptions, thought Cole.

One man missing an arm looked at Cole, trying to stare him down. With a friendly smile, Cole fixed and held his eyes on the man.

The man asked, "May I ask who the frig you are?"

The one-armed man was clean and dressed neatly. He wore a stained hat and sets of colonel's bars pinned to his shirt shoulders. He made no attempt to hide the stump of his arm. In fact, he pushed it into Cole's face.

"Sure, go ahead and ask, I'll tell you," said Cole, continuing his innocent smile.

"Okay, back up," said the man, "who the frig are you?"

One of the questioner's companions guffawed and slapped the back of the man sitting next to him. The others sat still, silent, and curious.

Cole picked it up. They're showing curiosity, not hostility, he thought. I'm doing okay. He looked over at the bar, as if contemplating a trip back to it. Still smiling and looking puzzled, he turned to his interrogator and asked, "Why back up?"

"Soldier, you carry a big number there in those pants. You got to be backed up somewhere." The one-armed man roared at his joke.

His companions rained down additional laughter. Cole joined in. The man pounded the table with his left hand, getting attention from the crowd for his witty response.

"My mother wouldn't appreciate your description of her son," Cole said with a chuckle. "But that's okay, 'cause she don't know who my company is, either. You from New York? Seeing I interrupted your game of insults, let me buy a drink."

"Accepted," said the man, reaching over with his good hand to grab Cole's. "Your guess is close." His face softened. "From Ohio, home of the Buckeyes, whatever they be, and I'm on my way west to get land and do some farming."

"A farmer. Me too." Cole's face lit up. "Cole's the name, Cole Mason, and I'm out of Vermont. On my way west too, to get free land for farming."

Cole was given a place at a table. He was soon friendly with each of the men and another round of drinks was ordered.

The banter continued among them. They talked of the strength, size and prowess of a soldier's maleness. War experiences, campaigns, battles, skirmishes and long marches were other topics. Tough officers, easy officers, and dumb officers were brought up too. Problems with Indians, outlaws, and religious fanatics were touched upon. Cole listened intently and laughed when he was supposed to. Even if they were enlarging on their stories, he was surprised at the encounters they had on the trail and how easily they were able to convert deadly situations into humorous stories.

Trail horses came up in the discussion and Cole saw an opening for himself.

"This little horse I got bred in Vermont is the strongest horse in the territory. I'd put that little rascal's pulling power up against any horse in St. Bartow."

"Any size horse?" asked a man at the next table, surprised.

"Any horse," answered Cole, nodding his head. "Who owns that big roan out front?"

"Why, is it stolen?" deadpanned Jason, a short man at the next table.

"The roan, which roan," another asked, "the one that just took off for Mexico?" The man slumped back into his chair, slapped his leg and roared heartily.

"No," said Cole. "Big roans like the one out front have speed but little strength. I had one. It looked majestic charging around town but for pulling strength, forget it, it's not in it. My beauty had trouble pulling an empty sled over ground covered with snow."

"That's mouthy, farmer boy," said a scornful, deep voice. "What you riding now, you say, a burro?"

The saloon grew quiet. The boots that were scraping across the worn wooden planks moments earlier were silent. Even the cowboys quieted down. Cautious patrons moved off to where they hoped the terrain was safer.

"Meant no offense, sir," said Cole, lightheartedly but not sounding repentant at all. "If that's your roan out there, I'm sure it's a fine horse. But we both know it's not bred to pull weight. They run like hell but just can't pull. I've owned one and pulled it against others, and I'm lucky right now I got this shirt right here on my back."

Cole turned to his new friends. They stared silently at him, mouths open. "How about another one, men?" suggested Cole.

A loud WHAM reverberated through the saloon. A heavy weight of some kind had been thrown onto a table or the floor. Cole heard the clock ticking over the bar. He hadn't noticed it before. The saloon had turned deathly quiet.

What made the noise? If it's a gun, Cole thought, I might have to back down. In no way do I want to go out in a gun battle, at least not now in this saloon. He hadn't gotten his word out yet, either. If it was a fist or a whiskey glass, a fight may be in order. That was more down his path. Cole looked over and the hell raisers were looking at him. Not one was smiling or even whispering. Just staring. All eyes were on Cole.

Cole looked over his shoulder at his challenger. He knew it was his challenger because a space had been cleared between them. The man was a gambler, dressed in black, with a rouged face. An officer, thought Cole. "Sir, I own a horse that's crossbred with a Vermont Morgan . . . you may not have heard of a Morgan or seen one." Cole's smile was gone, replaced by innocent earnestness. He sounded like a schoolteacher. "They're bred for strength." He spoke patiently, explaining why Rusty was superior. "He's probably not a beautiful horse like yours," Cole concluded, "but he is powerful. I'd like to leave it at that."

Cole turned to his table and smiled. His new friends remained silent. Cole could still hear the clock ticking.

The gambler raised his ante. "Were you old enough to serve in the War?" he asked as he stared into his cards.

"Yes, sir." Cole heard some patrons sigh their relief. The gambler was maybe attempting to soften his position. "Yes, sir," said Cole, placing an air of reverence into his response, "the 11th Vermont Infantry Regiment, sir. We worked with the Vermont Brigade. We were in defense of the north side of Washington. Saw fire at Spotsylvania, Fisher's Hill, Cold Harbor, and Petersburg."

"On a soldier's honor," said the gambler, eyes still on his cards, "are you ready to wager in a battle of strength?"

Pausing first, then looking puzzled and shaking his head, Cole answered meekly, "Yes, sir, you mean you against my horse?"

Laughter ripped through the saloon. Drinks were guzzled and spit out, backs were slapped, and spurs again struck out at the floor. Spittoons took a beating, as did the floors and the people near them. Legs were slapped, and faces howled at the ceiling in laughter.

Trembling, the gambler looked up and glared. He stepped to his feet and pointed at Cole. The saloon quieted a bit but it was nowhere near as quiet as it had been.

The gambler spoke loudly to be heard above the talk and laughter. "You're smart, boy. My roan against your nag. I wager five hundred dollars. Is your character as sharp as your tongue?"

Cole backpedaled. "Sir, I hurt your feelings." He extended both hands palms down, a sign of peace. "But I leave for the West in two days. I'm going to be roving scout for Al Witham's wagon train. I'll be on the north side. I'd like to accept your challenge but I cannot."

"You're a coward," the gambler yelled out loudly. His rouged face grew scarlet as he seethed in anger. "Boy, your honor is at stake. Soldiers of the Union Army do not run from a challenge."

Cole looked puzzled again. "Sir, I accept, given my honor as a soldier has been questioned. We must schedule the contest, though, so that my plans to go west are not affected. Are you in agreement?"

"Yes, of course," responded the gambler, relaxing for the first time.

Cole was pleased too. He didn't want a gun battle any more than the gambler. Cole continued, "I must limit the size of my bet to twenty-five dollars. I'm not a rich man, sir." Cole turned now to the crowd. "Are there others willing to cover the remainder of the bet?"

Intense wagering was instantly unleashed in the saloon as interest in the personal battle between Cole and the gambler quickly waned. Several of the patrons went outside to look at the two horses. A quick-witted gambler dragged a blackboard out from behind the bar. An associate collected bets while he was making odds. Everyone in the saloon had quickly become a part of a horse-pulling contest.

Still affecting an air of simpleness, Cole, smiling, went over to the gambler's table and offered his hand. "I don't know as I entirely understood your points but I'd like to remain your friend. My name is Cole Mason and I come from Vermont. My pa and brothers run a farm up there."

The gambler looked overwhelmed. Rouge ran in lines down his face. He accepted Cole's hand. "Sorry, kid, we met this way. I'm on my way west. San Francisco. Got an idea for a supply business out there, mainly hardware. My name's Johnson, Major Phil Johnson. You baited me, kid, I know that. You aren't as simple as you're trying to make out. But you'll be sorry for it. I got a good horse out there. You're going to need a machine to beat that roan."

The major was handsome, tanned, and his rouged face gave off a look of power, though the streaks in it now made him look silly. Like an Indian that hadn't learned how to apply war paint. His one-on-one manners were impeccable. His background must be private school, Cole guessed.

They shook hands. The major talked freely. He had commanded a Union Army unit, the 8th Virginia Regulars out of Alexandria. Although a native of Virginia, he had taken an oath as a young man in support of the Union and he kept it. Having fought north of Washington, Cole knew that Alexandria was on the south side of Washington.

"Didn't sit too well with neighbors who supported the Gray, but that's the way it was there. One family went for the North, another for the South. We'll get over it." He told Cole he was a graduate of the Army's top school, West Point in New York. "Tell me, soldier," he asked Cole, "what did you boys from Vermont do at Petersburg?"

"Sir," answered Cole, "we carried the flag around the left flank of Hastings and cut off his artillery. His center began to cave. It was a long, tough battle, though."

"Ah," said the major, obviously pleased with Cole's reply, "you Vermont boys earned your stripes that day, yes sir."

"Thank you, Major," responded Cole.

"Who was your commanding officer?" asked Major Johnson.

"Colonel and later General James Warner, sir, a West Point graduate himself from Middlebury, Vermont. A fine leader and well liked by all his men, sir."

"I agree with your assessment entirely. I knew James Warner. He was a couple years ahead of me at the Point. A fine soldier. One heck of a lady's man too. I'm glad we met, soldier," the major continued, "sorry I'll have to tan your hide tomorrow."

His smirk looked a little silly with the rouge running, thought Cole. He's going to be a tough loser. Winning is important to him. Born in Rebel territory, he picked to fight for the North. That may give an insight into him. He hates to lose.

The two men shook hands again. Major Johnson was not short but Cole stood at least three inches over him. They each selected a second to work out the details of the competition. Cole picked for his second, his new friend, the one-armed Donnie. The contest would be held across from the sheriff's office near Lady's, at a time just past noon the next day. Cole was pleased at the site selected.

Cole saluted the major and the major returned it informally, almost like a hand wave.

Cole and Donnie talked over the details of the contest for several minutes. They shook hands, and Cole headed out.

CHAPTER EIGHTEEN

Cole pushed open the doors of the saloon and inhaled the night air. He made sure he kept his back and shoulders straight, eyes ahead, and arms swinging evenly in military fashion. He smiled continuously, looking side to side. He knew that many sets of eyes were on him and he wanted them to see a confident man. The drinks he had in the saloon didn't help his performance.

The cool air refreshed him. When he had gotten clear of the saloon, he sighed, half-closing his eyes. He breathed lightly from one side of his mouth as though he didn't want anyone to hear the sigh. That was a close one, he thought. It took all his skills and some he never had. Good to be out of there.

He suddenly felt his left foot flap, slowly at first then more rapidly, then uncontrollably. Nerves. His left foot tapped, tapped, and tapped on the planks as he hobbled across them. Better get to Rusty before someone sees me crippled—a hero shouldn't have bad nerves. Upon reaching Rusty, Cole swung himself up and just as quickly started off to Lady's. He felt a burst of energy when he thought about beautiful Natalie.

Lady's? Why was he going to Lady's? Cole's head felt light. Did he want to see Natalie? Yes, he did. Natalie could help catch the sniper. What better place to pick up intelligence than in a whorehouse! That was it! That was why he wanted to go there. His head spun in circles. The alcohol was affecting his thinking. Or maybe it was the sudden cool air, he thought.

How do you go about it in a whorehouse, anyway, he wondered. The man and woman must talk to each other. I mean, there must be trust even though it's a business situation. Trust can hardly begin without conversation, right? Yes, that has to be it. They talk first.

As he rode down the road, Cole spotted campfires on the banks of the Missouri. They're starting west in the morning. They're talking over the tough trip ahead. And getting mite and mosquito bites. Probably learning English too, by listening to the trail master scream at them. Sonia's at one of those campfires. He hoped she was safe. His mind turned to the beast. Going to make her into a queen. He shook his head. He felt like he was sobering up.

He saw the lights of Lady's ahead. Easy to pick out—ornate roofline, not plain and sloping like the neighboring buildings. A lot of wrought iron used to trim that building. Must have kept a team of blacksmiths busy at least a year. Two gables, like some of the houses in Petersburg. Six horses tied up in front. Was he on time for dinner? He grinned. He kept feeling a little better. He was ready to feel a lot better. The spinning was disappearing. In fact he was beginning to feel giddy. That was the next step in his sobering process.

Cole slid off Rusty in front of a thick, planked entrance door. A siege door at Lady's, he marveled. Seems appropriate, I guess. He shrugged. Fancy kerosene lamps set off the doorway. The carved outline of a reclining naked woman graced the planks of the gate. I guess if you don't know where you are and can read pictures, you'd know where you are. He grinned. Do you knock or just wander in? I doubt you stand and yell. Cole was beginning to enjoy himself.

He chose to rap loudly. A small metal slide in the door opened and the fat face of a Negro man showed in the opening.

The expressionless face asked, "What do ya want, cowboy?"

"Cole Mason's the name. I want to speak to Natalie. Is she available?" he added, wondering whether that was appropriate to say.

The face scowled. "You been drinking, cowboy?"

"No, not really," said Cole, showing not a lot of confidence. "I want to speak to Natalie."

The face paused for a moment and then said, "She's done work at six o'clock. You can see her from nine in the morning until six. Come back tomorrow." The metal door slid shut.

"Tell her I'm here, please. Cole Mason," Cole screamed at the closed metal opening.

Cole could hear the man talking behind the metal screen. "I got rules, cowboy. I don't break 'em, otherwise, I got no job. You wanna get me in trouble with the Lady?"

Cole then heard another voice behind the door. This one was soft.

"Who is it, Napie?"

This is tougher than getting into an army fort, thought Cole. You'd think the whole Confederate Army was about to assault. He shook his head. The spinning in his head was gone.

The metal window slid open again and Natalie's face appeared. She had a pleased smile. Cole was relieved to see her. He hadn't planned what to say next. She opened the gate and walked out.

"Hi." He smiled shyly. "I didn't think I'd ever see you again. The security here is amazing," he added.

Natalie was laughing. She obviously found humor in his comments. She was wearing a long white dress cut and billowing at the shoulders, and woven black lace around her neck. Her black hair was pushed up and braided and held in place with multicolored, dyed wooden hair clips. Cole found himself staring at her and breathing heavily. There was a fragrance about her that turned the air sweet. He was pleased to have her laughing and beside him, but nervous in the presence of her beauty.

She grabbed Cole's arm and without a pause led him off down the boardwalk. They walked arm in arm.

Her sentences flew out as fast as bullets from a repeating rifle. "Napie is protective. I am Mrs. Talbot's business manager. I keep the books and make sure linens are fresh, that the food gets purchased, that cowboys' vomit gets taken care of." She laughed gently after her description, then stared at Cole. "You know," she said, "all the unspectacular duties."

He looked at her without expression; he was lost for words. "Oh," he finally said.

She stared again at him. They both laughed.

"When I left you yesterday, I was afraid you'd think I was one of the girls." She laughed. "I'm not." She paused and looked directly at him and laughed again. "Incidentally."

Cole felt the blood moving to his face. He tried to match the quality of her laugh but all he could get out was a groan and a forced grin. She tugged slightly on his arm and they resumed walking.

"I so much wanted to tell you that my work was on the business side." She laughed again. "But some of the girls, they are so very sweet." She turned to him and smiled mischievously. "Do you want a recommendation?" Her laughter was happy sounding and came in a slow flow.

"I 'preciate that," he responded, "but a sensitive, well-spoken lady like you would certainly hold a different kinda position. And about the recommendation. Should I need one, you're certainly the first one I'll come to." This time he smiled confidently.

"Oh," she said, mocking Cole's earlier comment and shaking her head playfully.

They both laughed again.

Cole was pleased with the visit but he at first couldn't remember why he was there. After it came to him suddenly, he explained the sheriff's plan to kill or capture the sniper.

She listened intently. When he finished, he could see in her eyes that her mood had changed. No longer was she the happy, playful Natalie.

"But why, Cole, why are you involved in this? Isn't it a lawman's job? It sounds so dangerous, you being the bait and all."

Cole was taken back. "Natalie, you're right, it's dangerous. But the sniper must be destroyed. I fought in the War. It is over. No one man can play God and pass out retribution.

Let peace come." He described how the sheriff had been nearly killed that morning. "And Natalie, I will be a lawman. Sheriff Lawton will deputize me. I'll get reward money, maybe as high as two thousand dollars." That was high, he knew, but he wanted badly to impress her, justify his personal risk, and bring her over to his side.

"Cole," she exclaimed, shaking her head, "you'll be a bounty hunter! They have reputations not much higher than the girls at Lady's."

Gosh, she was beautiful—even when angry, he thought while watching her mouth move. But what had happened to that easy, fluffy disposition? Her mood was deteriorating, thought Cole. She stepped in front of him and he stopped short.

"There's evil in St. Bartow, Cole. Men, women and children are found dead in fields and by the side of roads, anywhere and everywhere, with puncture marks in their necks. I saw evil as a child. The force doing these killings is a menace, much greater than the sniper, much greater. The whole population is imperiled. The killer is evil, evil, evil, Cole." She stared into Cole's eyes, her hands grasping his shoulders.

"I understand," responded Cole, feeling her mood and knowing that the fun part of the walk was over.

"You don't understand," she cut in, "the evil in New Orleans was set loose by the War. It is here! We must do something about it."

She was disturbed, he thought, to shift moods so rapidly.

"My master was flushed out by the fires. Yesterday I saw his face. There may be one or more lairs of evil right here in St. Bartow. We must stop them. They'll overwhelm us." Tears rolled down her cheeks.

She's back on the beasts, he thought. He had somehow put her back on the beasts. She wants me to get the sheriff to focus on the beast problem. Cole shrugged to himself. Convincing Lawton to go after the beast before the sniper would be like convincing Abe Lincoln, were he alive, to become the president of the Confederacy. Particularly since the sniper just tried to kill the sheriff.

They walked in silence. He heard a gunshot far off, and wild animals posturing for battle up in the backlands. He also heard dogs running by in search of food. An occasional lamp attached to a building attempted to cast a circle of cheer. Both of them were upset but neither wanted to go back before making up.

Natalie touched Cole's shoulder. "Look, Cole, over there, what's that?"

Cole looked where Natalie was pointing. A hanging lantern was picking up a reflection of something on the ground, beside a mud puddle.

Cole walked down the steps of the boardwalk and made his way across the road. Natalie followed close behind. The closer he got to the form the more human it looked. A dead body, maybe? It was a body. Cole bent down to investigate. It was the body of a young man. Cole reached down, picked it up, and carried it gently over to the light of a flickering lantern on a nearby building.

"Is he dead?" asked Natalie.

A mother out late with two children stopped to peer over Cole's shoulder. The body's arms flopped open as Cole laid it down on the boardwalk. The boy's hands were badly mauled. There had been a struggle, thought Cole. A big struggle. Not a natural death.

"Oh, come children, let's move along," said the woman, her curiosity satisfied, "not for children's eyes." She scurried off ahead into the dark, the children jabbering questions in her wake.

"He's dead," Cole said calmly.

The boy's face was white, as if his blood had been drained. There was a smell about the body, like it'd been sitting a while. Was the smell on the boy's clothing? Cole guessed that if he'd been in a puddle, he might smell like that. Bodies on the roadside might not be collected quickly in St. Bartow.

Natalie was silent, content to have Cole take the lead. She shivered in the cooling night air. "Look," she shouted suddenly, "Cole, look, his throat, punctures on his throat. Oh my," she whimpered, holding her hands to her face.

Cole breathed in rapidly. He placed his arm under the neck and raised it. Natalie was right, two purple blotches on the neck. Flickers of light from the lamp lighted the boy's face. Now it was Cole's turn to gasp. "Oh my, it's Carl," he whispered. He slowly pulled himself a few inches away from the boy.

Natalie trembled and moved in close to Cole's side. "Oh, I'm so afraid," she moaned. "I thought I'd left evil behind but it follows me, it threatens me. And no one understands."

Cole wasn't listening. He felt disoriented. Too much to observe and take in at one time. The sniper, the beast. Maybe evil is here affecting everything.

"Wait, wait," he said, standing up. He removed his hat and shook his head, trying to give off a sense of levity. He breathed slowly in and out. "This is Carl and he's been killed by a wild animal."

"No, no, no!" screamed Natalie. "He was killed by an evil beast that behaves like an animal sometimes and a human at other times. Cole, you are as unthinking and unreasonable as all men are." She broke from him and ran up the boardwalk back toward Lady's.

Cole's eyes followed her, then he looked down at the young man. He liked Carl, despite their problems. Had he unwittingly had a hand in his death? He felt unconnected. He needed understanding and there was no one to give it.

He ran after Natalie. He could barely see her up the boardwalk as she ran past the lamps on the buildings. She reached Lady's about fifty feet ahead of him and was instantly behind the gate.

"Natalie, please, wait, let's talk," he yelled, banging on the door.

The metal window slid open and Napie's angry face showed. "Get out. You're upsetting the girls and the customers," he shouted, slamming the window shut.

"You Rebel shit," Cole yelled, "let me in." He banged on the door using both hands and kicking it with his feet. He picked up a large rock lying by the roadside and threw it at the door. It bounced off, falling harmlessly into the road. He wanted to take that smug frigging Napie in his arms and bust his head open. But the door remained closed.

Dejected, Cole started back to where he had left Carl's body. It was still there under the light, ignored. Where was Pete? Why was Carl singled out? Was he, Cole, somehow involved in Carl's death? Did Willoughby Marchess fit into this? And what the hell was Willoughby, anyway?

Suddenly it struck him. The voice on the boardwalk. Carl's body was only about a thousand feet or so from the place on the boardwalk where he'd spoken with the voice. The blood on the boardwalk. Was it Carl's? Was Carl already dead when the voice spoke to him? Did the voice plan to kill him as he had already killed Carl? Or did someone else, for some other reason, kill Carl?

Cole moved Carl's body farther off the road; he couldn't leave it out in the open. He must go for help. He wished Natalie were with him. He sheltered Carl's body as best he could, for he feared the return of the foraging dogs.

He mumbled a respectful good-bye to Carl, patted his arm lightly, and started for the sheriff's office.

CHAPTER NINETEEN

Finding his way in the semi-darkness to the sheriff's office, Cole thought about Carl, about beasts, and about Willoughby Marchess. Marchess was the key to the beast, being the link to every strange occurrence Cole had witnessed or heard of since he'd rode into St. Bartow. Beast sightings, attacks and killings had filled his life since having that drink with the man at the Silver Dollar Saloon.

Cole concluded that Marchess was a beast. Simple as that, no matter how strange it sounded. And that he was responsible for these strange events, including the killings. Lawton was wrong. The killer was not an animal. The little man smelled like death, like the dead air from an open tomb. But it would be difficult, he reasoned, to behave as though he thought Marchess was a beast, in front of anyone but Brave, Natalie, and the Josephsons.

A mosquito buzzed Cole's neck and ears. He slapped at it. It still buzzed. The insect was after his blood. So, was a mosquito a beast? Was there any difference in behavior between a mosquito and a beast? Are we dealing simply with a problem of scale? He still was searching for reasons not to accept the existence of beasts.

The pace of the sightings and the number of attacks had speeded up. Cole felt a chill in his body like a sliver of cold metal. He trembled. What was the meaning of it all? Are beasts flowing steadily into the area?

Maybe Stilkey was right, immigrants were the source of the beasts. As more immigrants showed up, there are more sightings. Immigrants have different beliefs and languages. Maybe some are beasts or they are smuggling in beasts. Maybe it's such that the immigrants don't even know they're doing it. Cole shook his head as if to clear it. This couldn't be. It was so easy to find blame in the immigrants. As

Lawton said, 'they can't fight back and they look and behave differently.' No immigrants to date were involved in his experiences with beasts, thought Cole. The Josephsons are immigrants and they are good people. Without evidence, identifying immigrants as beasts would do nothing but start a witch-hunt. Can't accept 'the immigrants did it' conclusion either.

At the sheriff's door he rapped twice. After a pause, the door swung open. He smiled when he saw Brave, gun in hand.

Brave flipped the gun back into its holster and smiled at Cole. "Don't always get friendly visitors on foot this time of night," he said lightly, "pays to be prepared." Brave noted the concern on Cole's face. "What's wrong?"

"Killing, Brave, bad killing down the road. The road boy Carl, found him dead near a puddle not too far up the road, his neck's a mess, two puncture wounds. He'd tried to fight the attacks off. He had cuts and bruises all over his arms. Every drop of blood, every drop was sucked right out of him."

Brave's face tightened. He suddenly looked drawn. His bottom lip trembled. Why the boy? Brave thought as he found the nearest chair and slumped into it. His eyes stared into nothingness as his thoughts overtook him: There must be a reason. Beasts vigorously protect their interests. The boy knew something the beast didn't want known, or he must have done something the beast didn't want done. It couldn't be a coincidence that he picked to kill a kid he'd likely been dealing with.

Oblivious of Cole's presence, Brave continued thought: The tribe fought against a beast many years ago. He was a young man, a member of his mother's tribe. The tribe was compact. It acted as a unit against the beast. They were successful. That cannot be the case with the white man. If the boy chose to combat the beast, he did it alone. He had no help. He worked alone. He was no match.

White men are free men. What does that mean? It means they are not prepared to combat beasts. White men are always going somewhere, never satisfied. Beasts easily hide among them. Beasts buy protection from the weak. Beasts peck away at white man's freedoms until one day the white man has no freedom.

Brave was now talking to himself in a whisper and staring at Cole. "They say the white men think 'there's no such thing as a beast. You're crazy. It's all in your head. It's an animal.' "

"What, what," said Cole, not understanding Brave's mumblings. Cole recognized the distinctive markings of a battle-ready warrior forming on Brave's face and forehead. He was preparing for battle. It must be coming soon, he thought.

"I'm sorry," said Brave, straightening himself out, "thoughts about Carl were running through my head."

"Carl's body is just down the road. I protected it, but there are hungry dogs out there. Won't take long for them to find him."

"Let's get over there and look at the scene," said Brave, turning his mind to current business. "Too late to get Lawton. How'd you find him?"

"I was out with Natalie, the business manager at Lady's. She saw him first, by the side of the road. Do you know her?"

"Yes, know her well," said Brave, smiling. "She has become a legend in St. Bartow. The cowboys take their pay to Lady's, thinking Natalie is one of the girls. She isn't. Some disappointed boys."

He was interested in her himself, thought Cole. He looked at Brave. Brave was handsome, strikingly handsome. He'd make a good husband for a Negro lady. Cole was surprised to feel pangs of jealousy.

The two walked in silence back toward Carl's body. The lantern Cole held reflected its light off the ground and to the clouds of mist gathering in the dark along the roadside. The boardwalk was empty. It was a sad walk for both of them.

The body lay unmolested. Brave immediately bent down and inspected it.

The kid was dressed as always, thought Cole, in his modified bib overalls obviously purchased to fit someone taller. He looked small lying there.

"He has two clean puncture wounds on the left side of the neck, three inches below the chin line," said Brave. "His blood was sucked clean. Unusually clean. The wound differs from that of other victims I've seen. Streams of blood are usually caked on the victim's neck. Sometimes the streams run down to the chest and even come through the clothes. Not so here. The lust was strong for Carl's blood. The beast was thirsty or he hated Carl. Hate can strengthen a beast's desires, as can lust. He cleaned every drop of blood out of the poor boy."

"What's your conclusion?" asked Cole.

"He was definitely killed by a beast." Brave turned to Cole, who said nothing. "Lawton would say he was killed by an animal, I'm sure. Hard to conclude it was an animal. I'd say the killing is unusual in that the beast may have had something against Carl. Had he just happened upon him, he would never have spent that much effort draining him. Two may have been attacking him at the same time, but his neck shows only one set of puncture wounds."

Cole was silent. He was still having difficulty talking about beasts in his midst. He cleared his throat and said, "Carl told me a story yesterday." Cole now told Brave all that he knew and experienced about Marchess since arriving in St. Bartow. He included Carl and Pete's story about Marchess turning into a bird in front of them.

"Interesting," Brave responded thoughtfully.

Cole felt increasing respect from Brave, who added, "We'll keep these things in mind."

Cole noted that he didn't say "We'll report these things to Lawton."

"The boy didn't go down easily," said Brave, moving from the light so that Cole could see clearly. "Boy's clothes are torn. Look here." He pointed at the ground. "Here's scuffle marks where the boy tried to free himself."

Cole looked over the body and the ground, and agreed that Carl had put up a ferocious battle. Perhaps he wounded the attacker or pulled clothes or feathers or whatever off him, he thought. He suggested, "Let's search the area closely, see if we can find anything that may be tied to the battle."

Cole moved about six feet away to the edge of the road gravel where the scuffle apparently had begun. Brave held the lantern close to the ground and walked over to him. They looked intently at every square inch. They crossed the ground in a search grid, holding the lantern to light the area.

Partway through the search, they each saw a reflection at the same time. Was it a marble, a mica rock, a piece of discarded tin?

Cole reached down and picked it up. He handed it to Brave, saying, "Feels like the outline of a clasp for a badge."

Brave held it close to the light. "This may be important," he said with excitement in his voice. "It may have been ripped from the attacker. Hasn't been here long. It's clean on the front and back. We've had much wet weather lately and mud is not caked to it."

Cole remembered clasps like it in the military. "It looks like it held a medal or a badge. It's bigger than the ones used in the military. Its production is not unique. I'd say it was made in a batch molding process."

Brave said, "Strange finding it here. Not that many medals around here. I'll show it to Lawton, see what he thinks."

"Yeah," said Cole, laughing gently, "he'll think Carl was maybe killed by an animal wearing a medal."

Brave looked at Cole, smiled but said nothing. After he searched the area a while longer, Brave said, "I think our work here is done. Won't do any good but I got to report this killing to the marshal. The sheriff keeps a proper relationship with him even though it does no good. That guy sure upsets Lawton. He has two fat deputies at his side, waxy looking, red-faced deputies, important as hell, they think. They spend days eating and nights doing what you'd expect. A sad operation for a government office," Brave concluded, shaking his head.

Cole laughed at Brave's description. It was the first time he'd laughed in a while. "Well, you're not fat or red-faced yet. Better stay with the sheriff."

Brave laughed. The two men stared at each other for a split second and then laughed again, understanding each other.

"I'll take the body to the undertaker," said Brave, "notify the sheriff and the marshal, and try to find a next of kin. Doubt I'll find one. The boy was always on the street. Tough to know where he came from. I'll put up notices of his death. I'll also put a watch out for his friend, Pete. And you," he shook his finger at Cole, "you better get rest. You have an important contest tomorrow."

"Right," said Cole, suddenly feeling very tired.

Brave picked up Carl's body and set off for the undertaker's.

Cole headed back to get Rusty. He had left him at Lady's. He must be getting lonely, he thought, it's been a long day.

CHAPTER TWENTY

Cole woke to the smell of dampness rising from the spring foliage as the sun poked through the trees. A spot of warmth settled on him. He pushed lower into his blanket. Too early. Sleep, he wanted sleep. Suddenly Carl's face stared down at him. It was white and bloodless, with lifeless eyes. Cole cast the blanket aside and shot up as though he'd heard a bugle.

With six-gun in hand, he was nearly naked, half-awake, and half-ready for anything. He blinked and looked about. He was in his campsite and nothing was out of place. Rusty grazed peacefully, secured to a scrub tree. The horse turned away, finding greater interest far off.

Cole had been dreaming. Everything came back to him as he stood there feeling silly. Carl's death, the Union Saloon, the sheriff's plan, his talk with Natalie, his talk with Brave, the voice from the boardwalk. . . . Had it all happened in one day? A week? No, he decided, it had all happened in one day.

As he prepared himself for the new day, he suddenly knew—the way that truth comes to a fresh morning mind—Carl's death was not the work of an animal. Sheriff Lawton was wrong. He was right last night. He needed no further proof. Natalie and Brave were right. There was a beast at work in St. Bartow. He would speak as though there were beasts in St. Bartow to everyone, even to Sheriff Lawton.

Cole poured coffee and sat cross-legged watching the valley lose its freshness and turn a lighter shade of green. The scene was serene and far removed from his experience of the night before. On the valley floor, he saw a wagon train preparing to depart as smoke plumes from twenty or more campfires wafted their way up into the morning air. He heard not a whisper of sound from the scene. So different from his last day, he thought.

Did the beast have a goal? Take over the territory? Take over the West? The Union? Or was it without purpose, interested only in humans as nourishment? After listing the possibilities he shook his head as if erasing them. How long had the thing been here? Had it influenced history? How was it able to get humans to help it? Did the beasts have a way of growing in number?

Cole knew he had to leave for St. Bartow. He had to get ready for the pulling contest; he had to review the rules. He was reminded of his father's words: "He who makes the rules usually wins the contest." That warning was particularly appropriate, he thought, if your opponent was a Major Johnson. He smiled.

Cole finished his coffee, cleaned and stored his gear, saddled Rusty, and warily began another roundabout trek into St. Bartow.

* * * * *

Nearing town, Cole heard guns shooting off as rapidly as the barking of packs of wild dogs. Drunken cowboys? Lawton must have his hands full, he thought. The gunfire got louder as he got closer to the contest site. When he turned onto the main road, the purpose of the noise became clear. Men were lined up on the boardwalk firing off revolvers, one after the other. Frontier advertising, thought Cole, surprised by the racket and the interest it was drawing.

The odds board from the saloon had been set up in front of the sheriff's office. Two rouged associates of the major's, dressed in their blacks, were accepting wagers. More than three thousand dollars had been bet so far, Cole could see on the tally board as he rode past.

The contest was a town-wide celebration. Drunks, soldiers, settlers, immigrants, cowboys, town Indians, freemen, and farmers were milling about and watching the odds board. Others stood around eating popcorn and drinking sarsaparilla. Several road boys were engaged in battling with fists, feet, sticks, and handfuls of mud and dirt.

Cole looked for Pete but he was nowhere to be seen. Cole saw Donnie near the official's center.

Donnie saw Cole at the same time and he quickly headed toward him with a broad smile on his face. "I told the major you'd be here," Donnie sang out.

Sounds a mite bit relieved to see me, thought Cole.

"The major's telling everyone that you are going to skip out. He's offering bets on your skipping out." Donnie laughed. "The major would take a bet on his grandma's time of death."

Cole grinned and spoke with confidence. "Thanks for getting here early, Donnie, and for working this out. Quite a circus, eh? Must lack entertainment here. Any trouble with the major, other than a runaway mouth?"

Donnie relaxed. "No, he's confident, though he keeps talking about the size of his roan and the puniness of your horse. Says your horse has arms and legs like a hardware supply salesman. Sorry about those remarks. They are his exact words. But on the rules, he's like a starving dog searching for a bone. The man is always working for an angle or an edge."

"He knows nothing about Morgan-bred horses. He comes out of Virginia where everything is size and speed. Morgans are confined mostly to the Northeast. They have an endless amount of determination and an equal amount of strength. Their weight is low to their leg muscles. That makes them losers in speed races but winners pulling weights. The good major will be educated by afternoon's end." Cole thought how good it was to be free of beasts for a while.

Donnie smiled wanly. "I don't know dung 'bout horses, Cole, 'cept how to ride 'em and how to feed 'em and kiss 'em when they're good. I want you to beat that gambler's red ass though." Donnie laughed his apology.

"Well, Donnie, old man, you get me a fair pull and you'll soon see a beet-red ass." Cole laughed and Donnie joined in. He's gaining confidence, thought Cole. The wager board showed a lot of money riding on the major. It's bound to affect temperament, Cole reasoned.

The two men moved to the official's center where the major and his second were talking to anyone that would listen. The crowd was growing larger, Cole noted, and it showed no signs of leveling off. More spectators were here today than live in the whole of Franklin, Vermont, he thought. A lot of them must be up from the staging area. He saw several ladies dressed fashionably, coyly seeking eye contact with men. That wasn't difficult to achieve with the ratio of men to women, about twenty to one, he thought. He looked around for Natalie and wondered whether any of the ladies on the boardwalk were from the house of ill-fame.

Donnie and Cole pushed their way to the official's center.

The major saw them approaching and came forward with his hand extended and a smile of a rascal. "Well, you made it. I was some worried. A town like this is good for rumors. Some had you halfway to Lowry, hell bent." The major put his head back and roared.

An extra long fusillade of gunshots pierced the air as the major and Cole shook hands. The major's face was fully rouged today and he grinned widely.

He must have spent all night cleaning his face and getting ready for today, thought Cole. "No way in hell, Major, I'd put earth between me and teaching you a little humility." It was Cole's turn to laugh, a gentle, confident giggle.

"Humility. Mighty big word for a private. Learn it from your mama?" The major held a stare and a smile at Cole.

"No, I learned it in the War, writing about skirmishes with the Rebs down there in Virginia."

The two stared at each other for a few moments, eye to eye, smile to smile.

The major's mustache was shaped perfectly, not a whisker out of place. It was waxed, too. Rouge and cosmetics are big in his life. I can't picture him behind a plow leading a team of mules.

The two walked side by side toward a sled at the beginning of the course piled high with logs. Their seconds followed in step a few yards behind. The sled would be weighed down with the weights, and successive weights that Donnie and Cody had agreed upon.

"So this is the horse I'm going to own," said the major, casually taking Rusty's reins and looking at his teeth. Rusty turned his head, pulling away.

"What are you talking about?" demanded Cole. "Let that horse go." He grabbed the horse's reins from the major.

"Well," said the major, "hoss pulls are claiming pulls 'round here. The winner takes the loser's horse for wagon pulling or whatever. I'll claim your horse when I win. Now, if you want to up the wager, we can take this out of the claiming category. Make the pull worth my while and when you lose, you lose the money but keep the nag. I got no use for him anyway."

Cole was visibly upset. He glared at the major and brought his face down to within six inches of his. "You touch this horse . . ." Cole's voice trailed off.

The major got the message; he needed no more clarification. Major Johnson averted Cole's stare. "Take it easy, private, you haven't lost yet."

"Claiming a horse and taking ownership, Johnson, may be your custom, but where I come from it takes a bill of sale. Otherwise it's stealing and for that, there's a remedy."

The major's smile receded. Being accused of being a horse thief was not to be taken lightly.

An official in the center of the crowd shouted, "Okay, if everything is in order, let's throw the wood to the fire and get it underway."

"Things look fine," said Cole, nodding to Donnie.

Donnie nodded back.

The major stated, "I hear Morgans are skittish, unsure and unsteady on light weights. I hope you're able to settle that guy down. He is nervous." The major looked directly at Cole and added, "Private, you should address me as Major

Johnson. I led your army for five years, and to victory. I believe I deserve your respect."

Cole turned away. The man was irritating. He's a pole-cat, he thought. I'm not in the military. The Union is a democracy. I'll treat the man as he deserves. And I'll beat his ass today, bright red or whatever color it is underneath that rouge. That's that!

Cole looked over the crowd. He picked out Natalie in front of Lady's. She was wearing a fancy hat with a long, curved feather. It looked like a hat that would be worn in New York or Paris. Her dress bloomed outwardly from her knees and she twirled a parasol stylishly to free her of the heat and mosquitoes. Several men gathered around her trying to get her attention. Cole again felt a tinge of jealousy.

"The big guy," Cole said as he pointed toward the official's center, "the guy that's screaming, he's the judge?"

"Yes," Donnie said. "He'll settle challenges or disagreements."

"He sure is big," said Cole. "What's his reputation?"

"His name is Grimson. He's tough and fair. He's a blacksmith and has refereed at least six pulling contests. Major Johnson doesn't scare him. Crowds don't scare him either. I picked him out of three qualified and the major agreed. The guy is as honest as you'll find."

"Not at all in the major's pocket?"

"No. He likes to be known as honest and he's big enough to enforce his decisions."

Cole asked, in a near-whisper, "No money bet on the pull?"

"It doesn't look like he does. But that is something hard to tell."

"Donnie, another duty, please. Get over to the judge and with both Johnson and his second present, make sure they all understand that this is not a so-called claiming race."

Donnie nodded and walked toward the official's center. Cole rubbed Rusty to help relieve tension. Rusty was not used to crowds, thought Cole, nor gunshots.

Cole heard the crowd at the official's center laughing and singing. He could make out the words "When you lose, you can take your horsy home." The refrain was catchy and soon spectators were chanting it.

Wow, thought Cole while looking toward Natalie and being pleased to see she hadn't joined in, the major sure knows how to unsettle opponents.

Shaking his head, Donnie returned to Cole. Laughter continued in the background. "Sorry, Cole, didn't see that one coming. The major's boys were primed to sing. Anyway, Grimson says it is not a claiming race. That would have to be agreed upon between you and the major. The singing was just more major bull."

"Thanks, Donnie." Cole smiled, holding out his hand.

Donnie shook it firmly. He gave Cole a hard stare and a smile that told Cole, "You can count on me."

Cole signaled he was ready. The major did the same. Grimson stood up, completing last-minute paperwork.

Cole looked at the crowd. It was in excess of eight hundred people, he guessed. The road boys were still raising hell, now spitting at each other. Cole looked for Pete again. No luck. Is he hiding in fear or is he dead?

Cole glanced at the gambler's board. About five thousand dollars had been wagered, more than he expected.

Grimson looked up. He took a metal hammer and gave a mighty blow to an anvil on a flatbed wagon next to him. The contest was about to begin.

CHAPTER TWENTY-ONE

A short deformed man stretched his tired body on the stairway leading up to the boardwalk at Lady's. His left leg was crippled badly. He frequently would use both his arms to move it around as though the leg was paining him. Apparently, he was waiting for the contest to begin. Close up the man was calm and content, but from a distance he would be taken for a drunk, mainly because of his worn and dirty clothing. He listened closely to the crowd around him and occasionally he'd experience a happy moment and beat with his right foot to the rhythm of the gunshots coming from farther down the boardwalk.

Half of the man's face was covered by a heavy cloth draped like a cap, making his head appear, at a quick glance, mummified. The cap was pulled to one side of his head, making his features impossible to discern. On close observation, his left leg was severely damaged and its condition defined his movements.

The man's mind was a ferment of activity: Them Yankees got 'selves a short life to go. They'll find a quick end and hard soil out here. Yes, suh. No more horse-pulling, boys, yes, suh.

Dust rose from the road as wagons and spectators passed by. The crippled man coughed and spit. But he appeared unruffled. He listened to the cheering that rose and fell around him like he was on a safe boat watching waves on a sea.

"Hey, you, masked man, want to bet on the pull?"

The little man was startled. No one had talked to him for a month. It was the call of a wager man making his way through the crowd, collecting all potential bets.

"No suh. I'm for both horses and against both men." A grin spread across the small, exposed portion of the man's face. The man turned to the runner and pushed his cap back, exposing his disfigured face.

"I'm sorry, sir," the runner mumbled, "sorry I bothered you." He hurried off in search of other last-minute bets.

* * * * *

The thankless lout tore my coat. He was a vicious boy. I wrestled him. His thrashing body didn't get him free. His soft throat didn't evade for long. I held tight. I sipped his blood deliciously. He weakened. His thrashing slowed. His terrified eyes now stared blankly. His body relaxed and drifted. His heart pumped for me alone. I drained that vicious boy. He was unfaithful. It ended blissfully.

The boy in life was lovely. I offered to make him one with me. We could live and hunt together forever. Natalie could become our companion and slave. He showed himself without trust. He spoke secrets about me to others. He thought I wanted only to invade and use his body. I offered him eternal life. He chose disrespect and disloyalty. He chose the way of a barbarian instead of the life of a god.

I'll go to Natalie. Her heart will lovingly pump for me. She will become one with me. She is too beautiful for a human life. We'll become one together forever.

I leave now on my quest.

CHAPTER TWENTY-TWO

Grimson's voice rose like a foghorn above the noisy crowd. "People of St. Bartow and friends, welcome to the horse weight-pulling contest. The contestants today are—"

"Skip the talk," a voice yelled from up the boardwalk, "put the bridle on and start pulling. Got all my money on you, big boy."

Heads turned toward the source of the interruption and laughter gained strength as it worked its way through the crowd.

Another drunk called from a closer point, "Whooee, I want to bet my money on the fat man nag."

"Funny," Grimson responded, staring out at the source of the heckling. "Let me talk, then we can settle later who's going to do the pulling." The big blacksmith kept staring into the crowd.

The hecklers turned quiet and the laughter quickly subsided.

"The contest is between a mixed Morgan owned by Cole Mason of Vermont, and a gray roan owned by Major Phillip Johnson of West Virginia. Procedures have been agreed upon. Start pull weight is seven hundred pounds. The contestants have agreed upon a length of course containing several difficult sections and one crease near the finish line. The winning horse will successfully pull a weight that the other failed at. The horse that fails first has one additional try to equal or exceed the weight pulled by the competitor horse. Failing again, that horse is the loser. Succeeding, the contest continues until there is a winner. Are there any questions, Mr. Mason, Major Johnson, or the seconds?"

A ripple of laughter spread through the crowd.

The man's dance continues, thought Cole.

Grimson resumed, unfazed. "By winning a toss of the coin, the major chooses to go first."

Cheers erupted, flags waved, and boots beat on the boardwalk planks. One drunk chose that moment to roll off the boardwalk. He crashed down onto the roadbed. "He won, he won," they yelled. Several spectators went over to help him up but he signaled them away. He wanted to rest.

Major Johnson waved lightly and smiled to the crowd as he guided his horse to the starting position at the front of the sled. He steadied the big roan with quiet talk while hitching him to the load. He signaled his readiness to the judge. The judge dropped the flag. The major shouted his "go" command. The roan sensed the attached sled and lowered its haunches.

"Go, go, go," the crowd shouted, louder and louder.

Cole looked through the crowd while he had a chance. He was looking for a loner. One who fit his idea of a sniper and how a sniper would behave in a crowd. He didn't really know what a sniper would look like but he thought he'd know one if he saw one. He found not a single candidate, though.

He saw legions of immigrants, most standing mutely, watching the contest. They were experiencing Western-style horse-pulling and gambling for the first time. They don't look like snipers, any of them. They hardly have a motive either, thought Cole.

Lone drunks were plentiful, weaving in and out of the crowd. Any one of them could be a sniper, he guessed. But the drunks behaved as plainly as drunks, nothing more. They stumbled and panhandled and carried their bottles around as best they could.

Several spectators waved Union flags. They could be snipers using the flag as a cover, he thought. But no flag wavers looked like a sniper either. Cole was frustrated. It was like looking for a gopher in a rabbit hole.

He glanced over at Natalie again. Her dark face and husky lips stood out. She smiled occasionally and said words to those near her. Other women joined her. All were fashionably dressed. He wondered whether those near her were the girls of Lady's. One man near Natalie was dressed in cowboy garb. He was almost at her side. Cole decided the man was a good-looking cowboy. Once again, he felt the sting of jealousy.

A burst of cheers brought Cole back to the contest.

The major's roan had made short work of the run. Guns and cheers saluted his good work. Flags waved and the rumble of boots on the wooden boardwalk rose above the reverberation of the gunshots. Some spectators sucked greedily from the ready whiskey bottles they carried. Cole could hear from nearby spectators that the major's sled had been propelled nearly airborne over the course.

Cole smiled and smartly saluted the grinning and confident major. Showing my respect for a former leader during the "great war," he said to himself.

By the rules, Cole had five minutes to line up Rusty and begin his pull. The five-minute rule kept a competitor from delaying, never finishing and making a "no contest." Preventing a "no contest" could also prevent a riot among the gamblers. The rule also brought closure to the contest if a horse became injured. A horse defaulted if he was unable to pull for any reason within five minutes.

Cole signaled his readiness. Cheers sounded again—but they were not nearly as loud. They're going with the big horse, thought Cole.

"Little horse, little horse, go, go, go," a few cheers started up.

Rusty took off high-legged. There was no need for him to squat down; he was already there. The horse flew easily over the fifty-foot course. Cole was pleased and he patted Rusty affectionately. The crowd continued a low-level cheer.

Grimson signaled to both participants to come up to the contest center. "Look, neither of these horses is a palmetto plant, as we'd say in Carolina. Both are strong. I suggest that the weights be skipped to nine hundred pounds, and go by increases of fifty pounds. The spectators will be here until tonight if we don't speed up, and they'll be drunk and hell raising before long. If you agree, I'll announce it. What are your decisions?"

Cole said simply, "I agree."

The major hesitated. "Having the horses go through successive weights," he finally answered, "will be more difficult for the private's field horse. His horse lacks class and long-run stamina. I choose to continue as we have agreed."

"Wow, very technical," said Cole quietly. He laughed lightly. "Is that a West Point theory or is it officer corps poop?"

"It's your right, Major," said Grimson, reassuring the major. "I don't want nasty comments between you two. It is the horses that are competing here today. I'll announce that the competition will resume with no modification in the rules."

At that, Major Johnson said, "Okay, I change my mind. I agree to move to nine hundred pounds. The next weight will be nine hundred pounds and then nine hundred and fifty pounds. Is that correct?"

"That is correct, if you agree, Major," Grimson stared at the major, bewildered.

"I agree," responded the major.

The judge turned to Cole. "Do you agree?"

"I agree," said Cole, shaking his head, confused by the major's thought process. Perhaps he had become unsure of his approach to the contest. All his gamesmanship has resulted in this confusion, thought Cole.

Grimson announced to the crowd the change in procedure. The crowd booed. The weight was changed in the sled. The crowd cheered. A fickle crowd, thought Cole. The major nodded and Grimson dropped the flag.

The major's roan dug in and took off with every fiber and muscle in its body. It lowered its haunches to no more than two feet off the road. A real feat for a leggy horse, thought Cole. Slowly, the sled began to move. It slowed only when it reached the four-inch crease near the completion of the course. The roan made it to the finish but showed strain.

“Bravo, bravo,” screamed a mix of immigrant wagoners standing on the boardwalk near the finish line. Cole observed that they were all completely involved in the contest and were finding it exciting.

Cole took Rusty to the starting point as soon as the sled was brought back. He attached him quickly to the sled and nodded. Grimson dropped the flag.

Rusty took off. The sled moved almost immediately and never slowed. Rusty smashed across the four-inch crease as though it wasn’t a serious barrier.

Two men up on the boardwalk wearing hats pulled below their ears began to dance wildly. One was wearing a feather in his hat.

“Go, Yankee Doodle, Yankee Doodle,” yelled the crowd as the dancing men speeded up.

Rusty is winning the hearts of the immigrants, mused Cole.

It was the major’s turn. The comments from the crowd turned harsh. “Get that field horse moving,” yelled one animated spectator. “Give the dog a little whiskey,” yelled a second. “Maybe that horse pretty boy is a dolled-up dog,” yelled a third. “There’s a lot of dolling up here. You sure you didn’t use a little of that red stuff on him?” The last comment was aimed at the gambler’s wearing of rouge and it brought some laughter. Most spectators had bet on the roan and they were showing noticeable disappointment in his showing so far.

Cole sensed growing unease in the major’s camp.

“You got yourself there what we call in Illinois a jelly-ass horse. Give the dog some friggin’ leather.”

Some rouged faces had begun to turn red.

The losers were taking it personally, thought Cole.

Before resuming, the major went over and talked to his advisors. He was tense. He backed the roan up to the sled. His playing to the crowd was over. He nodded to Grimson and the flag dropped.

"Hayah, hayah, hayah!" the major screamed. Sweat rolled in streams down his face. His rouge was smudged and running onto his black coat.

He's beginning to look like a clown, thought Cole.

The roan strained gallantly and finally managed to take off. But he lacked a powerful thrust.

The poor horse is exhausted, thought Cole. He had performed his very best.

The roan backed off from the sled, and groans of despair arose from the crowd. The major brought his horse back, reset him, and again screamed his "go" command. Again the roan dropped his haunches, reared back and drove into his harness. Slowly the sled moved, picking up speed as it traveled along the course.

The groans turned to cheers. "Come home, big doggie, come home," yelled the crowd over and over. The guns along the boardwalk, silent for a while, resumed shooting.

The roan needs to get more speed to get over the crease line, Cole thought.

The horse dug in; its hooves kicked up clods of sand and dirt. He struggled heroically to maintain his momentum.

It was truly a gallant effort, thought Cole. He cheered for the roan himself.

With a final thrust, the roan pulled the sled across the finish line. The crowd let loose a tremendous roar. Screams of approval barreled down the main road of St. Bartow.

A relieved and smiling major raised his arms in a victory salute, spinning himself around on his heels for the crowd's approval. Gone was the crowd's disdain for the horse's earlier performance.

It was Cole's turn now. He hitched Rusty to the sled quickly and nodded to Grimson. The crowd had not yet stopped cheering for the roan's performance. The flag dropped.

"Okay go Rusty, go," Cole whispered and patted the horse lightly on the rump. The sled moved slowly at first, but then with increasing speed. It barely slowed moving across the crease, and the horse and sled easily crossed the finish line.

The crowd cheered again. The immigrants who had probably wagered little, thought Cole, were leading the cheering for Rusty.

"Little horse, big heart, little horse, big heart," they yelled in English and in other languages.

Cole looked over at a very somber major.

"We're going to win it," the major yelled above the noisy crowd, thrusting his fist into the air.

He was full of fire, but it was the last gasp of a defeated man. Cole had witnessed such verbal bravado in the past on the battlefield and in Saturday night fights at the dance hall back home.

Cole shrugged and held a finger to the wind, rotating it slowly as he stared up at it. He brought his finger down and rotated it again while he again stared at it. "Looks good to me," he shouted, straight-faced, to Major Johnson.

A puzzled look spread across Johnson's face. Cole intently eyed his finger again, pursed his lips, shrugged and nodded his head to the major. Let him figure that one out, he thought, smiling to himself. Getting beat by a crazy man won't be satisfying.

Cole surveyed the crowd again while the major hitched his roan for the next pull. The sniper must be a loner and he must be in the crowd somewhere. He wouldn't miss a major event like this.

But Cole saw no person that he thought was a sniper. He did not see Pete either. Where was Pete? Nor did he see Willoughby, for that matter. A man was sitting quietly alone on the stairs near Natalie. A hat was pulled down over his ears, covering part of his face. Was the man sick or asleep? He appeared drunk, showing no energy, thought Cole. Probably a drunk, he decided.

Cole turned back to the competition when he heard the cheers. The roan was ready, the flag dropped, and the major screamed his command.

The roan strained and pulled, and lodged its upper body forward against his harness. Cole saw a short moment of movement but that was all. The roan backed off. The horse looked as though it was pleading for rest. Perspiration was pouring from its body. The major dried him down quickly and gave him water.

The major looked the loser. Losing was a tough comedown for him. He was standing but hunched over, almost fragile looking, and his rouge had sunk deeply into his face and coat. The major re-set the roan and again gave the horse a forward signal. Without warning, the major grabbed a horsewhip from an associate and beat the horse hard, repeatedly, against his back legs.

Cole was stunned. Instinctively he ran at the major, grabbed his hand, and twisted the whip out of it. "You have no right to whip your horse. If artificial spurring was acceptable in the contest, it had to have been agreed upon." Cole stood on his toes, looking down on the major. "You broke the rules, you forfeit the contest."

"Who are you," screamed the major, all composure gone, his face looking wild, "I don't see your anvil. The judge didn't forbid it. I can use whatever means I want to make my horse perform. That's not contest rules, that's property rights."

Cole screamed back, "When horses are pitted against each other, the competition is between the horses, not the ability of an owner to whip or scare his horse into better performance." Cole's face was crimson.

The major fumed.

The crowd grew silent. A chorus of boos showed that the major lacked support from some spectators for his action.

The major looked to the judge. "It's your decision, Grimson, can I choose to motivate my property or not? Sometimes you whip an animal to get it to perform. The private here thinks horses are human. Suffering lets the beast display his true mettle. Tell the private I'm right."

The judge stood quietly but his mind was moving fast. There was nothing in the agreed rules approving the use of whips. He had never seen a whip used in a pulling contest except as a signal to the animal.

Only a decision worthy of a King Solomon, Cole thought, could save Grimson from the wrath of the major, his associates, and other disappointed bettors. What would the judge do? If Grimson was fair, the decision should be in his favor.

After a short pause, Grimson spoke. "I fall back on the rules negotiated between the two parties. Nothing is in the rules about artificial inducements, whips or the like. I have judged seven or eight pulling contests in St. Bartow and the issue has never come up. In all of these contests, whips and the like were not used. I conclude that an unstated rule exists that forbids the use of prods of any sort, except voice."

Grimson held up his hands to quiet the buzz of the crowd. "I see no reason to continue this contest. It is clear that the winner is the Morgan horse from Vermont."

The judge gave his anvil a mighty blow. The contest was over.

Many in the crowd roared disapproval. Some spectators moved menacingly at the big judge. "You're a dumb animal and a dead judge," yelled one. Screams and calls rose above the crowd suggesting the judge should lose his hide.

Grimson took a weighty blacksmith's tool and pounded it against his cupped hand and then against the anvil. The crowd began to move off. The judge's action and size quickly settled down the crowd.

Cole was praised by many spectators and congratulated in many languages. Rusty was held in awe; spectators ganged around to look him over. The admiring spectators had a difficult time understanding how a small horse could beat a large horse and by so much.

Donnie and Cole shook hands and smiled at each other.

The major had turned quiet. He looked like he was trying to slip away. His associates left his side and were helping pay off the winning bettors.

Cole was happy. He won the pulling contest and he made himself a top target for the sniper. But he was wary too. He hoped the sniper got the message, but he also hoped he wouldn't carry out an attack immediately. Cole would head west in the morning and fulfill his expected part.

CHAPTER TWENTY-THREE

Cole slept poorly that night; he tossed and woke up often. When awake, his mind repeated the same thoughts over and over. When asleep, he dreamed. He dreamed the same dreams over and over. He dreamed of horses pulling sleds, of crowds cheering, of rouged men, of guns shooting from alleyways, trees, and other high places. And Carl's face appeared over and over . . . silent, bloodless, stark white and sometimes glowing.

Cole finally gave up trying to sleep. He lay awake thinking through his finances. He was wealthier by twenty-five dollars because of his winnings from the pulling contest. His nest egg had dwindled to fifty, but add twenty-five and that gave him seventy-five. That was not enough money to get himself west, get land and start farming. That would cost more than his total, even though the land was free. Willoughby had been right on that score. Starting a business was costly.

He finally crawled out from under his blanket. He built and stared at the campfire, trying to focus his mind. After finishing coffee, he decided to begin immediately the trek into town. He was anxious to hear Stilkey's report on the young fellow killed up in Lowry. He hoped Stilkey's information would help him in his part of the plan. Besides, leaving in the dark would make it more difficult for the sniper to strike at him.

He saddled Rusty, broke camp, and headed into St. Bartow. He took the longest route in. He didn't want to be early and have to wait around for the meeting.

By the time he reached St. Bartow the darkness had begun to recede. He saw Lady's ahead, quiet, dark and stately. Yes, stately, he thought. He looked at the window where

Natalie had told him she often looked out. She was not there. A red tarp was pulled tightly about the window.

Cole thought of Natalie at the pulling contest standing on the boardwalk. She was beautiful, tall and poised. She sure knew how to dress. He wanted to let her know he agreed with her now, that a beast was loose in the area and it was a grave threat. Carl's grisly death had re-formed his opinion on beasts and even changed his opinion about the priority that should be accorded the two killers. He continued to look up at Natalie's window, but she did not appear.

Cole dismounted at the sheriff's office. He secured Rusty and rapped at the door.

The sheriff shook his hand. "That was a great job last night, Cole, very, very good! You have a talent that you hadn't shared! And at the pulling contest, your horse was superb. He's the talk of St. Bartow." Lawton beamed.

"Thank you, Sheriff," Cole said, feeling less tired. He accepted the sheriff's hand. "That was quite a turnout," he added, smiling. "The town loves a show."

"You're right," said Lawton, "and you proved it."

Brave and Stilkey stood by, smiling. The two deputies moved toward Cole and shook his hand.

Brave cuffed him friendly on the shoulder. "Two tins of Mom's coffee for you today."

They all laughed.

"This welcome sounds like you're setting me up for a new risk or you're going to make me drink a gallon of Brave's coffee."

They laughed again.

"We won't do that," Stilkey said. "The last guy we did that to ran off. He ain't been seen since."

More laughter.

Brave wagged his finger at Cole playfully. "I don't think my coffee is that bad," he said, still laughing, "but I did notice I'm not asked to make it often."

They laughed again.

The sheriff opened the meeting. "Jack, tell us what you learned up in Lowry."

"Sure, Sheriff. The kid, Randy Denny was his name, was taken down from about two hundred feet by a softball fired from a long rifle. It had to have been a rifle specially designed for sniping, unless, of course, the rifleman was very lucky. Denny spent the night before his death at a campsite a mile south of Lowry, just off the trail to St. Bartow. That information was from the sheriff up there, Farnsworth is his name. He says he's dealt with you in the past, Sheriff."

Lawton nodded. "Good man," he murmured.

Jack continued: "Denny came into Lowry that night and appeared at three different saloons. He made it clear that he liked a good time. He drank quite a bit and made cute passes at certain girls but always in a mild manner, from a distance, nothing crude. He laughed a lot. Didn't appear to have a serious bone, several told me. Two of the ladies he made passes at had men with them but they weren't upset at all. They were reasonable and they realized that Denny had been on the trail for a few weeks and had some catching up to do.

"In one saloon Denny got with a troop of actors and dancers, women, three or four of them, and volunteered to be in a comedy skit with them. The entertainers had been in Lowry before and all had good reputations. The sheriff vouched for them. Everyone thought the kid did real well. One or two said his acting was professional. He received a hand for his work and that seemed to please him. One of the girls in the troop liked him especial. You know, she smiled and giggled in his direction and rubbed her thigh a bit, you know what I mean. She was unattached. He showed little interest in her, though. By that time he was about washed out on the whiskey. He had been drinking since early evening.

"He announced at this point that he was a Yankee, that he recently left the army, that he disliked Rebels and that he won many citations for his soldiering. He described how he'd taken on and killed a few Rebels all by his self. He said he was westward bound, leaving for St. Bartow the next day. Several townsmen thought a lot of what he said was bull. He was drunk and responding to the cheers. When he left the third saloon, they thought he knew he'd done himself in with the alcohol. Most everyone thought he left town immediately. He wasn't seen in Lowry again.

"The next morning early, Farnsworth figures, 'bout two miles from his campsite, headed south to St. Bartow, in the mossy hills—that's what everyone calls it 'cause of the color of the hilly land—the boy was shot dead. Body was found at about five that afternoon. His camp supplies, money, everything intact. There was a partially written letter to his wife, maybe to his girl, in his pocket. I didn't see it. Farnsworth has it. That's how the sheriff got information on the boy's past. Doesn't look like he'd ever really been in the War. You guys know I don't read too well. But the sheriff up there said he couldn't see anything in the letter that would indicate that the victim was concerned about being ambushed. That's it, Sheriff.

"If you have any questions, I'll take 'em and tell you what I know or what I don't know, or what I think. From what I saw and heard up there, that boy was a good boy. He didn't deserve what happened to him."

Sheriff Lawton asked, "Was there any reaction in Lowry to his talk about Rebels? Any challenges, any tenderness on that score? Lowry has been home to heavy Southern sympathies, as you all know."

"Didn't hear of any, Sheriff," answered Stilkey. "I went through the town and it's solid Yankee now. If there were Rebs there, they been run out, gone into hiding, or changed their stripes. The War is over for the folks up there. They are all just trying to make a living."

Lawton said, "Did you hear of anyone seeing strangers about, hanging around the saloons or on the boardwalks that day?"

"I checked that," said Stilkey. "No reports of anyone of consequence in town at the time of the killing."

"What do you mean by 'of consequence'?" asked Cole, puzzled. "Was anyone seen hanging around there?"

"Well, you know, by consequence, I mean like a mountain man, a guy maybe carrying a long rifle, a guy quiet and drinking and listening, you know what I mean, someone guilty looking." Stilkey continued, "A guy did arrive in town about the same time as the victim. He was dressed in rags and was drunk most of the time and had little money. He was seen in a couple saloons and on the boardwalk steps a time or two. He may have been panhandling, although no one I spoke with saw it. Probably a wanderer. It's a small town so he kinda stood out. He made no impact, part of the scenery, sort of, you know what I mean."

"Any firm description of his appearance and dress?" asked Cole. His excitement was welling.

"Yeah, hat over his face, one side, I believe. I heard that you couldn't see his face because of his cover, so getting a description of him was impossible. One man who saw him up close told me he was disfigured, like from a knife or a rifle ball. The most noticeable thing was that as he walked he dragged a leg, the left one, I think. Unlikely a guy with that kind of ailment could get on a horse and get down here fast."

"That was him!" exclaimed Cole, jumping to his feet. "I saw the same guy at the contest. He was sitting on the steps leading up to Lady's. He wasn't doing anything but sitting and dreaming. I'll bet he's our man."

Stilkey shrugged. "Well, it could be, I guess, but the man I'm talking about was a sick burro. From descriptions, I doubt he could get himself together to bushwhack or to get himself to St. Bartow in time for the attack on you, Sheriff. For example, where would he keep a rifle? The guy behaved homeless."

"Jack," Cole said, "the man you describe fits exactly a man I saw at the contest. I made the same mistake as the people in Lowry. I underestimated him. I thought there was no way that man could pull off a sniper attack. We have to search through St. Bartow. We have to question him. He doesn't know we suspect him. He is probably still here."

Lawton interrupted. "Jack's got a point, Cole. It takes a lot of energy and discipline to pull off a string of sniper attacks. Does that wanderer possess these abilities? From your description, it's difficult to picture the man riding a horse, let alone riding a horse and carrying an enormous rifle. And speed—how would the man get here, get set up and attempt to bushwhack me one day later?"

"A sniper is crazy," Cole responded, his voice an edge higher. "You can't expect sane behavior in a sniper. As far as energy goes, his appearance and actions were perfect for a person wanting to fade into the background. I agree we should develop a reasonable idea of how he and his rifle get around. It may be there are two of these men, looking or acting alike and passing information and possibly living in separate towns."

"I have something to add," said Brave. "I ran into the guy you're speaking of while making security rounds during the contest. He was seated on the steps in front of the Talbot House. He acted drunk. I stood behind him and asked if he was all right. He jumped. Drunks aren't surprised like that. He raised his hat to me. His left cheek was scarred badly. I thought the viewing was done to get rid of me. He wasn't breaking any law, so I let him be. I concluded that there wasn't enough of the guy there to perform a string of sniper attacks. But I agree with Cole. There was something disturbing about the guy. He was very capable of manipulating people by showing his scars. We should look for him. He may still be here."

Cole said, "Sheriff, searching for him in town is worth our time. Brave is right, there's nothing to lose."

"Let me review," said Lawton. "The man in Lowry and the man in St. Bartow may be the same. But Jack's doubt is well placed. It takes considerable support to keep a sniper going . . . a gun, ammunition, a horse, food, shelter, money, and alcohol now and then. But if there were two snipers and they looked alike, it would be much simpler for them to succeed. The guy you describe, Jack, sounds confused, even crazy. He'd make mistakes and become a dead sniper before long. But I agree his appearance and behavior may be just an act. We have time before Cole leaves. I think we should look for him."

"We'll comb the town for him," Brave said. "We'll complete the search before Cole starts west. If we can't find him, he may not be the man, or he may have already left to set up his ambush of Cole."

The sheriff looked around the room. "Do we all agree?"

They were silent.

Lawton looked at each participant, nodding his head, and getting a nod in return. "Good," he said after finishing his round. "And Jack, that was a good piece of work. Thank you."

Jack nodded and smiled.

Tough guy, thought Cole. Did okay. He got good information in only a day's time.

"Okay, another point," the sheriff added. "You all know that Carl, the road boy, was killed last night. You know how he was killed." Lawton paused and cleared his throat. "You also know that a piece of metal that looked like a clasp was found on the surface of the road near where he went down. Given the condition of Carl's fingers, he may have pulled the clasp off the attacker while fighting for his life. Brave turned the piece of metal in to me. I called over Fred Ingals, the Wells Fargo man, and he gave the thing a close look using his new magnifying glass."

"What did he find?" asked Stilkey as he moved to the edge of his chair.

Lawton spoke slowly, choosing his words with care. "He believed the thing was a clasp made of bronze, a common bronze."

Stilkey showed impatience with the pace. "Give it to us, Sheriff, what's it about?"

"It's a clasp made to hold a medal to clothing. In a small indent on the back of the clasp the letter 'U' can be seen, as in U.S. There's room for a second letter but it didn't print. It wasn't worn off, it just didn't print. We decided that had the imprint been made, it would likely have been an 'S.' The clasp was meant to have the letters U.S. on it."

The sheriff shifted in his chair and continued. "Carl may have pulled the medal off the attacker in a struggle. Now, please note," he emphasized, "I say 'may.' The clasp was found at the location of the attack but may have been dropped hours or possibly even days before. But, then again, the clasp may have been attached to the attacker's clothing.

"If it was a clasp from a government medal, only military persons and government officials wear medals. Civilians aren't known to walk around with medals on. If anyone wants to comment, go ahead," said the sheriff. He sat silent, looking over the faces before him.

Cole asked incredulously, "Are you saying that the beast is a government man?"

"Not saying that, Cole," Lawton cautioned again. "I'm giving information about a likely source of the clasp and I emphasize the word 'likely.' In fact, I'm not sure the clasp came from the attacker. Might have been dropped somehow by a harmless civilian or by someone riding by on a horse. And whether the boy was attacked by a beast, as you call him, or something else, is still open to question."

The sheriff stretched his arms up and then leaned them on his desk. "Our belief is that the size of the clasp rules out its use as a military medal. Military medals are small in size, not like a sheriff's badge." Lawton pointed at his large badge. "Military medals are designed to be worn in rows. That clasp was made to fit a medal at least two inches wide."

"What does this all mean?" asked Stilkey, anxious for a conclusion.

"Well," said Lawton, "rule out the Texas Rangers, railroad inspectors and the military, and the only officials left who might use medals of this size are Treasury inspectors, U.S. Marshals and Deputy Marshals, U.S. Treasury agents and postal inspectors. The private agents that protect the president may wear them. I understand, though, that they are civilians."

"I never saw a Treasury agent," said Stilkey. "Don't know what they are or, for that matter, haven't seen a postal inspector around here, neither."

Cole whistled softly. "Do you think that's why the marshal behaves so oddly?" The inflection in Cole's voice implied he couldn't believe it.

A sudden disturbance out on the roadway interrupted the meeting. Horses were driving down the road at full speed, scattering the early morning traffic. Muleskinners and freight haulers were swearing mightily as they gave way to the galloping horses.

"Sheriff, come quick, we need you," came a voice from outside. What else the voice said was lost in the anguish of growling sounds. A horse halted in front of the sheriff's door and the rider's feet instantly hit the ground.

Stilkey was first into action. Gun drawn, he ran to the door and threw it open. The sheriff and Brave went into defensive positions, guns drawn.

"What the hell you all about, fat man," shouted Stilkey, his gun pointed at the rider. "You best got one good story."

"It's the major, sir, his arm's blown off. That's it, Sheriff. That's my story. His arm's blown clean off!"

The messenger, struck by the horror, was crying. The red rouge of a former army officer was running topsy-turvy about his face and onto the collar of his black suit. Sweat was pouring off him. He stood in front of Stilkey with his arms out, palms up.

"Tell your story," yelled the sheriff, moving out front. "I'm the sheriff in this town."

"Yes sir," said the rider as tears ran down his face. "The major, he was at Mrs. Pendalt's boarding house this morning, smoking a cigar on the porch, like he always does. The thing is in shreds, the bone's hanging there. Doc Bellow came over and said he's bleeding badly. Doc says he'll try, but nothing he can do."

Sheriff Lawton walked closer to the man. "Darn it, man, slow it down. Tell us what happened. Pendalt's is outside town. That's the marshal's domain. Have you contacted him?"

Cole's legs suddenly felt unattached. His job was going to be to flush out a sniper. He had no more security than the major had. He was putting his life on the line, and the sheriff was talking jurisdictions.

“We know, Sheriff,” said the second rider who had just pulled up, “we just come from the marshal’s. There was a sign in the window saying he was away and to see you, the sheriff.”

“He was sitting in the bushes, Sheriff,” the first rider went on. “He was up on the hill in front of Mrs. Pendalt’s porch sitting in the bushes. The major had just lighted up his cigar. Hadn’t taken two puffs, I’ll bet. I went out after I heard the rifle. The major was lying on the porch. His arm was upside down on the porch next to him. Just hanging there. The blood was just flowing from his arm. Oh Sheriff, it was terrible, terrible.”

The sheriff exploded, his voice sounding like an iron nail scraping across a dull saw blade: “And the marshal isn’t in again. What an irresponsible . . .”

Cole didn’t hear the rest. He was disconsolate, thinking: Did my pulling contest ruse bring the sniper onto the major? Maybe the sniper kills only Union officers. Both the sheriff and the major were Union officers. Both were targeted.

The sheriff turned to his lawmen. “I know some of you think jurisdiction is unimportant. I can see it on your faces. But it is important. I have no more authority to function in the marshal’s territory than does any other citizen, unless the marshal is away. We have laws and rules and regulations in this territory. I follow them. I’m responsible for the law. I follow the law.”

He rushed to the gun rack on the wall and grabbed a rifle. “Let’s go,” he yelled. “Let’s go out to Pendalt’s. Let’s see what we can do for the major and rid us of that crazy killer.”

CHAPTER TWENTY-FOUR

It was late and Cole was tired. He had arrived back at his campsite in the early evening after searching all day for the person he believed was the sniper. He'd looked for him as thoroughly as a comb moves through a fine beard. Cole now stared vacantly at the fire. He had not found him.

He felt that the day had been a waste. Today, both the beast and the sniper had scored one on him. It was wrong to take the hunt personally, he knew that. But what other way was there to take it? He needed sleep now. That's what he needed. Sleep to help him forget the day's disappointments. He sat with fixed eyes on the elegant and strangely comforting flames of the dying campfire.

Brave had worked with him in the search. Together they had questioned shopkeepers and bartenders, stared at faces in saloons, cornered road people and drunks, and stopped wagon drivers and muleskinners. They'd searched under the boardwalk where vagrants had been known to live and in places where vagrants had not been known to live. It was for not. They found no sniper.

Several of those they questioned had seen the man. One made a good case for having spoken to him. But no one knew the whereabouts of the crippled and maimed man. And no one who claimed he'd seen him, had seen him with a horse or a rifle. The man had always been seen either sitting or walking, and favoring his poor left leg.

At noontime Cole had learned that Major Johnson died. The word of his death spread rapidly though St. Bartow. Doc Bellow had failed to stop the massive flow of blood from the major's mangled arm. Cole felt strong remorse—close to guilt—over his death. He should have warned the major that the weight-pulling contest was a ploy to flush out the sniper. He had goaded him and his goading had led to his death. The major was a war veteran and an officer. He should have realized the major would be at risk even more than he would be.

In late afternoon, a disappointed and tired Cole left Brave and returned to camp. After an early supper of beans and fatback, Cole decided to get sleep.

With sleep, he dreamed. He dreamed of his mother. She sobbed and scolded him. "Too much risk," she groaned, and shook her head at Cole. "You promised me, nothing silly. You agreed. Too much risk." She groaned again. Next, he found himself behind Rebel lines. Natalie was standing beside him. "The beast is more important, Cole. The beast is the bigger threat, Cole. Go home, Cole. You're wasting it here." A stranger appeared. He was dressed in rags and carried a long rifle. He was faceless and his rifle fired without any reason. Smoke curled from the rifle's barrel. The man grinned. Cole's left arm went numb and hung limp. A doctor appeared, dressed in white, and stood next to him. The doctor reached down and felt his arm. "Hopeless," he said, shaking his head, "second one I've seen like this. I'm sorry." The doctor repeated over and over, "I'm sorry." The doctor flew off in a white cloud, shaking his head and repeating, "Should have listened to his mother. Should have listened to his mother."

Cole awoke several times, kicking off his blanket and rolling out of his saddle pillow. Once, he grabbed his left arm and became panicked when the arm was numb. Loud snorts from a dozing but disturbed Rusty woke Cole from his dream several times.

After one set of dreams, Cole awoke and saw streaks of light in the sky. Dawn was breaking.

"This is bull," he spoke aloud. He jumped up and startled Rusty awake. "I'm done trying to sleep, it's time to get on with it, start west."

He began now the task of breaking down his camp. Tonight he would be on a wagon train and camping in a new location. Or, he may be dead, he thought, shaking his head.

CHAPTER TWENTY-FIVE

Natalie too had trouble falling asleep that night. She changed sleep positions several times without effect, while half-listening to the banter in the front parlor. The parlor talk throughout the night was a distraction; she would have preferred quiet.

The beast was stalking her—she was sure of that. He had found her. He had made his way, somehow, from New Orleans to St. Bartow. Paralyzing dread and fear were eating at her again and overwhelming her. She must destroy him or find a way to get him destroyed.

She had no place to turn for help. Only Brave and she understood the horror of the beast. Could she find a way to get Brave and the law to help her? Certainly, the law was strong enough. The law could find a way to organize the power of the community to go after the beast. She felt a spark of hope for a moment but it disappeared as quickly. Her heart sank. White men just didn't understand. Their lives were devoid of things like beasts. For them, beasts were the stuff of nightmares—useful only to scare children into behaving.

Natalie understood beasts. She experienced them. They killed their victims but she knew they didn't have to. This was her biggest fear. Beasts could enslave their victims by taking only a portion of their blood and replacing that portion with the blood of the beast itself. That made the victim into a beast too. She knew that the beast after her had such a plan, she was sure of it. On the plantation, the other slaves told her the beast's purpose. He paid money to get information about her and told the other slaves of his intent for her. He would make her future nothing but a living hell, an eternity of hell.

The beast had to be destroyed. No one again would suffer the way she had. Who could she get to help her? Who?

Natalie slipped out of bed and opened her window to let in fresh air. She looked out onto the road below. Dawn had broken and the sky was coloring in the east. The road below was quiet. There were no wagons or riders out navigating the ruts and holes. The mud puddles caused by the recent rainstorms had dried up, leaving dry holes. The tranquil scene belied the terror building up in the town.

She smiled as she thought of Cole. He was so good, so human. She hoped his selfless attempt to get the sniper was successful. She'd grown fond of him in the short time she'd known him. He was so different, though. His experience in life had been so simple, clean and virtuous, so unlike her own.

A shadow moved across the roadside buildings. It caught her eye. She wondered if a breeze had stirred a shadow loose. Maybe it was a lonely tree, she thought. No, there was something moving on the other side of the road. It was early for a stroller. Probably a late-night drunk, she thought. Napie won't let him in here.

Natalie saw the outline of a real man, not a shadow. He was walking down the road haltingly, as though looking for something. His walk was somewhat familiar, she thought. She'd seen it someplace before. The man was dragging his leg behind him. His walk was so distinctive. Yes, she thought, she did remember, she had seen him and she knew where. It was on the steps of the boardwalk during the weight-pulling contest. The poor man. She had watched him walk away after the contest and he dragged his leg behind him. It was his left leg, she remembered. His cap was pulled low over his ears, hiding his face. He was a War victim probably. But what is he doing out there at this hour, she wondered.

Natalie watched the strange man plod along the boardwalk dragging his crippled leg. Though he moved slowly, she felt there was purpose in his step. He came to a stop in front of a group of several outhouses off the main road. He looked them over for a moment. Probably looking for the right one, she thought. He's fussy and very private, that's all. She felt lighthearted for the first time tonight.

But again her mind turned to the beasts. Carl was a target. In New Orleans, the beast preyed mercilessly on everyone. Perhaps Carl just happened to be at the wrong place at the wrong time. It was rumored that Carl had tried to fight the beast. You cannot fight a beast alone. You have to organize and fight as a group. Her people, unlike the people in St. Bartow, were not defenseless against a beast. Even as slaves, they were able to take him on. On the plantation, they isolated him in his mansion. The beast never attacked on the plantation. If he had, her people would have struck back and staked him. The beast knew that. Off the plantation, he was free to attack whom he wished. A slave could do nothing about that. The beast was protected off the plantation by white society. The beast was wise to be a white beast.

She grinned as she watched the crippled man leave the outhouse of his selection. But he came out carrying a long, slender package. She was surprised. He went into the outhouse with his arms empty and came out with a package. That truly is strange, she thought. The package must have been hidden inside the outhouse. The little man hobbled quickly now to the cover of a nearby building.

Natalie watched the place where he had disappeared. She was curious. She didn't have to wait long. The man soon came back out of the shadows near a public horse watering troth. She watched him place the package into the water of the stall and vigorously rinse it. She was disgusted. What could you take from an outhouse and rinse off like that?

The man moved quickly back into the shadows. He was hidden from her view again. Moments later he reappeared. He was leading a horse. Oh my, she thought, surprised, the man has a horse. She suddenly realized that the package he had retrieved contained a long rifle. He had hidden it in the outhouse. While Natalie watched, the man thrust the rifle into his scabbard and effortlessly swung up into the saddle.

“And he can ride a horse!” she exclaimed out loud, standing up with mouth open. “He must be the sniper,” she whispered, feeling the color drain from her face. “I must tell someone.”

She ran down the front steps of Lady’s and out the front gate, toward the sheriff’s office. Her fear had disappeared.

CHAPTER TWENTY-SIX

Early mist hugged the ground when Cole departed the camp for his appointment with Al Witham and the wagon train. He could hear the cheerful sound of morning songbirds as he rode across the damp valley floor. Smoke from the wagon train's campfires guided him to his destination.

As he got close, Cole made out two men riding side by side working to get the train underway. Both men were barking orders in rapid fire, their voices rising above the drivers' curses and the morning sounds of the cows and horses, oxen, mules and other farm animals that made up a homesteader's load.

That's Witham over there, he thought, recognizing one of the riders. He sounds a tad loud and a tad frustrated. He must be tired. Teaching immigrants English by shouting at them was not a job for the delicate, thought Cole, or for one with small lungpower. He smiled at his own humor.

"Morning, Al," Cole hollered out. It was lighter now and he easily saw his friend riding alongside the other man. Cole approached them and said, "Thought drinking at the Dollar was your day job. Good to see you sweat some, too."

Recognition crept slowly over Witham's face. "I got a joke about that," he said, "but I'll tell you about it later." He laughed and saluted Cole. "Lawton told me you'd be coming by. Been throwing any wise guys into puddles lately?"

"No, I gave up on that. Not enough challenge." Cole smiled. He decided not to tell Witham about Carl's death. He didn't know how to explain it without Witham thinking he'd gone ripe.

Witham grinned again. "My voice is whacked out. I was screaming my lungs out. I need a rest. What I've never been able to understand is why immigrants weren't born speaking English. Be so much easier."

“Well, at the Dollar Saloon, Al, you develop your throat power using alcohol. You need the immigrants now to help you develop your lungpower. You’re looking to become a full English teacher, Al.”

The three men laughed.

Witham said, “The immigrants come back in here yes’day aft’noon talking in five languages about the ‘little horse beat the big horse.’ Well, they all want a little horse. Couldn’t sell them a big horse now, no way. Is that the little horse you’re riding?” Witham looked Rusty up and down and didn’t wait for an answer. “He does look powerful. He’s got legs like my first wife. Your horse was sure the talk here.” Witham, still smiling, continued looking Rusty over.

The immigrants’ stories have obviously impressed him, thought Cole. He beamed and said, “Maybe I should forget about going west. Bring little horses in here and sell them to the immigrants. Become a rouged-up success of a businessman.”

That comment set off a roar of laughter from Cole, Witham, and his sidekick. Obviously, the red stuff that serious men put on their faces looked ridiculous to many people in those parts.

“No, you don’t want that,” said Witham slyly and still smiling, “you’d have to get a friggin’ tight-fitting suit from back East too, and there’s none your size. You’d look like that waxy guy you were drinking with in the Dollar, minus the rouge, of course. That fancy suit would shrink you right down to his size.”

They laughed again.

“Who was that guy, anyway, Cole? At first I thought he was your father. I didn’t say anything because he looked like he sold dead bodies. Then I decided he was there to get you drunk to pay you off for saving him from those road boys. Was I right?”

“No, he wasn’t in the body business, Al, far as I know. He did say he liked your looks. Sizing up your body, maybe. But you didn’t give him the time of day. You skedaddled right out the door. He was still measuring you when you left."

The three men roared again. With a wave of his hand, Witham's sidekick rode off, chuckling.

Cole and Witham got down to business.

"Lawton told me about you. Not a bad recommendation. How'd you become a right hand of the sheriff, having been in Bartow only a couple days? You one of those Washington magic boys, Pinkerton men?" Witham was serious and his smile was congratulatory.

"Thank you, but I'm just a simple country boy. He did explain what we are up to, right?"

"You bet he did. Tough situation. I'm all in favor of it and I'll help as I can. Rest assured on that."

"Thanks again, Al. Have you heard that the sniper targeted the sheriff the other day and Major Johnson, the guy I competed against in the pulling contest the next day?"

"Wow," said Witham, "did he?" His smile vanished and a mask of fear and outrage settled on his face. "Are they all right?" he asked, concern in his voice.

Cole explained how the sniper's attack on the sheriff was thwarted and how Major Johnson had died.

Al shook his head. "I'll do what I can to help. What a brazen piece of bull!"

"What kind of job do you have for me?" asked Cole, changing the subject.

Witham's trademark smile reappeared. "You're going to be a scout, Cole."

"A scout?" Cole was flabbergasted. How could he be a scout? "Al, I can ride a horse okay, but I'm no scout. I've seen scouts. Most of them are Indians, anyway, or half-breeds, or mountain men. They're tough like boot leather and their smell alone scares off trouble." Cole pictured himself sneaking up on a band of Indians to listen to them and then suddenly realizing he couldn't understand Indian. "No, Al, I'm really not scout material."

Witham laughed mightily and reared his horse up to punctuate his mirth. "Jeez, even old Tarball here don't like the idea of you being a professional scout, Cole. That's really not what I had in mind."

"Well, that's good." Cole felt relief. He was the subject of another of Al's jokes. Why would Al make me a scout? Those guys are like metal. Most have frontier and army experience. They'd probably do away with me if I went out there with them.

"You'll be a roving scout, not a professional scout. You'll look for problems close to the train. High water, sinkholes, prairie fires, wild animals, washed-out trails. You look for things like that."

"Who looks out for the Indians and renegades and the outlaws?" asked Cole, still doubtful.

"That's the job of the professional scout. We have six of them out there already. They are Indians, half-breeds, hunters, trappers and mountain men. Most of them have done work for the army. They usually stay six to eight miles in front of the train. Actually they surround the train. You'll travel two or three miles north or south and in front of the train. The professionals look out for Indians and outlaws and watch for renegades, white or red. They may also use you as a messenger to get an alert back to the trail boss."

"Well, that's a relief, Al," Cole said with a laugh. "How long do I stay out?"

"Each day you report back to the train boss. That's not necessary, though. It's not dangerous work, Cole, not like flushing out a sniper. The sniper job is more important than your job with the train. So keep your mind on that. A roving scout can't find too much wrong in the first couple days. And you may be with us only for a couple days. Once you get the sniper, you can continue on with us or return to St. Bartow, that's up to you. I won't hold you to anything."

Al discussed the work of a roving scout and the special perils of flushing out a sniper. He was experienced at both, having served in the War. He explained he'd seen infestations of Rebel snipers in the War. "Snipers terrorize an area, Cole. There's no freedom of movement, association, or even thought in places where they're active. Fear reigns. I'll do anything I can to help you. I hate 'em." Witham's smile vanished. "Lost several friends to 'em in the War. And I've lost business too in this venture. Because of fear of snipers, folks going west choose other starting points rather than leaving from here."

The men shook hands; it was a bonding moment. Cole felt pride in his renewed relationship. Men like Al and Lawton, Brave and Stilkey, and many others he had met were consciously building the West. He had become a part of it.

"On another matter," Al said, smiling, "wagon six, the Josephsons, will give you your grub this morning. Eat hearty, it's tough where you'll be and it may be some time before you get another square."

"The Josephsons." Cole's face brightened. "Do they have a daughter about twenty?"

"Man, you sure get around. You bet, the prettiest girl on the train. I wondered why she lit up so when she heard me tell the old man you'd be stopping by. What do you have there, anyway?"

Cole blushed. "I met her the other day. We took a shine to each other." He flashed a roguish smile and said, "I think we're in love."

"Kidding aside," Al responded, "that young woman got the muscle to plow fields, set a table, give a man fine sons, *and* look beautiful all at the time she's doing it. And that guy she'd be married to would enjoy the whole darn thing, from start to finish, yes sir!" Al hopped about on his saddle, his face in feigned ecstasy, rolling his eyes.

Cole smiled coyly. "Well, after we get hitched, Al, I'll make sure there's a place for you at the dinner table at least once a month. You can help with the plowing when you're not visiting. How's that?"

Al smiled and turned his horse away. He was still bouncing in his saddle as he rode away.

CHAPTER TWENTY-SEVEN

Sonia was standing by her mother near the campfire helping with the morning breakfast when Cole rode up. She was wearing her hair long, with matching pigtails that flowed to near her waist. Small yellow ribbons highlighted the pigtails at the very ends. Her hair was the color of rich corn and the ends of her pigtails swung back and forth as she puttered about with her mother.

His heart pounded as he climbed off Rusty near the wagon. Sonia smiled but made no attempt to greet him.

A little shy, he thought. Cole had never seen eyes as blue and he was enthralled by the dimple on her left cheek—he'd missed it before. The dimple had a separate smile of its own, he noted.

She'd be thought of as buxom, he reckoned, a big girl, but a big girl in very fine shape. A shape perfect for the onerous kind of work she'd face in the West. He realized how much he'd missed her presence since he'd last seen her.

Cole was given the place of honor at the breakfast sitting. Watching Sonia, he decided that she was the entertainer in the family and helped knit them together. A family needed a person with those skills, he thought; particularly on a long trip across the plains, living in such close quarters.

She showed a keen sense of humor and was a flirt too. She played little tricks on family members. Cole saw her place a small piece of hogback on her father's breakfast tin and ignore him when he asked for more. The father protested and acted as though her intention was to starve him. Sonia, of course, had no idea why her father was raising such a ruckus. Everyone understood the game and joined in with comments.

"Mr. Josephson," Sonia's mother commented seriously, "you eat too much anyway. Sonia is looking out after you.

Your pants get tighter and tighter. They go like balloons. Soon, we hire a seamstress to travel with us to make your pants bigger every day."

The family and Cole laughed.

"Who you get to sew, Mama, she be good cook too, and be pretty." Mr. Josephson was acting, but sounded serious. "If she going to take your place and take care of my pants, I gotta have her do everything." His voice rose on the word "everything."

There was light laughter but a stern look from Mother Josephson.

"Daddy," said Sonia, breaking in and sounding hurt, "that's not being nice at all. Mr. Mason doesn't want a whiff of your bad manners."

The family settled down now.

Cole asked a question he had been waiting to ask. "Sonia, have you been bothered by the bats or the man you met while you were out walking your dog?"

The family turned quiet. Cole knew that something had happened. Mr. Josephson looked over at him, caught his eye and looked away.

"Well, I guess nothing has happened," said Cole, holding his spoon up in his right hand, as if to end the discussion. "That's good," he added.

"Wait, Cole," said Sonia, "we see differently on this. I saw a bat several times. It flew after dark around the train. I stayed very close to the wagon at night, always with my dog, as you suggested. Daddy and Mama, they go to bed early. They see nothing. They told the story of the bats to an old man who was passing through and the old man laughed wildly at it. My mother and father thought my story was untrue because an old man laughed at it. They believed an old man rather than to believe their daughter."

Cole noted that Sonia was talking testily because she was obviously upset. He was alarmed but didn't want to scare the family. He asked, "Mr. Josephson, who was the old man?"

"He came traveling through visiting, a salesman, selling medicine. He said it was good for just about everything. I bought some for late-night pain," said Mr. Josephson.

"He was a horrible man," interjected Sonia, "simply horrible, horrible. And Cole, they listened to that horrible man. He smelled terrible and had a horrible, waxy face."

"Well, he was a gentleman," said Mr. Josephson, "he had on a gentleman's suit."

"He had a horrible, waxy face," Sonia repeated, her face flushed and full of anger. "His face wasn't real," she added, throwing her head back, "and he smelled horrible."

"And," said Mama, "he had on a gentleman's hat. Obviously a man of property, in addition to his medicines. And he spoke very well."

Sonia said, "Ya, such a gentleman. He was so sure the bats were in my imagination that he offered to go walk with me that night out among the bats! Can you imagine that, Mr. Cole? And my parents said okay. They sent me off for a walk with a stranger with a waxy face. And smell, that man had so much sweet smell on to cover up the bad smell that I was stomach sick. Even my dog growled at him all the time he was here. I absolutely refused to go."

"Sonia, my dear," Mr. Josephson said, "the man was a gentleman. He was trying to be nice."

"Nice? He asked three times if he could take me out there and finally you agreed. I'd probably be dead if I'd done what you wanted." Sonia burst into tears.

She was showing independence, thought Cole. It made her appealing and she was justifiably angry with her parents. Gosh, she could have ended up like Carl. Cole found himself trembling and so pleased for her independence.

"Sonia, you be quiet. Mr. Cole isn't interested in how you don't listen to your parents," said Mr. Josephson, staring hard at her, telling her in a father's way that he'd heard enough from her.

"Was the salesman's name Willoughby Marchess?" asked Cole. "Did he say he was from New Orleans?"

"Yes, that's the man," all three responded, staring blankly at Cole, surprised that he had heard of him and knew his name.

"You know him?" Mr. Josephson asked.

Cole believed he had to answer honestly and also make sure that Sonia was not put at risk in the future. "Well, I know of Mr. Marchess. He is being investigated by the sheriff's office in St. Bartow at this moment. I would be fearful of him. In fact, I'd be cautious of any stranger."

Cole's statement took Sonia by surprise. She hadn't expected support from him. She stared at him, mouth open, as if trying to read something more into it.

Mr. Josephson was hurt, Cole could see. He had taken Cole's statement as criticism of his attempt to get Sonia to face up to her fears by going out with Marchess.

Mrs. Josephson lifted her skirt slightly, stood up, and shook her head. While looking at both Sonia and Mr. Josephson, she said, "See, see, we must be more cautious. Not everyone is good. We do not know that Mr. Marchess is bad, but as Cole says, we must be extra cautious with our precious daughter." She turned toward Sonia, who ran into her arms.

"I probably make a decision too fast, my Sonia baby. I promise, I not do it again," said Mr. Josephson, going over and hugging her.

Cole prepared to leave. He promised the Josephsons that he'd be back. He explained his job as simply as he could, but did not tell them of his sniper mission.

"How could I not come by for some fine grub," joked Cole, "great food and a pretty daughter." He smiled his sweetest little boy smile and flashed his eyes at Sonia.

Sonia turned red, smiled too, and proudly thrust her breasts forward. She looked away and folded and unfolded her hands nervously.

"No trouble, you eat here, Cole," said Mr. Josephson. "When I need help change wheel, you be here to help."

He roared laughter and Mama joined in. Sonia was embarrassed by her father's humor, but she turned back and looked at Cole. She blushed her thanks and stood closer to him than she had before.

Cole swung up onto Rusty, feeling as though he was taking leave of family. In a very serious tone he warned the family members again about Marchess. As he waved good-bye, he saw Sonia by the wagon wiping tears from her eyes. He would have liked to run to her, take her in his arms, and hug and kiss her. But instead, he waved to her and rode off.

He signaled Witham, who was still out preparing for the wagon train's departure, that he was leaving to begin his scouting job. Witham nodded and waved good-bye.

A chill shot through Cole's body. He faced a serious challenge. He would succeed or it may be his last challenge.

CHAPTER TWENTY-EIGHT

Natalie slipped past a dozing Napie at the inside door and out the front gate of Lady's. She was wearing neither a hat nor a shawl but she didn't care what people thought of her appearance. Cole was in danger and she had information that could help him.

The boardwalk was empty at that early morning hour except for two crows that were dining on scattered refuse from the night before. The crows danced away from her as she ran by them, directly toward the sheriff's office. Two of the lawmen were out shadowing Cole—she knew that, but one would be minding the office. She'd get him to help her. She hoped Brave was on duty.

As she ran, she began to put things together in her mind. Cole had already left on his mission—it was too late to warn him. But maybe the identity of the sniper, his description, could be gotten to him. For him to know the "shape and color" of his enemy would better prepare him for the coming battle. She was sure of that. And she was determined to get the word out somehow.

And too, she thought, she had a duty to warn him. Although she knew the beast was more menacing than the sniper, she regretted how she had treated poor Cole the night before. She had made light of his interest in first focusing on the capture of the sniper. Besides, she could not ignore what she had seen right outside her window.

The day was unfolding rapidly as she made her way up and down the sets of steps of the boardwalk that led to the corner across from the sheriff's office. Off to the east, shades of color from the breaking dawn were showing through. The road was rapidly shedding darkness.

She almost ran into the man. He arose from the ground near the watering troth as she was about to cross the road to the sheriff's. Maybe he had spent the night under the boardwalk. She had heard that all kinds of strange people lived under there. Maybe he'd been sleeping or lying in wait by the water troth, or maybe just hiding. It struck her suddenly that she was not alone and that there was no one to yell to for help. She deftly sidestepped the man without a break in her stride. She believed she had left him behind.

He immediately recognized her. He quickly caught up with her and began to run beside her and plead with her. She didn't understand his talk. She tried not to look at him. She speeded up; her only purpose, she kept telling herself, was to get to the sheriff's office as quickly as possible.

"Who are you, what do you want?" she blurted out over her shoulder. She received a shot of confidence from a light she saw above the sheriff's window. She stopped running, caught her breath and looked sternly at her pursuer. She could scream for the sheriff now if she had to. This was not a man but a boy, a young man.

The boy circled her, jumped around and flapped his arms as though they were wings and he could fly. He fumbled his words: "Where's big man, little horse, strong horse, quick, I show him."

She realized it was Pete, Carl's friend. Cole spoke of him. The boy looked terrible, haunted almost. Cole had befriended the two boys, Pete and Carl. Maybe Pete knew something of Carl's ugly death. She felt panicky as she realized she was faced with both responding to Pete's entreaty and getting to the sheriff's office.

"I'm sorry but I must get to the sheriff," she said, trying to scurry around him.

But Pete kept one step ahead of her.

"Cole left town," she yelled out, looking toward the sheriff's office. "I'll tell him you want to see him," she added, and continued again running across the road.

He tackled her; not a rough tackle but a tackle nonetheless. It stopped her dash and brought her down roughly onto the gravel road. Her mouth flew open. He did not attack her when she was down. He tried to help her up.

"What are you doing?" she screeched, more in frustration than fear. She flexed her arm as if preparing to strike the man. She looked around for help but no one was on the road.

Pete raised his hands protectively as if expecting a wallop. Words came tumbling from his mouth like water in springtime over a river dam.

"Listen, listen, see, see," he said, pointing to his ears and eyes.

She saw a look of fear, anxiety and insistence on his dirty face. My gosh, she thought, he must have been through something terrible. Maybe he wants to tell me about Carl's killer, maybe about the beast. He must have been in hiding for at least a few days. This may be his first chance to be free from whatever he fears. She paused for a moment, giving more time to discern the boy's message.

He read her pause as a signal to plead anew. "Come, come, see, see. Show you, show you. You must see. Yes, come." His voice got louder and the words came out with more difficultly. He danced around and beckoned with his arms and fingers for her to go in a direction opposite of the sheriff's office. He spoke more slowly now, probably realizing that she was listening to him. "Please, please, you know big man, strong horse, you tell him, I show you, yes."

Obviously, his message was for Cole. Was he in some other kind of danger, she wondered, danger she knew nothing about?

"Come, must come see, before light, light no good, bad man all gone, must see before light come," Pete pleaded anew.

The word "light" struck a sensitive note in Natalie. Light was what a beast couldn't survive. Light or fire destroyed a beast. That was knowledge that had been passed to her by her forebears, those wise in the ways of the beast. She looked at the sky. In ten minutes, no less, sunlight would begin to inch its way through town.

She made a fateful decision; she decided to go with Pete. He hadn't acted evil or harmful, and he knew and obviously thought a lot of Cole. His use of the word "light" in his pleading convinced her. She grabbed his hand firmly, as if to say "Okay, let's go."

The young man was startled by her abrupt change. A look of relief and gratitude flooded across his face.

They took off and ran together down the boardwalk away from the sheriff's office.

"Here," he said as they came to a turn.

She needed no coaxing. She ran as fast as he did. They turned another corner, crossed two streets, and came to a stop at the back of a livery stable.

Pete reached down and found several loose boards on the back wall of the stable.

He knows the building, she thought.

He removed the boards, making a hole large enough to squeeze through. He went through the hole and beckoned her to follow. She did. It was dark inside and smelled of stale horse urine.

Not a clean livery, she thought.

The horses were neighing and jumping and making morning noises. Natalie paused and looked at Pete. He motioned her on. Pete's stature had grown inches in her mind but she still felt concern being alone with him in a dark livery.

Together, Natalie and Pete walked slowly and quietly to the front of the stable and the main entrance. Pete held his finger across his lips to indicate that she must be quiet. There were holes in the front wall with daylight shining through. Some holes were large enough to put a head through.

The stable man must look at arrivals through these holes, she thought, without having to swing the door open.

Pete stood beside her. It was still dark outside but the daylight was coming on rapidly. He motioned for her to move up to the holes in the front wall and he whispered to her, "See, see, soon now."

Natalie didn't know what she was looking for. Perhaps a hot poker would be thrust into her eyes. She looked out cautiously and was surprised to see that the livery was located right across the road from the marshal's office. She had seen the marshal's office many times before. She turned back to Pete, still puzzled. "What am I looking for?" she whispered.

"Very soon. Light come, look," he whispered, pushing her softly toward the hole.

She looked out again. What she saw curled her lips and convulsed her stomach. A giant bird, a bat, had taken roost on the roof of the marshal's office. It quickly transformed itself into a human shape and disappeared into an opening in the building. Two more bat figures flew down from the sky, landed on the roof and roosted where the first had been. The two new bats were in a flurry of activity.

God, she thought, the nest. The lair. It's in the marshal's office. They must hide there in the daytime and prey at night. The two bats changed into human forms. She was shaken by what she was seeing. She had heard as a child how beasts transformed from animal to human but she had never seen it happen. The beast near the Dollar Saloon had transformed from man to beast.

The human forms quickly disappeared into the building. They were gone. Moments later, the first rays of the morning sun struck the top of the marshal's office building.

Natalie raised her hands to her cheeks, disgusted. She looked over at Pete. He was grinning in celebration. He was letting loose, she thought. What a terrible knowledge he had kept bottled up! Carl must have known of this too, and that may be why he was killed. The beasts had since probably been trying to kill Pete as they did Carl.

She placed an arm on Pete's shoulder. "Let's go," she whispered.

She followed Pete though the livery to the back wall. The roof of the livery was not watertight and daylight was flooding in.

Outside the livery, Natalie motioned for Pete to come with her. He shook his head while grinning profusely. Natalie thanked him, gave him a hug, and watched him run off down the road. Now she must get to the sheriff immediately.

CHAPTER TWENTY-NINE

Cole gazed upward into the sky. He saw haze and more haze, and a hot, steamy sun. He'd been riding westward for two hours and the sun and heat filled his eyes with tiny droplets of fire. Perspiration soaked his shoulders, arms, groin and legs. His clothes stuck to his body. Sweat in rivers flowed down the creases of his face, back and legs. There was no relief from the heat in the grassy flatlands.

And the bugs. Mosquitoes and insects buzzed and bit him. He tried to ignore them but they assaulted relentlessly. They were everywhere. High in the sky, hawks and eagles sailed freely through what he suspected were drafts of cool air. Those birds dwelled in a different universe, he was sure of that. Ah, what he'd give for a steep dive into a draft of cool air. Or even just a drink of cold water. Cole pushed on.

He tested his guns again. He had done it several times. He drew his gun from its holster. Good, he thought, that was a good draw. He replaced the gun after checking its load. Then he yanked his rifle from the scabbard. He was pleased with the feel of it. He checked the load. Everything was okay. His guns were ready. He didn't expect to use them. Only in an emergency. He was the bait in the play. He was confident of being able to play the bait. But actually, being the bait was scary—he could become quite dead quite easily, quite quickly. He shrugged. He had accepted the position. He'd fulfill it. He was confident the sheriff and Stilkey would protect him.

Cole looked far ahead. The terrain was level until it reached the low hills, then it rose gradually. They weren't high hills. Lawton had told him he thought the sniper would strike in the low hills. The hills were the closest high ground to St. Bartow. He'd strike there because it gave good cover.

Cole glanced over his shoulder back at the wagon train. It was rolling, but slowly. He could make out twelve to fifteen wagons in the train. He couldn't tell exactly how many. Clouds of dust rose, swirled and gathered in layers around the train, making an accurate count impossible. Difficult to see on level ground, also.

Poor Sonia, he thought, in the heat and dust. She was struggling—a beautiful young lady. Going at it just like the other passengers. He was proud of her.

Cole expected to set up camp at the base of the first low hills. He'd reach there at about noon, maybe later. Those hills were critical to the sheriff's plan. It was the likely spot for an ambush. Without an attack, after the second day, Lawton and Stilkey would call the plan off. Cole could continue on with the wagon train or return home. It was his decision, Lawton had told him. He hadn't thought about what he'd do if the plan didn't work.

With a sweep of its majestic wings, a hawk dove into the low grass in the distance. Cole scanned again far ahead. Not a hint of a sniper. Nor a hint of the sheriff and Stilkey either. Lawton and Stilkey should be in the hills by now. Maybe they had taken care of the sniper already. If so, a pleasant surprise, he thought. He hadn't heard shots, though. Cole pushed on.

In the War, Cole remembered talking with sniper hunters for the Union Army. Two brothers from Tennessee. They spoke Southern but fought for the North. They were religious boys and prayed before a sniper hunt. When hunting snipers they looked for unnatural movements. A sniper was the cause of unnatural movements, they explained. They were sure of that. When they saw the movement, they knew the sniper was there and ready for killing.

"What's an unnatural movement?" Cole asked a brother early one morning before a prayer session.

"A movement unauthorized by God," he answered matter of factly, like he was reading it from a prayer book. He explained further. "Finding the exact location of a sniper is a matter of picking out a movement not of God's making. The maker of the movement is a sniper." Cole was assured that God hated snipers. The brothers got close to God by killing them.

Cole sat listening, rifle at his side.

"Yes, God detests snipers," a brother assured Cole.

"Snipers are evil," the other brother added, waking from a nap and preparing for prayer.

The brothers put a lot of faith in trail signs. They were unusually crisp at reading trail signs.

I guess trail signs are silent leads from God, Cole had thought.

Cole swatted at bugs buzzing his neck and ears. He was thirsty. He stopped Rusty, practiced sliding down him for a fast getaway, and drank some precious water from a leather bag. He treated Rusty to some. Rusty wants his own cold stream, he thought. None of this bagged water for him. There's got to be a stream for him soon. It rained plenty a few day ago.

He climbed onto Rusty and looked up at the horizon again. How close was he to the low hills? He felt the sweat stinging his eyes and blurring his vision. He saw nothing but haze right up to the horizon's edge. Haze and shimmering hills. He rubbed his eyes again for relief. His eyelids itched from insect bites. Rubbing did nothing to relieve them, nothing at all, he thought. He rubbed his sleeve across his forehead and trudged on.

Cole's mind flashed to Lennie. What a person to think of now, he said to himself. Lennie's life in Russia had been pretty meager, nothing like his own experiences growing up in America. Lennie's whole life was the czar. He still feared the czar way over here in America; he thought he'd pop up any minute from behind a tree. Lennie's life over there was limited. A person needs responsibility to make him a whole person. Hardships in a good cause, that's what you need. Lennie never had responsibility in Russia. Lennie came over here, running away. He would have found the responsibility he needed to grow in America. It's a darn shame he was killed.

* * * * *

Cole figured he'd been riding the grassy flatlands for hours. But it was only nearly high noon by the sun. The hills were a ways off but not far. No hint of the sniper. The last half-hour he'd concentrated on looking for unnatural movements. He tried to separate the unnatural from other types of movements.

The sound of birds fighting broke the quiet. Two bluebirds pecked at each other while in flight. Bluebirds warred here as they do back home. Mockingbirds were worse. Cole wondered, are humans like bluebirds and mockingbirds, born to battle each other? I don't think so. Humans cooperate. They are building the West, working side by side. People of different colors and religions working together. Well yes, that's so, but it took a war and a lot of hate to get them working together. The truth was still out. He decided.

Cole pushed on. He looked east. He was way ahead of the wagon train. Had Lawton and Stilkey reached their destination and set up camp? Maybe they'd been held up by something and he was out front. Out here alone? He had to have faith and trust in them. No need to revisit that, he thought. He put the idea out of his head. Lawton and Stilkey would perform their duty. He was sure of that.

Phillips, from New York, had asked the Tennessee brothers how they liked their work. They always paused before answering, like they were thinking deep. After a longer than usual pause, one said, "Shooting Reb snipers is like shooting squirrels, only the squirrels are prettier and smarter and better eating." The brothers smiled at that like it was a revelation from God. Or a call to dinner. The brothers liked to eat. When they weren't eating, sleeping or praying, they were sitting silent waiting for a call from an officer to rid the army of another sniper.

Lawton's plan of attack differed little from the brothers'. One brother served as decoy. The other put a rifle ball through the sniper. After an unnatural movement, of course.

Cole spotted movement up on one of the low hills. Something had moved up there. He was sure he'd seen a movement. He stopped and looked at the rock crevices for a few moments but there was no repeat movement. No reflections off metal and nothing appeared out of place. The birds had gone quiet. Could that be a kind of unnatural movement, he wondered. Then he saw it again.

A large animal was cautiously making its way through the brush. A false alarm. He pushed on.

* * * * *

Cole saw something ahead in the trail. A half-hour had passed and he was into the low hills. He pulled Rusty quickly to the side and slid down the horse's back, rifle ready. What is that in the trail? He peered ahead from the brush along the side of the trail. It looked like a small rock formation with a red flag hanging from the top. Was it an Indian sign? Were there Indians nearby? No, he thought, no Indians, the sniper built it. It was an unnatural movement. It was there because the sniper had become cocky confident after many successes. He wanted his victim to stop right in front of where his rifle was aimed.

Wide-awake, Cole trained his eyes up to the rock formation and at the rock crevices in it. He felt secure in his hiding place, and sure the sniper couldn't see him. Yet the sniper was close by; he could feel him.

He looked up above the formation again at a particular outcropping. Deep crevices in the rock made it an ideal place to hide. If he wasn't anticipating a sniper attack, he'd have walked right up to the flag, bent down to examine it and wham—his mother's son would be ready for a field of wild flowers.

Cole took Rusty firmly by the reins and led him over to a partial clearing he could see through the brush behind him. He tied him lightly to some bushes and patted him gently to let him know everything would be all right.

He then slid noiselessly through the high grass to get a better look at the crevices.

He peered again at the structure sitting in the trail as he thought that the sniper would have to move his rifle to target him. If Cole kept on the move, he'd be quite safe. And moving that big rifle would stir up a host of unnatural movements. He may instead decide to move on and attack farther on. Cole pursed his lips and wiped the sweat from his forehead with his sleeve. He blew breath through his mouth to cool his lips. The challenge had fully alerted him.

He waited for another unnatural movement—something to reveal the sniper's exact location. He waited half an hour. Nothing happened. No movement, no noise. Mosquitoes came down on him, buzzed and bit him. Sweat streamed off him. He waited silently.

Rusty was first to notice something amiss. Cole heard him jump lightly and snap his head around. It was out of place for him, thought Cole. He couldn't see him clearly; the brush was too thick. At first Cole wondered whether the heat was getting to him. Maybe he needed water. Did he smell another animal? The sniper's horse?

As the brothers predicted, it happened. An unnatural movement of a leaf caught Cole's eye. Something hit a leaf on a small branch up on the edge of a crevice. The leaf swung freely in the still air but failed to swing again. He looked at the location and saw something else out of place. A few inches of the barrel end of a rifle protruded over the bottom edge of the crevice opening. It was right there in the open. Cole wondered how he had missed it.

He looked up at the sky. Much past high noon, he guessed. His concern about heat, sweat, and bugs dissipated, replaced by the excitement of competition. Lawton and Stilkey would have put up for the day, but they couldn't be far away. He could crawl through the brush to them. Together they could come back and overwhelm the sniper. But he wasn't sure where Lawton and Stilkey were. And the sniper may get wind of his movements and leave before the three of them could return.

Why not attack the man alone? Attack him from the side or from above. The sniper wouldn't have much time to change the position of his weapon, particularly if Cole surprised him. Maybe if he got behind him or over him—he thought for a few seconds—that seemed like the best approach. He could drag himself through the woods and up the side of the hill, out of sight and hearing of the sniper. Cole could make his way out behind the sniper just above the top of the rock formation. He decided, yes, that was it—attack him alone.

He began immediately to inch his way away now, pushing himself and dragging his rifle. He went through the thick underbrush and grass, finding the openings he needed. Slowly, he thought, don't give it away.

He rested after crawling about forty yards—about half the way across a Vermont cornfield. Deciding to attack the sniper had re-energized him. After making his way about twenty more yards, he took another short break. The flies were as thick as ever but they bothered him not at all. He was not minding the heat either. He was concentrated on the task at hand.

Cole worked his way patiently up the hill, screwing his body around dead brush, under and through live scrubs, and around rocks. At any moment, he expected to be face to face with a friggin' snake or with the sniper himself. He was continuously alert.

The ground became steeper. He was careful not to grunt, but he had to push his body to make speed. He figured he was close to the level of the crevice. Once at that level or a little above it, he would be able to walk across to the outcropping. The sniper was holed up in the crevice right below the lip of the outcropping. Cole was surprised he had come so far so quickly while dragging and pushing his Remington.

Long ago he'd lost his dirty, sweaty hat. The loss only hurt his image. He had smiled and decided he'd look for it later.

* * * * *

Yankees aren't patient. I've hid quiet two days to shoot a Yankee. No food, no water. That boy is no officer but he's done damage. He must be put to rest.

Smeedsville! The man's mind exploded and visions erupted. Smeedsville! His hands flew up and his back trembled and grew rigid. He shook uncontrollably. He held a hand to his eyes. He looked out beyond the lip of the rock and saw vagueness and visions. He rose to a crouch, one hand holding the stock of the long gun and the other hand to his forehead.

The chase. The fire, he thought. Oh God, his face was numb and then it exploded with pain. His left leg began to flap. Was there a way out? They caught poor Rory. Rory was screaming. Oh, what had they done to Rory?

The man stood up and began to weave his way down the rock face. His left leg dragged behind him. "Smeedsville. Remember Smeedsville," he screamed. He shook his head from side to side as he slowly worked his way down the stone face.

Rusty was grazing in the small clearing just beyond the trail when the commotion began. He looked up, snorted, grunted, and danced. The horse saw the man making his way down the rocks, his right hand on a rifle about as long as the man was tall.

"Hey, bluebelly, remember Smeedsville," he screamed out several times. "There's few of us left. We won't forget. You burned our homes, buildings and fields, and stole livestock, remember?"

The little man inched his way along, stepping out on his right leg and dragging his left behind. He came close to tumbling with each step. To a lightly tethered Rusty, it was a worst fear come true.

Cole reached the high ground when he heard the commotion. What the dang, he thought. Was that Lawton and Stilkey? No, they wouldn't do that. He listened intently. If it's the sniper, he's gone loco.

Cole ran through the low brush at the high ground to the top of the rock. He bent down and peered over the edge. He saw the man he knew as the sniper headed down the rock face.

As Cole watched, Rusty managed to swing his powerful head and body back and forth and free himself from the light tether. He moved off a short distance and resumed grazing, one eye on the strange figure moving toward him down the rock front.

Arms trembling, Cole raised his rifle and sighted the barrel to the middle of the sniper's body. He locked in. The sniper was moving directly away from him. It was a simple shot. But Cole didn't pull the trigger. He couldn't. He'd seen battle-scarred Union soldiers behave in a similar way. He could not kill a person, even a sniper, if that person was not a direct threat. The man wasn't a threat to even Rusty anymore.

Mustering all the strength in his voice, Cole shouted, "Hey, hold it, you're under cover from three sides. Lay down the rifle, you're under arrest!"

The man instantly stopped his forward movement. His back stiffened. He turned toward Cole slowly. His lips quivered but Cole heard no sound. He could clearly see the sniper's face now. The cap covering was gone. One eye was set high. There was no second eye. There was one hollow, one hollow only, set into his head. There was no arch over one eye—it was gone and scar-sealed. It had been either blown off by a bullet or cut out by a knife. The big rifle carried by the man was useless in his shaking arms.

Yet he shouted up to Cole, "You did the burning, the raping? You killed little sister."

Cole panicked. Could he pull the trigger on the crazy man? He'd seen similar crazy men. "Get hold of yourself, soldier," Cole screamed, "everyone must deal with his devils."

Change suddenly worked its way through the man's appearance. A look of peace spread through him. His shakiness faded. He stared at Cole, almost with a look of understanding or recognition.

The man was slowly swinging his rifle toward Cole when a bullet hit him square in the middle of the chest. The impact picked him up and tossed him eight feet through the air into a heap at the bottom of the rock formation. He lay there quietly in a fountain of spewing blood.

Silence reigned, broken only by the sniper's rifle, the notorious rifle, bouncing down the rock face from barrel to stock to barrel.

"Mason, are you all right?" Sheriff Lawton screamed from off to the side.

Cole didn't answer. He sat with his head in his hands, his eyes staring down at the rock in front of him. "I can't kill," he whispered.

CHAPTER THIRTY

After leaving Pete, Natalie hurried to the sheriff's office. She wanted to alert Brave to what she had witnessed. Brave would be there if he had not yet left for his security round, she thought. "Oh Lord," she whispered quietly, "make him be there." Her legs pumped rapidly along the boardwalk, heedless of drawing attention.

How would she tell Brave? It was so grisly. He knew about her past bouts of melancholia; she had told him in a moment of frankness. Would he accept that the marshal's office was a hideout for beasts? Would he believe the sniper buried his rifle in an outhouse? Or would he think she imagined these things or was searching for attention like women sometimes do? She'd tell him quietly, her voice free of emotion. She'd sound rational and professional. He'd not dare disbelieve her.

She ignored the road traffic and pushed forward. When she was ready to cross the road, a Negro mule driver was passing by. He thought her too close to the edge of the road. She could see beads of perspiration dripping from his face. He smiled quizzically down at her from his high seat on the wagon. But he sped right by, shouting and whipping at his charging mules. He turned and waved his arms and hat wildly at her. Let him be upset, she thought, my mission is urgent. She ran across the road, choosing to spring from the dry spots, ignoring all else going on around her.

She stepped up the stairs to the sheriff's office as the morning sun reached seven o'clock in the sky. From the saloon district she heard gunshots heralding the new day. She raised the door latch and pushed. The door did not budge. In a burst of frustration, she flopped her full body weight against the door but just as quickly, bounced off. Her heart sank. The always-present fear in the pit of her stomach heightened. Brave was gone. She flopped her weight against the door once again, this time with every ounce of energy she could summon. The door was locked. Brave was not there. She was defeated. Anguish took control of her mind and body.

"Open, open," she screamed, fruitlessly beating her open palms against the dense boards.

Inside the office, Deputy Brave had awakened a little earlier. His night had been quiet. With the sheriff and Stilkey away, he napped anytime he had a free moment. The quiet wouldn't be long lasting, he knew that. Soon, somewhere out there, burly cowboy Johnson and tough farmer Svedson would let their fists fly and onlookers would rush to battle. Brave would be summoned.

It was quite a life, but he loved it. Enforcing the white man's law had given his own life a boost to first-class recognition. Dangerous, full of action, never boring, humorous at times, his life among his father's people was without rules as compared to what his life had been as an Indian.

He was rinsing his mouth when he heard the commotion at the door. He drew his gun and quickly walked to the door. He listened and heard Natalie's sobbing.

What the hang, he thought. He opened the door and there she was, her clothes spotted with mud and sweat beads running down her forehead, face and chin. Having never seen her the least bit disheveled, he was taken aback. He glanced about outside and saw nothing but morning light behind her. He reached down, took her trembling arms and gently but firmly walked her in.

Inside the door, she fell into his arms, sobbing and grabbing for his shoulders and neck. He remained silent and tried to comfort her. She backed off now and stared at him, tears tumbling down her cheeks. She tried to speak but she couldn't form the words. She was too upset even to begin to relate her story. Brave had her sit down, and he pulled up a chair next to her.

But bit by bit, stammer by stammer, word by word, now more forceful, now earnestly, Natalie managed to convey the night's events to Brave. He listened silently. Her story originated in two different worlds, he recognized. One was the tribal world of his youth where good and evil were real and clashes between them expected and understood. The second was the world of the white man, his father's world, where a man had been set loose as a sniper by the ferocity of a running battle between two competing lands—one of the North, the other of the South.

When she finished her story, Brave was silent for a moment, trying to come to terms with the enormity of it.

"Natalie," he finally said, choosing his words carefully, "we must distinguish what we can do from what we'd like to do. My opinion is that we can do nothing to influence the battle with the sniper. He is on his way to do what we hoped he'd do. He has likely singled out Cole and he intends to ambush him. We must hope that the sheriff and Stilkey and Cole will be prepared for him."

Brave got up, poured a glass of water from a pitcher and handed it to Natalie, all the while thinking of how to approach the next subject. He sat down and said, "The matter of the beast is different. We must move immediately to destroy it. We know his lair is the marshal's office. We know he probably has other lairs. But we must destroy the lair we know. Otherwise, he may learn of our plans and move to a safe house nearby or further west."

Brave paused to look at the clock. "We don't have much time. Only you and I know the enormity of the menace. We must act alone but we must act together as one."

She nodded in agreement. The fear residing in her was subsiding.

Natalie and Brave pulled their chairs close to the sheriff's desk and developed a plan. They drew from their experiences—Natalie from the memories of her youth on the New Orleans plantation, and Brave, from what he'd witnessed and the stories he'd been told by his tribal elders.

* * * * *

About an hour later, Brave knocked at the door of the marshal's office. "Marshal, are you in there," he shouted. "We need your assistance."

He was there ostensibly to notify the marshal of a report of a killing in the low hills east of St. Bartow, an area within the marshal's responsibility. As Brave expected, there was no response from the office.

He shouted again, "Marshal, please, if you're here, there is an urgent need for your presence east of St. Bartow, outside the town. Marshal, we have another problem. The Chief. U.S. Marshal in Washington is trying to locate you. He has contacted the sheriff in your absence."

Still there was no answer. Brave tried the door handle next but it was locked. A note was hanging in the small, barred, mud-caked window, placed so that it couldn't be blown away or destroyed by the sun, rain or wind. The edges of the paper were yellow with age. The note read:

MARSHAL SMITH HAS BEEN ACCOMPANIED BY HIS STAFF TO THE BANJA REGION OF THE TERRITORY TO INVESTIGATE A SERIES OF WANTON KILLINGS. PLEASE CONTACT THE SHERIFF IF YOU NEED EMERGENCY ASSISTANCE.

Brave knew of the note; he had seen it and similar ones, usually using a killing, a rustling, or an attack on a telegraph line or a trunk rail line as an excuse for his absence. Brave backed off and returned to his horse, grabbed the reins and started back up the road toward the sheriff's office.

On his way, he came upon Natalie peacefully strolling the boardwalk. She had donned hat and shawl, and had changed clothes since earlier.

Brave stopped his horse by the boardwalk and turned to Natalie. He smiled and tipped his hat. "Howdy, Miss Natalie, enjoying the weather?" He smiled broadly.

The sentence was prearranged. It meant to Natalie that there was no response at the marshal's office. The beast or beasts were probably asleep or in a trance in there. It was midday now. They had seven to eight hours to get inside the marshal's office and stake the beasts.

Brave knew he'd have to break into the marshal's office to stake the beasts. He knew that word of his forceful entry would get around town fast. It might draw a crowd of puzzled spectators and he didn't know how they might react. He wanted the town to know that he had tried hard to raise the marshal before resorting to a break-in.

He also wanted the word out that the marshal's superiors in Washington had instigated his action . . . not the sheriff's office. Once he got inside the office, an outside crowd wouldn't know he was staking beasts.

At that moment an unexpected ally appeared. Pete walked out from behind a building and shyly made his way onto the boardwalk near Natalie. Natalie thought he looked exhausted and his face and clothes were dirty as ever, but what a warm sight he was to her. They smiled at each other.

Brave swung down from his horse and walked up to Pete, who was cowering now beside Natalie.

"Look," Brave said softly and gently, "we don't know each other. Natalie is your friend and she is my friend too. I know her and she knows you, and I need your help to rid us of the evil birds. Do you understand me? Will you trust me and help us?"

Pete looked at Natalie. He was bent a little forward, his normal posture. She nodded to him.

Pete looked back at Brave. The young man's facial appearance had changed; he now looked resolute. He nodded his head and tried to say yes.

Perhaps, thought Brave, the beast killed his friend Carl and he wanted to help right it.

As the three talked together on the boardwalk, an observer would have thought that they were speaking of the condition of the aging structure. In fact, Brave pointed to spots in the framing several times while he spoke.

They agreed to the next step in Brave's plan. They each knew what they were expected to do. Back on his horse, Brave touched his hat with his finger and bowed his head to Natalie and Pete as he departed in the direction of the sheriff's office.

Natalie and Pete moved off to prepare for the attack.

Brave felt more confident now with Pete to help him, even though he knew the help would be limited.

CHAPTER THIRTY-ONE

About an hour later, Deputy Brave walked out of the sheriff's office to begin a fateful ride. He swung up into his saddle and headed for the marshal's office: fifteen minutes, several roads and centuries of history away.

Riding along the road, he watched and listened closely to what was going on around him. He did not want surprises. Traffic was about nonexistent, very light even for a hot weekday afternoon. That pleased Brave. He counted only six wagons on the road and two lone riders. Both of the riders were moving away from him. The wagons were parked at supply shops. Boardwalk activity was insignificant too. A few strollers and drunks were out. The quietness was reassuring. It was a ho-hum late spring day, nothing stirring, and very hot.

As he rode, several boardwalk drunks meandered in and out of the saloons. Some wavered for a moment at the swinging doors, marshaling the courage to go in. Nothing unusual here, he noted, probably just a few more panhandlers than usual.

Brave recognized several of them. He'd had run-ins with them in the past. Most drunks arrived innocently in St. Bartow on their way west. But they carried weaknesses with them often aggravated by War experience. And steady doses of alcohol further disabled them. They became unable to work and soon needed the alcohol to exist. That often brought them into conflict with the law.

"Af'noon, Sheriff, good see you, Sheriff. I been good Sheriff, you be proud of me, Sheriff." Brave had heard it all. They stood on the boardwalk today, bending and weaving, and nodding and waving emphatically at him as he rode by.

Brave stared ahead. He saw all and ignored all, and kept up his pace. He saw boys playing with a metal hoop on the corner. They were testing who could roll the hoop the fastest.

Drunks, road boys, nothing out of the ordinary, Brave decided. He felt more relaxed and confident.

He saw a drunk lying on the boardwalk in front of the Palace House. Though prone, the man looked familiar. Brave recollected him. He and a fellow drunk had spent several nights under lock. The drunk looked up at Brave as he rode by. He clumsily leaped up and limped off.

"My, I see the sheriff," he slobbered. "I gave up fighting, Sheriff, yes sir," he said, half-turning to Brave. The drunk staggered to the corner of the Palace. "Leaving for the wagon train, Sheriff, got a job there, yes sir. Thanks for putting a word in for me." He waved good-bye while turning the corner.

That man was a strange one, thought Brave. Babson was his name. What was the name of the man he hangs around with? Rabson, that was it. Babson and Rabson. They fight like they're serious, but it's really a show. Pick one up and lock him up and he calms right down. Before long, he's snoring. Never pick both of them up though. Brave grinned. Costs twice as much in grub and they keep fighting. Wonder where Rabson is? Babson wasn't as drunk as usual, the deputy noted. He'd kept his balance skeedadling around the corner. Very unusual, Babson being even a little sober. Brave grinned.

He picked up speed. The marshal's office was in sight. Not too fast, he thought, the trip must look public and routine.

He pulled up to the office, tied his horse, and walked up to the door. He banged loudly. "Hello, Marshal, this is Deputy Brave, back again. Are you here?" He hesitated a moment for a response. "Your superiors in Washington want to get in touch with you pronto. No bullshit. Extremely urgent. Keep getting dispatches in on it."

Brave banged loudly several more times on the door. He stepped over to the barred window at the front of the building and looked in. He could make out nothing. The glass window was filthy and streaked with dirt. No housemaids these beasts, he thought, as he shook the bars, showing his frustration to anyone who might be watching.

He walked around to the side of the building and then behind it. Out of sight from the main road, Brave took his time looking over the building's structure. The marshal's office apparently had a full foundation. That's odd, he thought. Pretty unusual in this town. The space below ground level could be a cellar and used as another room, he reasoned. It could be a hideout for the beasts.

Brave walked back to his horse and pulled an iron pry rod from his saddlebag. He wanted anyone watching to see that he was taking all reasonable steps to raise the marshal before breaking in.

He attempted to open a front window with the pry. It was impossible; the window was nailed shut. He shook his head in frustration and tossed the rod to the ground. He looked around and saw the livery stable across the way. He knew it was the stable that Natalie and Pete were in that morning. He also knew that Lester was the liveryman and was likely a paid informer for the beasts. With a look of total dejection, Brave crossed the road to the livery.

"Hey Lester, liveryman, you in there? Come on out, will ya. This is Deputy Sheriff Brave calling."

After a respectable pause, the door of the livery swung open and Lester walked out. "Hi Deputy." He was smiling broadly. "Don't see you down this way. Well, with the marshal next door, we don't get much bull here, no sir. What can I do for you?"

He's talking confidently, thought Brave. Was it real or a put-on? How could he run a business next to a beast's lair and not know what was going on?

Lester's eyes darted across the road to the marshal's office.

That glance just gave you away, my friend, thought Brave. "Well, Lester, it's 'cause of the marshal I'm here. Has he been around lately?"

Lester's face lit up. "I heard you calling earlier. He's real busy. He's in and out and into the backlands a lot. A murder, cow rustling, corralling a thief, you name it. Busy man, that marshal. Them Indians too, big problem." He smiled again at Brave.

Brave knew he was needling him. He got baited a lot by a certain element of the townspeople.

"Haven't seen him in a few days, no sir," Lester added, still smiling.

"Well, Lester, you hit on my problem. The sign on the door says he's investigating farther west, but Lester, that sign is at least three months old. I saw the same sign three times in the last three months. Government's having the same problem that we are having, Lester. They haven't seen hide or tail of the man. They telegraphed to the sheriff's office to see if we could dig him up."

"Can't help, Sheriff," Lester answered. "I learned when I was just a little Lester," he let out a laugh, "yeah, just a little sucker, I learned not to stick my nose in lawmen's duty." He laughed loudly at his own joke.

Brave turned and saw Pete scuffling down the road throwing rocks at buildings. He'd expected him to be there and he was. "Hey kid, come over here and help me," he yelled.

Pete stopped and stood, staring wide-eyed.

"Help me move a ladder."

Lester said, "Oh, no, no, no, better not do that, Deputy. I don't think the marshal would like that at all."

Pete came forward cautiously, scuffling his ragged, oversized boots.

"Don't worry, kid," Brave said, "I'll give you a copper for your troubles." Brave gave him a kind smile.

Pete looked pleased but remained cautious. He looked first at Brave and then at Lester.

The kid is a good actor if he's doing this on purpose, thought Brave. "Gotta use your loft ladder, Lester, for a few minutes." Brave scanned the livery. "That one will do, come on, kid." Brave walked boldly to a ladder, ignoring Lester's protests.

Trembling, Lester sputtered, "Well . . . the boss . . . Deputy . . . he doesn't want me to let anyone use the equipment. Those ladders are hard to make, ya know."

Brave gave him a stern stare, and Lester quickly added, "Well, seeing you're the law, I guess it'll be all right."

Suddenly Lester turned suspicious. "Why do you want to go up there? Tack a message on the door? When the marshal gets back, he'll find it." Lester looked quizzically at Brave.

"The marshal has been gone a long time, Lester. He may be dead or hurt in there or left a note on how to get in touch with him. A lot of lawmen's offices have escape hatches in the roof. If I can get in that way, I'll save busting up his door."

"Oh," said Lester, showing more strain.

He doesn't believe me, thought Brave. The beast probably pays him off. He doesn't act or look like a beast himself, though. He may not even know he's dealing with a beast. Probably happy as long as he gets his money on the first of the month.

"Come on, kid, help me move that ladder."

Pete slowly came into the livery, his eyes wide and a mark of terror affixed to his face.

Brave patted him on the back reassuringly. "Bring that piece of iron too, kid, over there. We may need it to get in."

Pete threw Lester a frightened look and picked up the iron rod. Brave looked up and down the road as he and Pete crossed the road carrying the ladder. Again he saw nothing unusual, nothing out of place. He felt his confidence surge.

After placing the ladder against the office building, Brave went back to his pinto and grabbed his rifle. By legend, rifles were ineffective against beasts, but he felt more comfortable having one with him. Besides, he thought, they may have humans guarding them in the daytime.

Brave looked down the road again. All was calm. The drunk, Rabson or Robson, was back, staggering about. A short career for his new career, thought Brave, smiling. He could hear a hammer pounding far away, probably beating on metal nails. It filled the early afternoon with noise. He felt uncertain whether or not to proceed but the quiet, calm road reassured him.

Brave was first up the ladder and onto the roof. Pete tailed him cautiously. The door opening in the roof was plainly visible. It was a three-foot by three-foot trap door located above where the marshal's desk would be below. About a six-foot drop from the roof to the desk, Brave figured.

Brave reached down to try the trap door. It was fastened tight and wouldn't budge. Must be unlocked at night while the beasts hunt or one stays behind to guard the lair, he reasoned.

A covering coated with a tar and felt-like composition was placed around the frame of the door. Brave worked quickly to rip it off. After removing it, he noticed a space between the frame of the door and the roof. He forced the iron rod into the space, and using the frame as a lever he pried up the trap door. It opened easily.

Brave glanced at Pete and after a look below, he swung down from the roof, holding onto the frame and landing squarely on the marshal's desk.

A ghastly odor hit him; it was sickening. He felt faint for a moment and his eyes watered. The smell was of putrid and rancid air. Pure evil. Without any doubt this was a beast's lair.

Should he get reinforcements before going further? Wait for the sheriff's return? No, he decided, it was too late in the day and he'd come too far to put it off. The beasts would find the broken door and swarm the community like wild bees. We must attack while the element of surprise is on our side, he thought. Besides, he didn't know when the sheriff would return. Best get at it. That's what he was paid to do anyway, he thought.

Pete motioned that he wanted to come down. A courageous young man, thought Brave. Scared to death up there but he still wants to come down. He must smell the air and know what he'll be getting into.

Brave lowered himself to the office floor, making room for Pete. Pete swung down, landing on the desk. He immediately jumped down next to Brave. Brave heard him gasp for breath when he hit the floor. Brave grinned at him in admiration and placed a hand on the boy's shoulder.

They stood side by side on the office floor for a moment, neither saying anything. They were having difficulty with their eyes adjusting to the gloomy atmosphere.

As his sight improved, Brave saw several cloth rugs scattered about the floor. They don't look decorative, he thought. He remembered when he was outside, he'd thought there must be a room below the main floor. He kicked at one of the rugs and then at another. Under the second rug, the outline of a trapdoor was perceptible. The door had been built with care, he could see, unlike the door leading into the office from the roof. This must be it, he thought. The lair must be down below.

Brave took a small knife from his belt and cleared debris from around the frame of the door. He tried the door and, strangely, it was unlocked. He felt Pete's hand grabbing his arm. The boy was terrified. Brave nodded and looked confidently at him. Pete appeared to grow steady.

The deputy pointed at himself and at the trap door. He brought his finger up and ran it across his neck; he was telling Pete that he was going below to destroy whatever was down there. Pete stared back with a mixture of fear and astonishment.

Slowly, Brave pulled the door open. When it was partway up, he heard an unusual noise, a kind of squeal, and saw Pete's head move at the same time. The sound came from somewhere over on the left. In the near-darkness, Brave made out a human form standing there in the dark, observing them. The rifle in its hands was pointed directly at Brave.

Pete ducked instinctively, making room for Brave to swing his rifle around.

Brave recognized the form—Rabson, the drunk—an instant before a bullet ball plowed into his chest. Brave bounced once off the wall of the marshal's office and he lay gasping on the floor. Pete stood near him, screaming. There was no place for him to run.

CHAPTER THIRTY-TWO

Natalie watched Brave and Pete from a boardwalk position up the road. She saw them carry a ladder to the marshal's office. She saw them climb up onto the roof. She waited. Time passed so slowly. She was startled to hear a gunshot; she hadn't expected that. Had something gone wrong? Maybe she imagined she heard a gunshot. She waited about fifteen more minutes. Was it taking them longer to stake the beasts than expected? Were there more beasts than they expected? Were the beasts putting up a fight? She must do something.

She was terrified. She had no place to go for help. No one would understand; they would think she was just raving. Her stomach jabbed her with pain again. She couldn't concentrate. She wanted to run and hide. She must do something, but what? She watched the liveryman leave the stable, go get the ladder, and drag it across the road back to the livery. How dare he do that! Brave and Pete were still in there.

"Oh my," she whispered aloud. As blood rushed from her face, her stomach pained worse. She felt defenseless.

She decided to walk down the road to the livery. When she reached it, she strode right in, mindless of her fears. She faced Lester, the attendant. "I am looking for Deputy Sheriff Brave. Do you know where he is?" she asked.

"Hold on, ma'am. Who?" His face screwed up in feigned heavy thought.

"Deputy Brave. He was here a few minutes ago and got a ladder from you," she explained quickly, attempting to hide the terror in her voice. "He took it across the road."

"Oh that guy, yeah, he was here about an hour ago, I think, don't know exactly. He borrowed my ladder, kid was with him, I just went over myself and got the ladder back.

Was that a sheriff, you say? Not very polite leaving my ladder over there. Is he on bad terms with the marshal, do you know? Looked to me like he was trying to break into the place. Funny you should say he was a sheriff, I was going to call the sheriff to report his behavior."

Natalie asked, "Did you hear a shot?"

"A shot? Is that what you said, ma'am? I hear shots all the time. The saloons are over there." He pointed across the livery toward the saloon district and laughed.

"That's his horse over there. He wouldn't just leave it there," she argued.

"Oh, you're right," Lester said, "I see his rifle is gone. He took his rifle. That's good. I'll put the horse in the stable for him. He'll show up. Can't get far without a horse around these parts. Thanks for straightening me out, ma'am. Don't you work up at Lady's, ma'am? You sure are pretty. I may just see you up there some day." He left Natalie standing there and he started across the road to where Brave's horse was tied.

My God, she thought, the beasts have Brave and Pete and I have no way to get them help. Feeling herself begin to tremble, she ran from the livery.

CHAPTER THIRTY-THREE

The three rode silently down the main road into St. Bartow. They passed within twenty feet of a crowd forming along the boardwalk. Swirling dust, the product of three rainless days, rose up and clung to the brown oilcloth coats they wore. Sheriff Lawton was first in line; Cole and Deputy Stilkey followed. A riderless horse carrying a tied-down load came last. Deputy Stilkey held the horse's reins.

Road traffic pulled to the side to give the procession clear way. Pedestrians on the boardwalk slowed, stopped, stared and pointed at the passage. The bright silver stars worn conspicuously by two of the three riders caught and held the interest of the spectators.

The riders were bedraggled; they were unshaven and their clothes were torn and soiled. The ponderous gait of the horses reflected the weariness of the march. Yet the riders showed sparks of vigor too. Each held his head high and cast his eyes at the boardwalk crowd as if in an odd kind of military review.

Deputy Stilkey guided the trailing horse easily. The remains of the sniper were on the horse, tied down and covered by a brown tarpaulin. Lifeless limbs stuck out grotesquely from under the cover and bounced to the beat of the horse's movements. The procession wound its way steadily toward the sheriff's office.

"Nice work, Sheriff," tolled a voice from up on the boardwalk. Scattered cheers erupted. The cheers turned to a low rumble of approval but then quickly tailed off.

They want to know what happened and who got killed before giving full approval, thought Cole.

"One of us or one of them, Sheriff?" yelled a voice from the boardwalk. A laugh kindled mild cheering that spread delicately through the expectant watchers.

"Plant 'em on the boot, Sheriff, say a prayer and maybe we'll get rain." A few tired laughs lifted sullenly into the dry air but they too quickly died out.

Cole shook his head and wiped the dust and grime from his face. He spit out what had found its way into his mouth. Cole thought back to his first experience with road dirt in St. Bartow. The dryness hadn't helped the stuff's flavor. Still that plain vanilla I have to get used to, he thought. A good drink of water was on his mind but there'd be no break for water, he knew that. For security, the procession had to move rapidly to the sheriff's office.

The sniper had been a former Confederate military officer. There were still many Grays in the area, some of them not nice people. Lawton was convinced, though, that the dead sniper had been working alone.

More and more people were arriving and watching as the group made its way down the road. The word of their arrival seemed to move faster than their pace, marveled Cole.

A young boy, excited by the moment, ran down the steps of the boardwalk and up to the trailing horse. "Who is it, mister?" he shouted at Stilkey while grabbing for a dangling stirrup. "Did he rob a bank? Can he really bring us rain, you think, if you plant him?" The kid was enthralled.

Lawton turned in his saddle, pointed at the boy, and growled, "Clear back."

The kid scurried back to the shelter of the boardwalk. "A dead hand, I saw it," he screamed. "It was just laying there and there was bullets in it," he added, underlining his newly achieved authority. "And blood all over it! He was a bank robber or a Johnny Reb, I think!" he concluded, knowledgeable and basking in his sudden wisdom.

"I saw his pants, blood all over 'em," yelled another boy, not to be outdone.

"You weren't even out there, donkey head," yelled the first boy, protecting his turf.

The procession soon closed on the sheriff's office. When they reached the crossroads leading to the Rebel Saloon, they shifted their glance from side to side and up onto the boardwalk to down the street toward the Grays' saloon. Lawton had said "If we're going to have trouble, it'll come there." But they encountered no trouble. The entry was going to be eventless. That's good, thought Cole.

The sniper's name was Jeremy Nichols. He was a Confederate Army captain. His home was in Georgia and he'd served in an intelligence unit attached to an infantry regiment made up of Georgia draftees and enlistees. Later on in the War, when a shortage of soldiers developed for the Confederate front, Nichols was shifted into artillery. Lawton found war records on the sniper's body that confirmed that progression.

During Sherman's march, Nichols was authorized to abandon his artillery unit and fight with guerrillas that were forming for the purpose of picking off supply wagons at the end of Sherman's convoys. Nichols apparently got his comeuppance at a small town called Smeedsville. Sherman had loaded some supply wagons with infantry soldiers and purposely put the wagons in harm's way. The group Nichols was a part of was ambushed when it attacked. The Yankees chased, captured and shot most of the guerrillas as they ran away after realizing their plight. How Nichols got away was not clear. From his writing, it was evident that he was badly hurt in the escape. He experienced real hell, thought Cole.

Riding down the road, the sheriff thought of the letter of notification he'd have to compose. The letter would be addressed to Nichols's next of kin. In this case, his mother in Georgia. Lawton would have to describe the circumstances of his death. He hated to write those letters. Not because he had to admit to killing someone, but because he believed he couldn't write well enough to describe the situation right.

Lawton had composed several letters of notification over the years and he kept a copy of each of them in an office drawer. He also had copies of the letters composed and sent by previous sheriffs. He'd learned from reading them that you tried to say something nice about a deceased, even if you had to fib a little, especially if the letter was going to a mother, a wife or a child. Sometimes it was difficult to do that. Lawton had seen some likely lies in several letters sent out by previous sheriffs. Well, he thought, maybe the sheriffs had writing problems similar to his—not being able to express yourself in writing. You got to do what you got to do, thought Lawton.

However, he was happy to write this letter because it meant the ordeal was over. The soldier's mind had been destroyed by the War. That was apparent from the notes Lawton had found in the sniper's possession. "Saw too much, felt too much, left too much of himself on the battlefield." That was how Cole had put it. And he pretty much spoke for all, thought Lawton.

The procession reached the sheriff's office without incident. Lawton nodded to Stilkey, and the deputy rode off with the body to the undertaker's. Cole and the sheriff swung down, took off their coats, and staggered wearily into the office.

Each swigged long on the water in the bucket near the fireplace.

Even warm water tastes right when you're this thirsty, thought Cole. This dryness in my mouth will take a long time to go away. "I need coffee now," Cole said, tossing out the old stuff and reaching down to rekindle a fire. "Looks like this stuff was left over from this morning."

"Agreed," said the sheriff. "I'm going to submit papers for your reward money right away, Cole. I was pleased with your work. You know that, but I have to tell you. I don't know your plans, but it'll probably take about a month to get the reward. I can have it forwarded west through Wells Fargo if you would like. Brave must be out on a security round," he added matter of factly.

They were interrupted by a beating on the office door and a voice pleading, "Cole, please, Cole. They've killed Brave."

It was a woman's voice. Was it Natalie? It sounds like she's done for, Cole thought. He ran to the door, and the sheriff was a step behind him.

Cole flung it open and found Natalie, terror stricken. She moaned. Her eyes failed to settle on either one of them or on anything, in fact.

"Natalie, what's wrong? What did you say?" Cole grabbed her and held her, hoping he hadn't heard her say what he thought she said. He couldn't have heard right, he thought. "Brave killed?"

Natalie sobbed uncontrollably in Cole's arms. "Oh Cole, so much has happened. We know where the beasts stay. Brave went to destroy them. Brave and Pete were captured or killed by the beasts, they both have been killed, I think."

Her voice rose in disbelief as she said the word "killed." "It's probably too late to save them. The beasts have protectors. The protectors are human and they control everything. One runs the livery across the road. Oh . . ." She tried to talk and failed. She clung fiercely to Cole.

Cole gently sat her down.

The two men listened to her story. Lawton had never lost a lawman. Now Natalie was possibly telling him about the first one. And he had been killed by something she described as a beast. Her story was impossible to believe on first hearing.

Once Natalie calmed, Lawton pressed for more detail.

Both men listened as she again described the events of her day. When she concluded, Lawton and Cole stared at one another, their faces expressionless. There was no doubt in either of their minds. Killer beasts were in St. Bartow.

It was six o'clock, early evening. Shadows from the wooden buildings had begun to darken the roadway. Full darkness was two hours off. The traffic on the dusty road was moving slowly, unaware of an impending crisis.

CHAPTER THIRTY-FOUR

Natalie's account of her day shocked Cole. The likely death of his good friend Brave was unnerving. And with the mind-numbing battle he'd had that morning with the sniper, he wondered if his mind and body were up to an immediate strike at the beasts. For the first time since the Beaudin affair, Cole wondered whether he had confidence enough in himself to deal with what was going on around him. He tried now as best he could to put the pressure out of his mind and to think through the best approaches for going forward.

If Natalie's account was accurate—and Cole believed it was—Brave was dead. It had happened as sudden as if a sniper had picked him off out on a lonely trail. Poor, simple Pete's fate was less clear but he was probably dead too. The sheriff would want to strike back at the beasts immediately. Brave and Lawton were as close as you get in the West. The sheriff wouldn't leave Brave there, possibly alive but under the domain of even one beast. He wouldn't take that path even if there was only a very slim chance that Brave was alive and could be saved.

In his training and attitude, Lawton was a military man. His reaction would be vintage General Grant—when a situation is dark but there are a few elements of light—attack, but remember to keep critical resources in reserve. For most Union officers, that was a big lesson of the War.

But Cole questioned the wisdom of an immediate response. Daylight was fading. By the time they could organize an attack, the beasts would have departed their lair and be out for the night preying. The lawmen might end up doing a lot of planning, making a lot of noise, but attacking and burning an empty lair.

Returning before the first rays of the sun, the beasts would easily discern a burned-out, empty lair. Seeing it, they might instead fly off to another lair. Natalie had told him that the beasts were intelligent. They had been preying on and fighting off humans for thousands of years. They always built an alternative lair for when times got tough. They might just choose to disperse as they had after being burned out of New Orleans. Or, for all Cole knew, the beasts might choose for a while to burrow, burrow deep into the ample, tall grass around St. Bartow and stay there until the threat receded. Some might even have enough wax on hand to protect them from the sun's rays and slip right through the people.

Cole shook his head. Burning the lair may be a solution for St. Bartow, but it wasn't a solution for the general problem of beasts in this new country.

If instead the group set up an ambush, surrounded the marshal's office, and broke in after the beasts returned, they could stake and destroy them all. The beasts would be vulnerable in the morning. A staked beast was a dead beast. A dead beast would never show up farther west. Not possible, thought Cole.

Burning up the lair, though, did have a disadvantage. The whole town was vulnerable to catching fire. Fire would spread easily in freshly cut timber, passing from structure to structure. Buildings around here were built practically one on top of the other. Many frontier towns had burned up after a fire started in a single building, Cole had heard.

Thinking further, an ambush after daylight had weaknesses too. Keeping preparation for an ambush quiet would be difficult. The word of it would pass fast through the town. Beasts and their human patrons would learn of it. Cole didn't know what their reaction would be, but for sure it wouldn't be mild.

Cole felt as though he had worn himself out from thinking over the possibilities. The problem with all these potential solutions, Cole thought, was that they didn't have enough information about beasts and their behavior to make a truly good decision. A best solution required them to understand the scale of the problem. They didn't know that at all. They needed to know the number and the location of lairs and the number and location of the beasts in the area. Some idea of the number of humans helping them would also be useful. With that, they would know the resources needed for a complete and total retaliation—one that would knock out all the lairs and destroy all the beasts at one time and before they could disperse.

Without that intelligence, their plan would be only as sophisticated as a plan to take on a gang of bank robbers holed up in a bank. The sheriff really needed intelligence of the same quality as an army would need planning an attack: how many soldiers, wagons, weapons, etcetera.

Cole decided that in the meeting he'd follow the sheriff's lead. Lawton had to weigh all this information and make a final decision. He'd give the sheriff support and provide his best opinion. But the decision was in the sheriff's hands.

CHAPTER THIRTY-FIVE

"They're out there," the sheriff said. His words snapped as if from a whip of a muleskinner. "They're well juiced on Brave and the boy. I say burn up their lair tonight, right now. With their lair gone, from what we understand, when they return in the morning, they'll fry in the heat of the sun." Lawton's eyes narrowed as he looked around the group. "Any comments?"

Stilkey grabbed the flag. "I have no comment, Sheriff. Dynamite or kerosene or both, you say the word and I'll be there, doing what's right."

"Wait, let me talk," said Natalie, her face drawn and showing strain. "In New Orleans the beasts were burned out. The fire sent them to the four winds. Burning them out may not solve the problem. It may just disperse it."

Seeing an opening, Cole moved in. "How many lairs? We don't know. How many beasts? We don't know. How many paid protectors? We don't know. We know little about these monsters and their living habits. We need better information to plan effectively. With better information we could answer Natalie's question about dispersal as a problem if we burned up a single lair."

"What are you suggesting, Cole? That we wait until daylight after they return and go in and stake them to death? Maybe capture one and get information out of him? Or do you think that the problem may be so severe that we should hold off. Maybe shift the problem up to a higher level. Say, let Washington determine whether it's a local or territorial or a regional or maybe even a national problem. Is that what you're saying?"

Cole thought Lawton looked disgusted as he spoke.

Stilkey cut in, "Yeah, let's buck it somewhere, somewhere out of our reach. Buck it to the same guys that are going to come up with solutions for the coming range wars. Maybe buck it to the guys that appointed the marshal here. The same guys that started the War." Stilkey shook his head and threw his hands up.

"Look, Sheriff," said Cole, backing off, "it's your call. If there's a chance Brave and Pete are alive, I say we must go in tonight."

"I don't understand," said Stilkey, "we're sitting here talking and the beasts are out sucking on humans! What's to talk about? We're wasting time! We are the law, the only law the town has! In the end you know we'll have to go in and get those mangy beasts anyway, Sheriff."

The sheriff paused. "Any other positions or ideas?" He looked around the group.

He's anxious to get moving, thought Cole. He's made his decision.

"Something has bothered me," said Natalie. "Is our force the right makeup to take on the beasts? Rifles don't work against beasts. In my culture, medicine men fought beasts. Should we include members of the clergy and religious icons in our arsenal? Should we fight ultimate evil with ultimate good?"

"You make a point, Natalie," Lawton said, rubbing his forehead impatiently. "I'm confident that fire and rifles and dynamite can win. I admit, though, that we don't know that much about the beasts. A few days ago I thought beasts resided only in heads. Perhaps we should broaden our force. Take on a religious tone. We don't know why the beasts are here. It may be because of the destruction around us recently, wars and battles with Indians and among ourselves. I'd never be able to do my job if I spent time thinking about these things."

"Or," interjected Stilkey, nodding his head, "the number of immigrants flooding through our area."

Lawton said, "Anyway, Natalie, meeting your concern would require us to change our approach. We don't have the time for that. We must consider the lives of Brave and the boy. That is my basic responsibility. I have listened," the sheriff concluded. "I have heard your points, but my decision stands. We attack now. We destroy the beasts that are in the marshal's office. We capture the humans that have been protecting them, if any are there. They'll face justice and the wrath of God. We'll search for and find Brave and Pete. When we're done, if it makes sense, we'll burn up the lair."

The room was silent.

"Let's go," Lawton said, rising.

CHAPTER THIRTY-SIX

It was eleven o'clock at night. Lawton and Cole left the sheriff's office together and rode down the road to a building near the livery stable across from the marshal's office. The newly installed gas lanterns lit the night air brighter than usual and gave off a unique sound of rushing air.

They sound like flapping wings, thought Cole, trying unsuccessfully to check his imagination.

The two dismounted and walked quietly up the boardwalk to the side of the stable. They stumbled their way through the hard clay and weeds to the back. It took no time to find the hole that Natalie and Pete had used hours earlier. The men crawled through and stood silently for a moment at the back of the stable getting their bearings and listening to the horses claw and bang against their wooden stalls.

Lawton and Cole didn't have to wait long. Deputy Stilkey started banging on the marshal's door across the road. They heard him clearly.

"Marshal, this is Deputy Sheriff Jack Stilkey, are you in there? We may have a man down. We need your assistance." He waited silently.

There was no response.

"Marshal, are you in there, we need your help."

Still no response.

The two men heard a stirring in the front of the livery and knew it must be Lester. A glow from Lester's lantern lit the front of the stable. The door creaked and swung outward.

"Deputy, hello there, I heard you yelling. I'm the liveryman, Lester. Can I help you?"

Stilkey called back in a loud, annoyed tone, "Maybe. Where's the marshal, Lester? What's going on? He's never here. Would you believe an empty marshal's office? What's with the guy?"

"The marshal is away. If it was light, you'd see the note. He's up north going after a pack of rustlers, I think it says. Yeah, rustlers maybe."

"Oh," said Stilkey. "Have you seen anything of Deputy Brave? We got back from the hills and he's nowhere. Disappeared, horse and all."

"Well, you know half-breeds." Lester laughed knowingly. "You're lucky the guy stayed as long as he did. Those breeds don't know whether to steal and run like a white man or to steal and hide like an Indian." He laughed again, louder, obviously pleased with his wit. He added, "You're lucky the Wells Fargo shipment didn't go with him."

Lawton and Cole could hear Lester laughing uproariously.

He's on dangerous ground, thought Cole. Stilkey and Brave are close friends.

Stilkey walked down from the entrance to the marshal's office and crossed the road to the front of the livery, drawing his gun as he got close. "I think you know more than you're telling me, Lester. What'd you do with his horse?"

Panic swept though Lester when he saw the gun. He tossed the kerosene lantern at Stilkey but Jack saw it coming. He jumped to the side and the lantern passed by him harmlessly. A five-foot geyser of fire rose from the lantern and lighted up the area around where it landed. Stilkey moved quickly again, this time landing near a surprised Lester. He cracked Lester on the side of the head with his gun barrel, and Lester sunk to the ground.

Hearing the commotion, the sheriff and Cole came running to Stilkey's side.

"I guess he's no friggin' beast," said Stilkey, his eyes on the prone Lester. "Just does the beast's bidding, I guess," he said, sounding surprised.

In the light of the burning kerosene, Cole looked around the livery and found another lantern. Natalie now walked into the circle of light from a position down the road. Lawton explained to her what had happened.

"Let's first find Brave's horse," said the sheriff. "Lester picked it up from outside the marshal's office, right, Natalie? So it should be in here somewhere. Jack, you stay outside with Lester. Keep your eye on him and look for trouble coming up or down the road."

Lawton, Cole and Natalie went into the stable and began examining each horse for markings that would prove it to be Brave's. After twenty minutes of searching they had gone through the whole stable and not found Brave's horse. They changed sides and followed the same routine, thinking that they had missed a horse. The result was the same. Brave's pinto was not in the stable.

A note of concern entering his voice, the sheriff asked Natalie, "Do you think you made a mistake?"

"No," she said firmly, "it was Brave's horse. The liveryman led it right past me and into the stable. He must have moved it out of here. That's the only answer."

"Do you think Brave came back and picked it up?" The sheriff was thinking out loud and beginning to wonder if he had overreacted.

"No," Natalie responded with hardened firmness. "I saw Lester take the horse into the stable."

Cole raised the lantern over his head to get a better look around the stable; he was searching for a hidden door. He noticed a raised mound in a corner of the stable covered with loose hay. Could it hide a trap door or a hidden entrance into another section of the stable?

"What's that mound over there?" he asked, pointing with his free hand.

Lawton walked over and kicked the mound. His kick sounded strange and his foot didn't slice through or bounce off the way he would have expected. He reached down to sweep off the top hay and expose what was underneath.

"What's this?" he murmured. He worked feverishly to expose the straw-covered object. "It's the body of a horse."

Cole and Natalie stood mute. The sheriff uncovered the object fully—it was Brave's pinto. Shaking his head and murmuring to himself, Lawton inspected the dead animal.

"How'd he die, Sheriff," asked Cole. "Did he shoot him? Why would he do that?"

"Shirr," murmured the sheriff, trying to hide his anguish. After a few moments Lawton arose, shaken. His voice trembled and his eyes moistened as he stared down at the dead horse. "Well, we know what we're up against, for sure."

The sheriff forced out his words: "There are eight to twelve incisions on the animal's neck. There are bruises on his ribs, thighs and legs, probably made by the horse himself trying to get free from his attackers. All the incisions are surgical in appearance. And they are about the distance apart of a human's eye teeth."

In the quiet stable Lawton's voice rose to a loud wail: "The beasts had a party here tonight," he lamented. He covered his eyes with his right hand and staggered backward a couple steps.

Cole went limp and his mouth flew open, the sheer horror of the find overwhelming him.

Natalie grabbed Cole's arm, sobbed, and looked away. She quietly pleaded, "Will it ever end!"

A gunshot from out front of the livery broke into their anguish, the sound echoing down the dark road and through the stable. It brought the three back to their purpose.

The sheriff drew his gun and they ran together to the front of the livery. They found Stilkey standing over and looking down at a prone Lester.

"What happened?" asked the sheriff, holstering his gun. He bent down to examine Lester.

"He went crazy, honest, Sheriff, he did. When he heard you scream in there he started to shake. He went for my gun. I think he wanted me to shoot him. I don't know, Sheriff. It happened so quick. He started to cry too. He was going crazy. That's all I can say."

The sheriff rose. "Lester's dead," he said, his eyes focused across the road at the marshal's office. "So be it." Lawton told Stilkey about the dead horse in the stable.

Stilkey was shocked into a moment of silence. "What are we waiting for," he then yelled. "No wonder he killed himself. He was in on the pinto's death. He knew we'd fix his ass for him. I'm getting kerosene so we can do the job right." Stilkey disappeared into the depths of the livery stable.

"Before we attack, see this." Natalie drew several six-inch pointed wooden spears and a silver crucifix from beneath her cloak. "We may need these."

"Okay, let's go," said the sheriff, rifle in hand and leading the way across the road.

Cole and Natalie followed, and Stilkey, carrying a container of kerosene, caught up with them.

At the front door of the office, the sheriff calmly drew his six-gun and fired away at the lock. Three shots rang out and the lock shattered. Lawton pushed the door in.

The stale and inhuman odor that greeted him was the same as had repulsed Brave and Pete hours earlier. It hit them all with the force of a wet plank.

The smell of death, thought Cole. He recognized the odor as a more intense version of the one that had engulfed Willoughby Marchess the day they'd had a drink at the Dollar Saloon.

"Ugh, what the hell," queried the sheriff, his eyes watering and his left hand pinching his nose.

Cole stepped forward, lantern in hand, ready to lead the way in.

"No," the sheriff said brusquely, "I'm going in first. Give me the lantern, you take the rifle. Cover me."

Lawton grabbed the lantern from Cole and pushed his way through the open door. The smell now hit the sheriff full force.

"What is this—a tomb?" he asked, staggering and answering his own question.

Lawton made his way to the marshal's desk in the flickering light. He set the lantern on the desk and stepped back, still holding his nose. Tears engulfed his eyes. It was like walking into the mouth of a serpent. Shadows from the lantern danced grotesquely on the office walls.

Stilkey, Cole, and Natalie moved in behind Lawton. Stilkey carefully placed his kerosene on the desk, but away from the lantern. The three began looking for hiding places.

"What's this here," said Cole, noticing the outline of a trap door in the floor.

It was out in the open, the same door Brave uncovered earlier. The dirt from Brave's scrapings still laid in little piles beside the frame. The three inspected the door. The sheriff knelt down to open it. It was unlocked.

Natalie was the first to hear the sound. It was a squeaky sound like from a rusty hinge. She didn't know it but Brave and Pete had heard the same sound earlier. She turned in the direction of the noise and saw a section of the wall swinging open. A human form appeared with a rifle in its hands.

"Aaah!" she screamed, pointing at it. "Over there, look!"

The form swung its rifle toward the men on the floor. Natalie instinctively knew that the men would be unable to react in time so she lunged toward the form while drawing a wooden spear from under her bodice. Her speed was of desperation and athleticism.

The form, sensing the threat, swung the rifle away from the men and toward her. The rifle exploded at the same moment the sharp spear plunged into the form's heart. Natalie staggered and fell to the floor.

It happened so swiftly that the sheriff, Cole and Stilkey, standing near the trap door, could only watch in shock.

"Natalie!" Cole screamed.

He ran to her. She was gasping for air and her arms lay limp at her side. Cole picked her up as blood poured from her mouth and ears and from a giant wound in her chest. Her beautiful eyes were lifeless in the lantern's light. She was dead, just like that.

Cole held the beautiful woman close to him. He rocked her as though she were a child asleep. He cried and grieved.

The dying beast with the wooden spear lodged in its chest jerked and quivered on the office floor. Strange, inhuman sounds arose from its wide-open mouth. Wisps of smoke came up from its ears and nose. Its body contorted.

Sheriff Lawton kicked away the beast's rifle. "That thing is going nowhere but to its maker," he screamed. Horrible, he thought, shivering in distaste at its appearance.

The thing's eyes had bugged out and flashed like little beacons. Blue pus oozed from beneath it.

The sheriff stared at the squirming, obviously dying beast. The sight was horrible but fascinating. The beacons of light coming from its eyes were slowly dying. Lawton kept staring at what was left of the beast. He was amazed to recognize the face of the marshal on the beast, a face he'd seen only twice in his years as sheriff. If there was a question whether the marshal was a beast, he thought, the answer lay withering there on the floor of his office.

Cole continued to cradle Natalie's lifeless body. He spoke not at all but he was thinking about what he could have done to save her life.

Deputy Stilkey moved closer to look at the beast's remains. He saw the viscous liquid flowing from under it and spreading on the floor and he railed, "Look, the friggin' thing's melting!"

The sheriff took command. He turned to Stilkey. "We must get moving. We must find Brave and Pete. There may be other beasts hidden here. Cover me, I'm going below."

Lawton went to the trap door, Stilkey following. He raised the lid again. It lifted easily, revealing steps leading down to a dirt floor. The odor from below was more putrid and more intense than Lawton had yet experienced.

Without a word, he slowly inched down the stairs, lantern in one hand, gun in the other. As he walked down the stairs, the burning kerosene acted to purify some of the outrageous smell rising from the basement. He knew not what to expect or how useful his gun would be. His eyes watered unbelievably from the foul air. "Filthy beasts," he whispered.

The space below was a dirt floor cellar. He saw Brave's body in a corner of the room. Plainly, a chunk of his chest had been blown out. Died instantly, Lawton decided. Pete's body was thrown beside Brave's like a sack of garbage. Total horror was pictured on his drained, white face. Poor kid, the sheriff thought, he must have suffered terribly.

Lawton raised the lantern and looked around the cellar room. He counted six coffins. Five looked like they had been built recently and a sixth had ancient markings carved into it and was set on an ancient carved stand. Resting places for five other coffins were set up in another section of the cellar. They must have been planning to expand soon, he thought. The marshal's must be the fancy one. He has been plaguing the human body and spirit for a long time.

The sheriff was repulsed. He had given his life to the law and had seen gruesome things, particularly during the War. But nothing matched this. How could the office of a Federal United States Marshal have been used in this way? A wild thought went through his mind. What if Washington is involved in this? A secret federal policy to feed the beasts with immigrant blood? First, entice immigrants to the country and then move them West for the beasts. He shook his head. That's absolutely crazy. This beast thing is unnerving me.

"Let's get out of here, we've seen enough," Lawton yelled to Stilkey, who was standing at the middle of the stairs, kerosene at the ready. "The other beasts must be out preying. Let's give them a bad day of sleep tomorrow."

Stilkey started down the steps with his bucket of kerosene. "This place can be cleansed only by fire," he shouted.

He's smiling, Lawton noted. Well, this is what he's wanted to do for three days. Lawton was smiling too. It was a release amidst the horror.

When he reached the bottom step, Stilkey tossed what was in the container onto the coffins and around the room.

"Throw some on Brave and the kid. We don't have time to get them out," yelled Lawton.

Finished, Stilkey and Lawton ran back up the stairs. They found Cole still cradling Natalie.

"Cole," shouted Lawton, trying to bring him around, "take Natalie and get out. This place is going up in flames."

Without a word, Cole picked up Natalie's body as though it was a doll and carried it to the front door. Lawton followed. A crowd had formed outside the office. Stilkey stood inside for a moment and tossed the lamp down the steps to the cellar floor.

Moments later, the building was ablaze.

EPILOGUE

The burning of the marshal's office gave the newly formed volunteer fire organization in St. Bartow its first experience at containing a major in-town fire. It was successful, and no other buildings were lost. The marshal's office itself was completely gutted; nothing was salvageable.

Reports were that the fire had taken the lives of several citizens. These citizens had gone to the fire hoping to save the building but instead they were killed. One person killed was a deputy sheriff and a second was a member of the staff at the Talbot House. It was also reported that the marshal was killed in the fire but there was no confirmation on that, although he never did return to St. Bartow after his office was burned.

The volunteer firefighters observed a strange phenomenon while fighting the fire. They witnessed what they believed were numerous birds flying over the building. Several volunteers thought the birds looked and flew more like giant bats, though several others reported that they were larger than any bat they had ever seen. All the volunteers agreed that the birds screamed and flipped their bodies and wings in flight as if in fear of the fire or the heat of the flames. None of the volunteers or observers had ever seen or heard of such a thing. As dawn broke, the birds appeared to tire. The volunteers agreed that the birds eventually flew away, toward the west.

Natalie was buried just outside the Hill section, not far from where Jeremy Nichols, the sniper, was buried. She was the first Negro free person to be buried on the Hill in St. Bartow. The sheriff, Stilkey, and Cole attended her final service, leading a procession of townspeople. Lady Talbot, Napie, and several other friends of Natalie's from Lady's attended the service and participated in the procession.

Cole gave a eulogy that impressed the attendees for its sensitivity. In death, he said, she looked as though she had finally achieved the peace and freedom she had been searching for. He spoke of Natalie with all the dignity usually accorded a white person. He also spoke kindly of Deputy Brave, of his young friend Pete, and the other people lost that day.

Several months after the fire, Cole joined a wagon train going west. He had received a bounty payment of six hundred dollars for his role in the capture of the sniper—an amount greater than he had anticipated. He used the reward money to settle down and begin homesteading on new farmland in Nebraska.

After two harvests, as he had promised, Cole notified Angela, his girl back in Franklin, Vermont, of his success. He did not clearly invite her out. She responded quickly and kindly, explaining that she had decided to remain in Vermont. He never saw or heard from her again.

Cole met up with Sonia. The Josephson family, too, had selected to settle in Nebraska. Cole and Sonia renewed their love and got married. On their farm in Nebraska, they raised four children, three of them boys. One boy graduated from West Point Academy and was awarded a Silver Medal for bravery in 1899 in the War with Spain. In 1918 Cole, then a well-to-do Nebraska farmer, died of natural causes.

Seven years after the destruction of the marshal's office, a drunken cowboy ambushed and killed Sheriff Lawton while he was on an afternoon security round. The citizens of St. Bartow memorialized the sheriff for his selfless work by placing a bronze plaque on the front of the sheriff's office. It is still hanging there today.

Deputy Stilkey never recovered from the stress of the burning. Although he remained a deputy in St. Bartow, many of the townsmen thought his personality had changed—he grew to be quiet, distrustful, and had a haunted look about him. In public, he talked out loud to no one in particular and told stories about strange things that no one quite understood. Some thought the loss in the fire of his good friend,

Brave, had affected his personality. The deputy left St. Bartow in 1874, moving out West. There, he turned increasingly to alcohol for solace. He died penniless in 1902 in a flophouse in San Francisco.

The presence of beasts in St. Bartow was never again an issue.